JOURNEY
TO THE
CENTER
OF THE
EARTH

JOURNEY
TO THE
CENTER
OF THE
EARTH

Jules Verne

MEDIA

Published 2024 by Gildan Media LLC
aka G&D Media
www.GandDmedia.com

Front cover design by David Rheinhardt of Pyrographx

Interior design by Meghan Day Healey of Story Horse, LLC

Library of Congress Cataloging-in-Publication Data is available upon request

ISBN: 978-1-7225-0401-4

10   9   8   7   6   5   4   3   2   1

JOURNEY
TO THE
CENTER
OF THE
EARTH

I

It was on Sunday, the 24th of May, 1863, that my uncle, Professor Lidenbrock, came rushing suddenly back to his little house in the old part of Hamburg, No. 19, Königstrasse.

Our good Martha could not but think she was very much behind-hand with the dinner, for the pot was scarcely beginning to simmer, and I said to myself:

"Now, then, we'll have a fine outcry if my uncle is hungry, for he is the most impatient of mortals."

"Mr. Lidenbrock, already!" cried the poor woman, in dismay, half opening the dining-room door.

"Yes, Martha; but of course dinner can't be ready yet, for it is not two o'clock. It has only just struck the half-hour by St. Michael's."

"What brings Mr. Lidenbrock home, then?"

"He'll probably tell us that himself."

"Here he comes. I'll be off, Mr. Axel; you must make him listen to reason."

And forthwith she effected a safe retreat to her culinary laboratory.

I was left alone, but not feeling equal to the task of making the most irascible of professors listen to reason, was about to escape to my own little room upstairs, when the street-door creaked on its hinges, and the wooden stairs cracked beneath a hurried tread, and the master of the house came in and bolted across the dining-room, straight into his study. But, rapid as his flight was, he managed to fling his nutcracker-headed stick into a corner, and his wide-brimmed rough hat on the table, and to shout out to his nephew:

"Axel, follow me."

Before I had time to stir he called out again, in the most impatient tone imaginable:

"What! Not here yet?"

In an instant I was on my feet and in the study of my dreadful master.

Otto Lidenbrock was not a bad man. I grant that, willingly. But, unless he mightily changes, he will live and die a terrible original.

He was a professor in the Johannaeum, and gave the course of lectures on mineralogy, during which he regularly put himself into a passion once or twice. Not that he troubled himself much about the assiduity of his pupils, or the amount of attention they paid to his lessons, or their corresponding success. These points gave him no concern. He taught *subjectively*, to use a German philosophical expression, for himself, and not for others. He was a selfish *savant*—a well of science, and nothing could be drawn up from it without the grinding noise of the pulleys: in a word, he was a miser.

There are professors of this stamp in Germany.

My uncle, unfortunately, did not enjoy great facility of pronunciation, unless he was with intimate friends; at least, not when he spoke in public, and this is a deplorable defect in an orator. In his demonstrations at the Johannaeum the professor would often stop short, struggling with some obstinate word that refused to slip over his lips—one of those words which resist, swell out, and finally come forth in the anything but scientific shape of an oath. This put him in a great rage.

Now, in mineralogy, there are many names difficult to pronounce—half Greek, half Latin, barbarous appellations which would blister the lips of a poet. I have no wish to speak ill of the science. Far from it. But when one has to do with rhomboidal crystallizations, retinasphaltic resins, galena favosite, molybdates of lead, tungstates of manganese, and titanites of zircon, the most nimble tongue may be allowed to stumble.

The townsfolk were aware of this pardonable infirmity of my uncle's, and they took advantage of it, and were on the watch for the dangerous passages; and when he put himself in a fury laughed at him, which was not in good taste, even for Germans. His lectures were always very numerously attended, but how many of those who were most regular auditors came for anything else but to make game of the professor's grand fits of passion I shouldn't like to say. Whatever my uncle might be, and I can hardly say too much, he was a true *savant.*

Though he sometimes broke his specimens by his rough handling, he had both the genius of a geologist and the eye of a mineralogist. With his hammer and steel pointer and magnetic needle, his blowpipe and his flask of nitric acid, he was a master indeed. By the fracture, the hardness, the fusibility, the ring, the smell, of any mineral whatever, he classed it without hesitation among the six hundred species science numbers to-day.

The name of Lidenbrock was consequently mentioned with honor in gymnasiums and national associations. Humphry Davy, Humboldt, and Captains Franklin and Sabine, paid him a visit when they passed through Hamburg. Becqueul, Ebolmann, Brewster, Dumas, Milne-Edwards, Sainte Clarice Deville, took pleasure in consulting him on the most stirring questions of chemistry, a science which was indebted to him for discoveries of considerable importance; and in 1853 a treatise on Transcendent Crystallography, by Professor Otto Lidenbrock, was published at Leipsic, a large folio, with plates, which did not pay its cost, however.

Moreover, my uncle was curator of the Museum of Mineralogy, belonging to M. Struve, the Russian ambassador, a valuable collection, of European celebrity.

Such, then, was the personage who summoned me so impatiently.

Fancy to yourself a tall, spare man, with an iron constitution, and a juvenile fairness of complexion, which took off a full ten years of his fifty. His large eyes rolled about incessantly behind his great goggles; his long thin nose resembled a knife-blade; malicious people declared it was magnetized, and attracted steel filings—a pure calumny; it attracted nothing but snuff, but, to speak truth, a superabundance of that. When I have added that my uncle made mathematical strides of three feet at every step, and marched along with his fists firmly clenched—a sign of an impetuous temperament—you will know enough of him not to be overanxious for his company.

He lived in his little house in Königsstrasse, a dwelling built partly of brick and partly of stone, with a crenated gable-end, which looked on to one of those winding canals which intersect each other in the center of the oldest part of Hamburg, which happily escaped the great fire in 1842.

The old house leaned forward slightly, and bulged out towards the passers-by. The roof inclined to one side, in the position a German student belonging to the *Tugendbund* wears his cap. The perpendicular of the house was not quite exact, but, on the whole, the house stood well enough, thanks to an old elm, firmly embedded in the façade, which pushed its flower buds across the window-panes in spring.

My uncle was pretty rich for a German professor. The house was his own, and all its belongings. These belongings were his godchild Gräuben, a Virland girl; seventeen years old, his servant Martha, and myself. In my double quality of nephew and orphan, I became his assistant in his experiments.

I must confess I have a great appetite for geological science. The blood of a mineralogist flows in my veins, and I never grow weary in the society of my beloved stones.

On the whole, it was possible to live happily in this little house in Königstrasse, notwithstanding the impatience of the owner; for though he had a rough fashion of showing it, he loved me for all that. But, the fact was, he was a man who could not wait, and was in a greater hurry than nature.

When he used to plant mignonette and convolvuluses in his terracotta pots in the spring, every morning he went regularly and pulled their leaves, to hasten their growth.

With such an original, there was no alternative but to obey, so I darted into the study immediately.

II

The study was a complete museum, every specimen of the mineral kingdom was to be found there, all labeled in the most perfect order, in accordance with the three great divisions of minerals—the inflammable, the metallic, and the lithoid.

How well I knew this alphabet of mineralogical science. How many a time, instead of loitering about with boys of my own age, I amused myself by dusting these graphites, and anthracites, and pit coal, and touch-stones; and the bitumens, and the resins, and organic soils, which had to be kept from the least particle of dust; and the metals, from iron up to gold, the relative value of which disappeared before the absolute equality of scientific specimens; and all those stones, enough to build the little house in the Königstrasse over again, and an extra room besides, which I would have fitted up so nicely for myself.

But when I entered the study now, I scarcely thought of those wonders. My mind was entirely occupied with my uncle. He had buried himself in his big arm-chair, covered with Utrecht velvet and held a book in his hands, gazing at it with the most profound admiration.

"What a book! What a book!" he exclaimed.

This reminded me that Professor Lidenbrock was also given to bibliomania in his leisure moments, but an old book would have had no value in his eyes unless it could not be found anywhere else, or, at all events, could not be read.

"What! don't you see it, then?" he went on. "It is a priceless treasure! I discovered it this morning while I was rummaging about in Hevelin's, the Jew's shop."

"Magnificent!" I replied with forced enthusiasm.

Really, what was the good of making such a fuss about an old quarto volume, the back and sides of which seemed bound in coarse calf—a yellowish old book, with a faded tassel dangling from it?

However, the professor's vocabulary of adjectives was not yet exhausted.

"Look!" he said, asking himself questions, and answering them in the same breath; "is it handsome enough? Yes; it is first-rate. And what binding! Does it open easily? Yes, it lies open at any page, no matter where. And does it close well? Yes; for binding and leaves seem in one completely. Not a single breakage in this back after 700 years of existence! Ah! this is binding that Bozerian, Closs, and Purgold might have been proud of."

All the while he was speaking, my uncle kept opening and shutting the old book. I could not do less than ask him about the contents, though I did not feel the least interest in the subject.

"And what is the title of this wonderful volume?" I asked

"The title of it?" he replied, with increased animation. "The title is 'Heims Kringla,' by Snorre Turleson, the famous Icelandic author of the twelfth century. It is the chronicle of the Norwegian princes who reigned in Iceland."

"Indeed!" I said, doing my best to appear enthusiastic. "And it is translated into German, of course?"

"Translated!" cried the professor, in a sharp tone. "What should I do with a translation? Who cares for translations? It is the original work, in the Icelandic—that magnificent idiom at once grand and simple—which allows of the most varied grammatical combinations and most numerous modification of words."

"Like German," I said, making a lucky hit.

"Yes," replied my uncle, shrugging his shoulders; "without taking into account that the Icelandic language has the three numbers like the Greek, and declines proper names like the Latin."

"Does it?" said I, a little roused from my indifference. "And is the type good?"

"Type? Who is talking of type, you poor, ignorant Axel. So, you suppose this was printed! You ignoramus! It is a manuscript, and a Runic manuscript, too."

"Runic?"

"Yes. Are you going to ask me to explain that word, next?"

"Not if I know it," I replied, in a tone of wounded vanity.

But my uncle never heeded me, and went on with his instructions, telling me about things I did not care to know.

"The Runic characters were formerly used in Iceland, and, according to tradition, were invented by Odin himself. Look at them, and admire them, impious young man!—these types sprang from the imagination of a god."

The only reply I could think of was to prostrate myself, for this sort of answer must be as pleasing to gods as to men, since it has the advantage of never embarrassing them. But before I could do this the current of the conversation was changed in an instant by the sudden appearance of a dirty parchment, which slipped out of the old book and fell on the floor.

My uncle pounced on this treasure with avidity, as can easily be supposed. An ancient document, shut up in an old volume, perhaps from time immemorial, could not fail to be of priceless value in his eyes.

"What is this?" he exclaimed, carefully spreading out on his table a piece of parchment, five inches long and three wide, on which some incomprehensible characters were inscribed in long transverse lines.

I give the *exact facsimile*, for great importance attaches to these fantastic marks, as they led Professor Lidenbrock and his nephew to undertake the strangest expedition of the nineteenth century.

The professor looked at the queer characters for some minutes, and then pushed up his spectacles and said:

"It is Runic! these marks are exactly like those in the manuscript of Snorre Turleson. But what can they mean?"

As Runic appeared to me an invention of learned men to mystify the poor world, I was not sorry to see that my uncle could not decipher it. At least I judged so from the convulsive working of his fingers.

"Yet it is the ancient Icelandic!" he muttered to himself.

And Professor Lidenbrock could not but know this, for he was considered a veritable polyglot. Not that he could speak fluently the 2,000 languages and 4,000 dialects used on the surface of the globe, but he was familiar with a good part of them.

A difficulty like this, then, was sure to rouse all the impetuosity of his nature, and I was just expecting a violent scene, when two o'clock struck and Martha opened the study door and said:

"Soup is on the table."

"Pitch the soup to the devil and the cook too, and those who eat it."

Martha fled and I scampered after her, and hardly knowing how, found myself in my accustomed seat in the dining-room.

I waited a few minutes. The professor did not come. This was the first time to my knowledge that he has ever neglected the grave business of dinner.

And what a dinner, too! Parsley soup, a ham omelette, and sorrel *à la muscade*, a loin of veal, and a *compôte* of plums; and for dessert, *crevettes au sucre*, and all washed down with sparkling Moselle wine.

All this was what my uncle was going to lose for the sake of an old paper. Really, as a devoted nephew, I felt obliged to do his share of eating as well as my own, and I did it conscientiously.

"I never saw the like of this!" exclaimed our good Martha, "Mr. Lidenbrock not to come to dinner! It is incredible! This bodes something serious," went on the old servant, shaking her head.

In my opinion it boded nothing except a frightful outbreak when my uncle found his dinner devoured.

I was just finishing my last *crevette* when a loud thundering summons tore me away from my voluptuous enjoyment. I made one bound into the study.

III

"It is evidently Runic," said the professor, knitting his brows, "but there is a secret in it, and I will discover it, or else—"

A violent gesture completed his sentence.

"Sit down there," he added, pointing to the table with his fist, "and write."

I was ready in an instant.

"Now, then, I am going to dictate to you each letter of our alphabet which corresponds to one of these Icelandic characters. We shall see what that will give us. But by St. Michael take care you make no mistake."

The dictation commenced. I did my best. Every letter was called out one after another, and formed the following incomprehensible succession of words:

m.rnlls	*esreuel*	*seecJde*
sgtssmf	*unteief*	*niedrke*
kt,Samn	*atrateS*	*Saodrrn*
emtnaeI	*nuaect*	*rrilSa*
Atvaar	*.nscrc*	*ieaabs*
ccdrmi	*eeutul*	*frantu*
dt,iac	*oseibo*	*Kediil*

When I had finished it my uncle snatched the paper from me and examined it attentively a long time.

"What can it mean?" he repeated mechanically.

On my honor I could not tell him. Besides, he did not ask me, he was speaking to himself.

"It is what we call a cryptogram, where the meaning is concealed by confusing the letters designedly, and to make an intelligible sentence they must be arranged in proper order. To think that here perhaps lies the explanation or indication of some great discovery!"

For my own part, I thought it was absolute nonsense, but I was wise enough to keep my opinion to myself.

The professor took up the book and the parchment again, and compared them.

"The two writings are not done by the same hand," he said. "The cryptogram is of later date than the book. On the very face of it there is an irrefragable proof of it. The first letter is a double *m*, which would be sought in vain in Turleson's book, for it was only added to the Icelandic alphabet in the fourteenth century. Consequently, there are at least 200 years between the manuscript and the document."

This certainly seemed logical enough.

"I therefore come to the conclusion," continued my uncle, "that these mysterious characters were inscribed by some one who came into possession of the book. But who on earth was it? Could he have put his name, I wonder, in any part of the manuscript?"

And my uncle pushed up his spectacles, and taking a powerful magnifying-glass, began to examine carefully the first pages of the book. On the back of the first leaf he discovered a spot, which looked like a blot of ink. But, on closer inspection, sundry letters, half obliterated, could be distinguished. My uncle saw instantly that this was the chief point of interest, and fastened on it furiously, poring over it through his big magnifying-glass, till at last he made out these marks, Runic characters, which he read off immediately.

"Arne Saknussemm!" he cried, in a triumphant tone. "Why, that is a name, and an Icelandic name, too; that of a celebrated alchemist, a *savant* who lived in the sixteenth century."

I looked at my uncle with a feeling of admiration. "These alchemists," he went on, "Avicenna, Bacon, Lully, Paracelsus, were the true, the only savants of their times. They made discoveries that may well astonish us. Why should not this Saknussemm have hidden under this incomprehensible cryptogram the secret of some surprising invention? It must be so. It is."

The professor's imagination was enkindled at this hypothesis.

"No doubt," I ventured to reply; "but what interest could the savant have in concealing a wonderful discovery?"

"Why? Why? Ah, don't I know? Didn't Galileo act so about Saturn? Besides, we shall soon see. I will get the secret of this document; I will neither eat nor sleep till I find it out."

"Oh!" thought I.

"No more shall you, Axel!"

"Plague it!" said I to myself. "It's a good job I have had a dinner for two to-day!"

"The first thing to be done," said my uncle, "is to find the language of the cipher."

I pricked up my ears at this. My uncle continued his soliloquy.

"Nothing is easier. In this document there are 132 letters, in which there are 79 consonants and 53 vowels. Now this is just about the proportion found in the words of southern languages, while the northern idioms are far richer in consonants. Consequently this must be in a southern language."

His conclusions were very just.

"But what language is it?"

It was this I waited for him to tell me, for I knew he was a profound analyst.

"This Saknussemm," he went on, "was a learned man, and since he did not write in his mother tongue, he would be sure to employ the language in common use among the cultivated minds of the sixteenth century; I mean the Latin. If I am mistaken, I could try the Spanish, the French, the Italian, the Greek, the Hebrew. But the learned in the sixteenth century generally wrote in Latin. I may rightly, then, say, *à priori*—this is in Latin."

I started, for my recollections of Latinity revolted against the pretension of this assemblage of uncouth words to belong to the soft tongue of Virgil.

"Yes, Latin," repeated my uncle; "but tangled Latin."

"So be it," thought I. "And if you disentangle it, my uncle, you'll be clever."

"Let us examine it thoroughly," he said, taking up the sheet again on which I had been writing. "Here are 132 letters in evident disorder. In some words there are nothing but consonants, as in the first, *m.rnlls*; others where the vowels, on the contrary, abound—the fifth, for example, *unteief*, or the last but one, *oseibo*. Now this arrangement has, clearly, not been designed. It is the mathematical result of the unknown law which ruled the succession of these letters. It seems to me certain that the primitive phrase has been written regularly, and then turned upside down, according to some law I must find out. Any one who had the key of the cipher could read it fluently. But where is the key? Have you got it, Axel?"

I made no reply, and for a good reason. My gaze was fixed on a portrait hanging on the wall opposite me, the portrait of Gräuben, my uncle's ward, who was just now at Altona, on a visit to her relations, and her absence made me very unhappy, for—I may as well confess it now—the pretty Virlandaise and the professor's nephew loved each other with true German patience and placidity. We were betrothed, though unknown to my uncle, who was too much of a geologist to understand such sentiments. Gräuben was a charming young girl, a blonde, with blue eyes, rather inclined to be grave and solemn, but loving me none the less for that. For my part, I worshiped her, if there is such a word in the Teutonic language. The image of my little Virlandaise transported me in an instant from the world of realities to a world of fancies and memories.

I could see my faithful companion in labors and pastimes. Every day she helped me to put my uncle's precious collection of stones in order and put on the labels. Indeed Miss Gräuben was quite a mineralogist. She would have put more than one *savant* to the blush. She loved to dive into the deepest questions of science. What delightful hours we had spent in studying together, and how often I had envied the unconscious stones handled by her charming hands!

And when our tasks were over, how we used to go out and wander along the shady walks by the Alster, and then repair to the old black, tarred mill, which looks so picturesque at the far end of the lake, chatting all the way and holding each other's hands! I used to tell her droll stories which made her laugh heartily, and beguiled the time till we reached the banks of the Elbe, and after saying "Good night" to the swans, which swim about among the tall white irises, we returned to the quay of the steamboat.

I had just got to this point when my day-dream was rudely interrupted by a violent rap on the table from my uncle's knuckles, which recalled me to reality.

"Look here!" he said, "it seems to me that if one wished to mix up and confuse any sentence, the first thing he would think of would be to write the words vertically instead of horizontally, in groups of five or six."

"Indeed!" thought I.

"We must see what that makes. Write some sentence on this bit of paper, but, instead of putting the letters one after the other, put them in vertical columns, grouping them in numbers of five or six." I understood what he meant, and immediately wrote from top to bottom.

*J	m	n	e	G	e
e	e	,	t	r	n
t'	b	m	i	ä	!
a	i	a	t	u	
i	e	p	e	b	

"Very good!" said the professor, without reading it. "Now arrange these words in horizontal lines."

I obeyed, and this sentence was the result:

JmneGe ee,trn t'bmiä! aiatu iepeb

"Perfectly so," said my uncle, seizing the paper from my hands. "This has the look of the old document already. Vowels and consonants are grouped in the same disorder. There are even capitals in the same way in the middle of words, and also commas, exactly as in the parchment of Saknussemm."

I could not but think these remarks very ingenious.

"Now, then," said my uncle, addressing me, "I don't know what sentence you have written, but all I need to do to enable me to read it is

---

* I love thee well, my little Gräuben.

to take the first letter of each word in succession, and then the second, and then the third, and so on."

And to his great amazement, and certainly still more to mine, my uncle read:

Je t'aime bien, ma petite Gräuben!

"Eh, what?" said the professor.

Positively, like a love-sick fool, I had written this tell-tale sentence, without knowing it.

"Ah! you love Gräuben," resumed the professor, in a thoroughly magisterial tone.

"Yes—No—" I stammered out.

"Ah! you love Gräuben," he repeated, mechanically. "Well, well, let us try my method with the document in question."

My uncle was completely absorbed again in his subject of contemplation, and had already forgotten my imprudent words. I say imprudent, for a *savant's* head cannot understand *affaires du coeur*, but fortunately the great business of the document carried him away completely.

Professor Lidenbrock's eyes flashed like lightning through his spectacles, and his fingers trembled as he took up the old parchment again to make his important experiment. He was greatly excited. At last he coughed violently, and in a grave tone read out the following letters, naming successively the first of each word, and then the second, and so on as he had done in my unfortunate sentence.

mmessunkaSenrA.icefdoK.segnittamurtn
ecertserrette,rotaivsadua,ednecsedsadne
lacartniiiluJsiratracSarbmutabiledmek
meretarcsilucoIseffenSnI

I must confess I felt excited as I ended the series. The letters themselves, named one by one, sounded perfectly meaningless, but I fully expected to hear my uncle come out in a pompous style with some magnificent piece of Latinity.

But who could have thought it! instead of this a tremendous thump of his fist sent the table spinning, jerked out the ink, and made my pen fly out of my hands.

"That's not it," he thundered out. "It does not make sense."

Next minute he was off like a shot, rushing down the stairs with the speed of an avalanche, and away out into the street as fast as his legs could carry him.

IV

He is gone!" cried Martha, running up to see what the noise was about, for the door closed with such a bang that it shook the house from top to bottom.

"Yes," I replied, "clean gone."

"And without his dinner?"

"He won't have any!"

"Nor supper either?" said the old domestic.

"Nor supper either," I said.

"What!" exclaimed Martha, clasping her hands.

"No, my good Martha, he will neither eat any more himself, nor allow any one else in the house to eat."

"Goodness me! Then there is nothing for us but starvation?"

I did not dare to say that with such an autocrat as my uncle this was our inevitable fate.

The old servant was evidently alarmed, however, and went back to her kitchen sighing.

Now that I was alone, the thought came into my head, that I would go and tell Gräuben the whole affair. But how could I get away? The professor might be back any moment. And suppose he called me, and wanted to recommence his logogryphical labors, which old Œdipus himself would not have undertaken? And if I am not forthcoming, what would be the consequence?

The wisest plan was to stay, and I had plenty to do, for a mineralogist in Besançon had just forwarded us a collection of silicious nodules, which had to be classified. I set to work, picking out, labeling, and arranging in their glass-case all these hollow stones, full of small glittering crystals.

But this occupation did not engross me entirely. Strangely enough, I could not get the old document out of my mind. My brain was disturbed, and an uneasy feeling began to steal over me. I had the presentiment of some approaching catastrophe.

In the course of an hour, all the stones were in their right places, and I ensconced myself in the large velvet easy-chair, swinging myself, and throwing back my head. I lighted my "hookah," the carved bowl of which represented a Naiad reclining carelessly. I amused myself with watching the progress of carbonization which was gradually turning my Naiad into a thorough negress, and kept listening for footsteps on the stair. But there was not a sound. Where could my uncle be? I fancied him striding along the road to Altona, among the beautiful trees, gesticulating, and making cuts at the wall with his stick; thrashing the grass vigorously, nipping off the tops of the thistles, and disturbing the tranquility of the solitary storks.

Would he come back triumphant or dejected? Would he master the secret, or give it up? As I was thus questioning myself, I mechanically took up the paper on which I had written the incomprehensible series of letters, and I said:

"What can this mean?"

I tried to group the letters so as to form words. It was impossible. Let me arrange them as I might, putting two or three, or five, or six together, I could make no intelligible sense. True, the 14th, 15th, and 16th would make the English word *ice*, and the 83rd, 84th, and 85th would make *sir*, and also, in the middle of the document, I noticed the Latin words, *rota, mutabile, ira, nec, atra.*

"Hang it!" I said to myself, "these last words certainly do go to prove my uncle is right about the language in which the document is written." And in the 4th line again, I noticed the word *luco*, which means the *sacred wood*. On the other hand, I read in the 3rd line the word *tabiled, a.* thoroughly Hebrew expression, and on the last, the vocables *mer, arc, mère*, which are pure French.

It was enough to craze one. Four different idioms in this meaningless sentence. What connection could there be between the words *ice, sir, colère, cruel, sacred wood, chair, grant, mère, arc*, or *mer*? The first and the last might easily be brought together since there was nothing astonishing in finding a *sea of ice* mentioned in a document written in Iceland. But as for understanding the remainder of the cryptogram, that was quite another thing.

I fought and fought with this insurmountable difficulty, gazing fixedly at the document till my brain grew giddy, and the letters seemed whirling round my head.

A sort of hallucination came over me. I felt stifled, as if from want of air, and involuntarily began to fan myself with the sheet of paper. The back and front of it alternately met my eye, and as it waved rapidly to and fro I fancied I could see on the back some perfectly legible Latin words, amongst others *craterem* and *terrestre.*

Light broke in on my mind instantly. I caught a glimpse of the clue. I had found the key to the cipher. To understand this document it was not even necessary to read it through the back of the page. No, just as it was, exactly as he had dictated it to me, it could be spelled out easily. The professor was right in his arrangement of the letters, and right about the language of the document. A mere nothing would enable him to read the whole sentence fluently, and this mere nothing chance had just revealed to me.

It may be imagined how excited I was. My eyes began to swim and I could scarcely see. I had spread out the paper on the table, and one glance would make me possessor of the secret.

At last I managed to calm myself somewhat. I made myself walk twice round the room to quiet my nerves, and then dropped again into the capacious arm-chair.

"Now, then, we'll read it," I exclaimed, taking a long breath.

I leaned over the table, and, placing my finger on each letter in succession, read the whole sentence aloud.

But what stupefaction, what terror seized me! I sat motionless, as if paralyzed. What! Had any one really ever done what I had just read? Had any mortal man been bold enough to make the search?

"But no, no!" I cried, leaping up from my chair; "my uncle shall not know it. He would not be satisfied with the mere knowledge of the fact. He would undertake the journey for himself. Nothing could hinder him. Such a daring geologist as he is would start off in spite of everything, come what might! And he would drag me with him, and we should never return. Never! Never!"

I cannot describe my state of agitation.

"No, no, that shall never be," I said, passionately, "and since I can prevent my tyrant from getting such a notion into his head, I will. If he were to begin twisting and turning the document about he might chance to discover the key. We'll destroy it."

There was still a spark of fire in the grate. I snatched up both the sheet of paper and the parchment of Saknussemm, and, with a feverish hand, was just going to fling them on the hot embers, and make an entire end of the dangerous secret, when the study door opened and my uncle appeared.

V

I had only just time to replace the unfortunate document on the table. Professor Lidenbrock seemed absorbed in his own meditations. His ruling thought allowed him not a moment's respite. He had evidently been poring over the subject and analyzing it, and bringing all the resources of his imagination to bear upon it during his walk, and he had come back to try some new combination.

In fact, he was no sooner in than he seated himself in his arm-chair, and taking up his pen, began a fresh formula, which resembled some algebraic calculation.

My eyes followed his trembling hand; not one of his movements escaped me. What unhoped-for result was he suddenly about to produce? I trembled, and yet needlessly, for since the right combination and the only one had been already found, all further search must of necessity be useless.

For three long hours my uncle continued his labors without speaking or even lifting his hand, blotting out and doing again, erasing and making a fresh beginning a thousand times.

I knew quite well that if he succeeded in arranging the letters in all the relative positions they could occupy the right sentence would come out. But I also knew that twenty letters only can form two quintillions, 432 quadrillions, 902 trillions, 8 billions, 1,175 millions, 640,000 combinations. Now there were 132 letters in the sentence, and these 132 letters would make a number of different sentences, composed of 133 ciphers at least, a number almost impossible to enumerate or adequately conceive.

I therefore reassured myself on the score of this heroic method of solving the problem.

However, the time passed away and night drew on. The noisy street had become still, but my uncle, still stooping down over his task, saw nothing, not even his good old Martha, when she ventured to open the door partially and say:

"Will you take any supper, sir?"

He never heard her, and the worthy old servant had to go away without getting an answer. For myself, I held up as long as I could, but at last weariness overpowered me completely, and I fell sound asleep on the end of the sofa, while my uncle still continued his calculations and erasures.

When I woke next morning the indefatigable worker was still at his task. His red eyes and wan face, and wild disordered hair, through which he was constantly drawing his feverish fingers, and the crimson spots on his cheeks, all told the story of a terrible struggle with the impossible.

Really he moved my pity. I could not but feel for him, much as I might justly blame him. The poor man was so completely engrossed with one idea that he forgot to put himself in a passion. All the vital powers were concentrated on one single point, and I began to fear the long strain on them, without any escape by their usual safety-valve, would positively end in some internal explosion.

I could have relaxed this tension by a single gesture or word, and yet I did not.

Still, I was acting from a kind motive. For my uncle's sake I remained silent.

"No, no," I said to myself, "I won't say a word. He would want to go then, I know he would. He would risk his life to do what no other geologist has done. I'll say nothing about it, I will keep this secret chance has revealed to me. It would be the professor's death. Let him guess it if he can. I'll not have to reproach myself, at any rate, with having disclosed it."

My resolution taken, I crossed my arms and waited. But I was not prepared for a circumstance which occurred some hours later.

When Martha went to go out as usual to market, she found the door locked. The great key was gone. Who had taken it? My uncle must, of course, when he returned from his hasty walk the night before.

But had he taken it purposely, or through inadvertence? Did he really want to subject us to the horrors of starvation? This seemed to me going too far. Were Martha and I to be victimized for what did not concern us in the least? No doubt of it, for I remembered a precedent which might well frighten us. Some years before, when my uncle was engaged on his great mineralogical classification, he ate nothing whatever for forty-eight hours, and made his entire household feed on this scientific diet. I well remember the sharp twinges in my internal regions I got through it, for such diet was not very satisfying for a boy like me, naturally inclined to be rather voracious. It certainly appeared we would have to dispense with breakfast, as we had with supper the preceding night However, I determined to be heroic and stand out in spite of hunger. Martha was quite distressed, and looked very grave over it. What troubled me most was that I could not get out of the house. That was a great grievance, as may easily be supposed.

My uncle still labored on. His imagination was wandering in the ideal world of combinations. He lived above the earth, and really above earthly wants.

Towards noon the pangs of hunger made themselves seriously felt. Martha, innocently enough, had eaten up all that was left in the larder the night before. There was nothing whatever in the house. I still stood out, though; I made it a point of honor.

Two o'clock struck. The thing was becoming ridiculous, and even intolerable. I began to see matters in a different light, and thought I had been exaggerating the importance of the document; that my uncle would not believe in it, that he would consider it a mere hoax, and that even if the worse came to the worst, and he wished to attempt the adventurous journey, he could be prevented by main force; and finally, I thought he may, perhaps, discover the secret for himself, and I shall only get my fasting for my pains.

These appeared excellent reasons to me now, though the night before I had rejected them indignantly. I even thought I had been acting absurdly in waiting so long, and determined to give the solution of the mystery without further delay.

I was just waiting for a suitable opportunity, not wishing to be too abrupt, when the professor got up, and taking his hat, was about to go out.

What! Was I going to let him leave the house, and shut us all in again? Never.

"Uncle!" I said. He did not seem to hear me.

"Uncle Lidenbrock!" I repeated in a louder tone.

"Eh? What?" he said, like a man suddenly roused from sleep.

"Well! Have you got the key?"

"What key? The key of the door!"

"No," I replied; "the key of the document."

The professor looked at me above his spectacles, and no doubt noticed something unusual in my face, for he seized my arm sharply, and, without saying a word, gazed at me inquiringly.

Never was question put more plainly.

I nodded my head.

He shook his in a pitying sort of manner, as if he thought he had to do with a fool.

I made a still more affirmative gesture. His eyes sparkled, and his grip became threatening.

This mute conversation of ours would have interested the most indifferent spectator, and really I hardly dared to speak now, for I was afraid he would stifle me with embraces in his joy. But he became so pressing, that I was forced to reply.

"Yes," I said, "this key has by chance—"

"What are you saying?" he cried, with indescribable agitation.

"Here! Take this," I replied, handing him the piece of paper on which I had written what he dictated. "Read."

"But there is no sense in that!" he said, crushing up the paper.

"No, not if you begin at the beginning, but if you begin at the end—"

Before I had time to finish the sentence, the professor gave a cry, or rather I should say a perfect roar. A revelation had come to him. He looked transfigured.

"Ah! ingenious Saknussemm!" he exclaimed. "Your phrase was written backwards then!"

And, snatching up the sheet, he read in tones full of emotion, the entire document, beginning at the last letter. It was as follows:—

In Sneffels Yoculis craterem Rem delibat umbra Scartaris Julii intra calendas descende, audas viator, et terrestre centrum attinges. Kod feci. Arne Saknussemm.

Bad Latin, which may be translated thus:

Descend the crater of the Jokul of Snäfell, that the shadow of Scartaris softly touches before the Kalends of July, bold traveler, and thou wilt reach the center of the earth. Which I have done. Arne Saknussemm.

My uncle gave a leap as he read this, as if suddenly touched by a Leyden jar. He was magnificent in his joy, and daring, and conviction. He went up and down the room, clasped his hands over his head, moved about the chairs, piled up the books. It seems almost incredible, but he began to toss about his precious specimens of stones; he gave a thump with his fist here and a tap there. At last he grew calmer, and sank down in his arm-chair as if exhausted.

"What time is it?" he asked, after a brief silence.

"Three o'clock," I replied.

"Stop! I have had no dinner! I'm starving. Let us go and have it at once, and then afterwards—"

"Afterwards?"

"Pack my trunk."

"Eh? What?" I cried.

"And your own, too," added the merciless professor, as he passed into the dining-room.

VI

These words made me shudder, but I restrained myself, and resolved to put a good face on it. Only scientific arguments would be of any avail with Professor Lidenbrock. But such arguments there were, and good ones, against the possibility of such a journey. To go to the center of the earth! What folly! However, I reserved my dialectics for a fitting moment and concerned myself about dinner.

It would be useless to repeat my uncle's imprecations when he found a bare table. All was explained and our worthy domestic was forthwith liberated. She hurried immediately to the market, and made such successful purchases that, in about an hour, my hunger was appeased and I was able to realize my situation fully.

During the meal my uncle was almost merry. He then indulged in a few jokes—very harmless ones certainly. After dessert he beckoned me into his study.

I obeyed. He seated himself at one end of the table and I took the other.

"Axel!" he said, in a rather gentle tone, "you are a very ingenious fellow. You have done me a noble service just when, weary of the struggle, I was about to give up the combination. What wrong tracks should I have got into then? Who can say? I shall never forget this, my boy, and you shall have a share in the glory we are about to gain."

"Come," thought I, "he's in a good humor; now's the time to discuss the glory."

"Above all," continued my uncle, "I enjoin upon you the most absolute secrecy. You understand me. There are *savants* who are envious of me, and many would undertake this journey who will never know of it till we return."

"Do you think there are so many bold enough to venture?"

"Certainly. Who would hesitate to win such fame? If this document were known, a whole army of geologists would rush after Arne Saknussemm."

"That is just what I doubt, uncle, for there is no proof of the authenticity of the document."

"What! Didn't we discover it in the book?"

"Yes, and I grant that Saknussemm wrote those lines; but does it follow that he really accomplished the journey, and may not this old parchment be all a hoax?"

This last word was rather hazardous, and I almost regretted I had said it. The professor knitted his brows, and I was afraid I had seriously damaged my cause. Fortunately no remark was made. A faint smile, indeed, was discernible on my stern interlocutor's lips, as he replied:

"That is what we shall see for ourselves."

"Ah!" said I, "but perhaps you will allow me to exhaust my stock of objections to the document?"

"Speak your mind freely, my boy. I allow you perfect liberty of opinion. You are no longer my nephew, but my colleague. Go on, then."

"Well, I should like to know at the outset what this Jokul, and Snäfell, and Scartaris are. I have never heard of them before."

"I have no difficulty in telling you that. I happened, just a short time ago, to get a map from my friend Augustus Peterman, of Leipsic, and it could not have come more opportunely. Fetch the third Atlas, in the second row of the large library, list G, plate 4."

I got up, and, thanks to these precise directions, found the atlas wanted. My uncle opened it and said:

"Here is one of the best maps of Iceland—Handersen's, and I daresay it will solve all our difficulties."

I leaned over it, and the professor said:

"Look at this island, composed of volcanoes, and notice that they all bear the name of Jokul. This word means *Glacierus*, Icelandic; and in the high latitude of Iceland most of the eruptions break out through sheets of ice. The name Jokul applies, therefore, to all the eruptive mountains in the island."

"Well, and what is this Snäfell?" I replied.

I hoped he would not be able to answer this query, but I was mistaken; my uncle began again:

"Follow me along the western side of Iceland. Do you see Reikiavik, the capital? Yes. Well, go up the innumerable fiords on the shore, and stop a little below the 65° of latitude. What do you see there?"

"A sort of peninsula, like a long bare bone, ending in an enormous knee-pan."

"A very good comparison, my boy. Now do you see nothing on this knee-pan?"

"Yes, a mountain, which seems to have risen out of the sea."

"Well, that is a Snäfell."

"Snäfell?"

"Its very self. It is a mountain 5,000 feet high, one of the most remarkable in the island, and assuredly the most celebrated in the whole world, if its crater leads to the center of the globe."

"But that is impossible!" I exclaimed, shrugging my shoulders.

"Impossible?" repeated the professor sternly; "and pray why?"

"Because the crater is evidently blocked up by lava, burning rocks, and because—"

"And what if the crater is extinct?"

"Extinct?"

"Yes. The number of active volcanoes on the surface of the globe is only about 300, but extinct volcanoes are to be found in far larger numbers. Now, among these last is Snäfell, and the only eruption on record took place in 1219. From that date the rumblings began to die away gradually, till now it is no longer ranked among the active volcanoes."

To positive declarations like these I had absolutely no reply to make. I had, therefore, to pass on to the other obscurity in the document.

"What does this word *Scartaris* mean? and what have the Kalends of July to do with it?" I asked.

My uncle took a few minutes to think, and I began to hope. But only for an instant, as he soon went on again, and said:

"What you call obscurity is to me light. This proves the ingenious pains Saknussemm has taken to make his discovery clear. Snäfell is composed of several craters, it was therefore necessary to indicate which one led to the center of the globe. How has the Icelandic *savant* done it? He has remarked that 'as the Kalends of July approached,' that is to say, about the end of June, 'one of the mountain peaks, the *Scartaris*, projects its shadow over the opening of the crater in question'; and this fact he states in the document. Could any one imagine a more exact indication, and the summit of Snäfell once reached, could there be the least doubt which road to take."

Positively, my uncle had an answer for everything. I soon saw all attack against the words of the parchment would be useless. I therefore ceased to discuss the subject, and went on to the scientific objections to the journey.

"Well then," I said, "I am obliged to confess, the sentence is plain enough, and leaves no doubt on the mind. I even grant that the document appears perfectly authentic. This *savant* has been to the bottom of Snäfell; he has seen the shadow of Scartaris fall softly over the edges of the crater, towards the Kalends of July; he has even heard legendary tales, that this crater leads to the center of the earth; but to believe that he has reached it himself, that he ever made the journey, or came back if he did, no! a hundred times no! I say to that."

"And your reason?" said my uncle, in a peculiarly bantering tone.

"My reason is, that all the theories of science prove the impracticability of such an enterprise."

"All the theories say so?" replied the professor good-humoredly. "Ah! those tiresome theories! How they hamper us, those poor theories!"

I saw he was making fun of me, but I went on notwithstanding.

"Yes," I said. "It is well known that heat increases about 1° in 70 feet below the earth's surface. Now, at this rate, the temperature at the center must be over 20,000°, since the radius of the earth is about 4,000 miles. Everything in the interior must consequently be in an inflamed gaseous state; for metals, gold or platinum, and even the hardest rocks, could not resist such a heat. I am justified, therefore, in asking if it would be possible to get there?"

"So it is the heat, then, Axel, that stumbles you?"

"Undoubtedly. If we even only reached the depth of the earth's crust, we should find the temperature was above 1,300°."

"And you are afraid of passing into a state of fusion?"

"I leave you to settle that question," I said crossly.

"This is what I settle," replied Professor Lidenbrock, mounting the high horse; "that neither you, nor anyone else, knows anything certain that is going on in the center of the earth, seeing that we scarcely know the 12,000th part of its radius, that science is eminently perfectible, and that each theory has constantly to give way to a fresh one. Was it not believed, till Fourier's time, that the temperature of the planetary spaces was constantly decreasing, and is it not known now that the greatest cold does not exceed 40° or 50° below zero? Why should it not be so with the internal heat? Why should there not be a certain limit beyond which it cannot increase?"

I could not reply to this, since my uncle now placed the question in the regions of hypothesis, and he went on to say:

"And now let me tell you that many learned men, Poisson amongst others, have proved that if the temperature of the center of the earth was 20,000°, the incandescent gases, arising from the molten materials, would acquire such elasticity that the crust would burst like a steam boiler."

"That is only Poisson's opinion, uncle, that's all!"

"Certainly; but other distinguished geologists agree with him in thinking that the interior of the globe is neither formed of gas nor water, nor of the heaviest minerals known, for in that case the earth's gravity would be twice less."

"Oh, figures can be made to prove anything!"

"And facts, too, my boy. Is it not unquestionable that the number of volcanoes has considerably decreased since the early days of the world; and if great central heat existed, would it be likely to get less powerful?"

"If you enter the field of suppositions, uncle, I have nothing more to say on the subject."

"And I have to say that my opinion is supported by that of very competent judges. Do you remember a visit Sir Humphry Davy, the celebrated chemist, paid me in 1825?"

"Not the least, since I only came into the world nineteen years afterwards."

"Well, Humphry Davy came to see me, in passing through Hamburg, and, among other topics, we had a long discussion on the hypothesis that the center of the earth was in a liquid state. We both agree that this liquidity was impossible, for a reason to which science can find no reply."

"And what is it?" I asked in surprise.

"It is this—that the liquid mass would be subject, like the ocean, to the moon's attractions, and that, consequently, twice a day there would be tides which would heave up the earth's crust, and cause periodical earthquakes."

"But still it is evident that the face of the globe has undergone combustion at some period, and it is allowable to suppose that the exterior crust cooled first, and the heat took refuge in the center."

"It is erroneous," replied my uncle. "The earth has been heated by the combustion of its surface, not otherwise. This surface was composed of a great quantity of metals, such as potassium and sodium, which have the property of igniting by mere contact with air and water. These metals take fire when the atmospheric vapors fall on the ground in the form of rain, and as the water gradually penetrates the cracks in the earth's crust, they cause fresh fires, which burst out in explosions and eruptions. This is why volcanoes were so frequent in the early ages."

"That certainly is a clever hypothesis!" I could not help exclaiming.

"And Humphry Davy made me see it by a very simple experiment. He made a metallic ball of those metals, chiefly which I have just mentioned, which perfectly represented the globe. On this he squirted a sort of fine dust, and the surface began to puff up and get oxidized, and assume the shape of a little mountain. A crater opened in the top, and an eruption took place, which communicated such intense heat to the whole ball that it could not be held in the hand."

Positively I began to be shaken by the professor's arguments, heightened as their effect was by his usual fire and enthusiasm.

"You see, Axel," he added, "geologists have raised diverse hypotheses about the earth's center, but nothing has been less proved than the existence of great heat. According to me it does not exist, it cannot exist, but we will go and see, and, like Arne Saknussemm, find out for ourselves who is right."

"Yes, that we will!" I exclaimed, carried away by his enthusiasm. "We shall see, that's to say, if we can see at all there."

"And why not? May we not reckon on some electric light, and even on the atmosphere, for the pressure, as it approached the center, would render it luminous."

"Yes, it is possible after all."

"It is certain," replied my uncle triumphantly. "But silence, remember; silence about the whole business. Let no one take it into his head before us to try and discover the center of the earth."

VII

So ended this memorable conversation. It had put me in a perfect fever. I was quite giddy when I left my uncle's study, and there was not air enough in the streets of Hamburg to revive me. I went along the shore of the Elbe, beside the little stream which conveys passengers to the Hamburg railway station.

Was I convinced by what I had been hearing, or was it merely the professor's power that had conquered me? Must I treat this project seriously? Had I been listening to the mad speculations of a fool, or the scientific deductions of a great genius? And in it all, where did the truth end and error begin?

A thousand contradictory hypotheses floated before my mind, and there was nothing I could lay hold of.

However, I recollected I had felt convinced, though my enthusiasm began to cool down, but I would have liked to start immediately, before I had time for reflection. Yes, I could have strapped my portmanteau and set off that moment.

But, I must confess that, within an hour, this unnatural excitement left me. My nervous tension relaxed, and I was able to ascend from the depths of the earth to the surface once more.

"It is absurd!" I exclaimed. "It is not common sense. It is not a rational proposal to make to a sensible lad. Nothing of the sort exists. I have not slept well, and I have had a bad dream."

Meantime I had followed the shores of the Elbe, and got past the town. After I came out of the harbor, I took the road to Altona, in obedience to a presentiment which after events justified, for I soon descried my little Gräuben tripping along on her way home to Hamburg.

"Gräuben!" I shouted in the distance.

The girl stopped, rather put about, I should imagine, at hearing her name called out on the public road. A few steps, and I was beside her.

"Axel!" she said, in surprise. "Ah! you came to meet me; I know you did, sir."

But when she looked at me she could not but notice how upset and worried I looked.

"What is the matter?" she said, holding out her hand.

"The matter, Gräuben?"

A few brief sentences told her the whole affair. She was silent for a minute. Did her heart throb like mine? I didn't know, but the hand I held in my own did not tremble in the least. We had gone a hundred steps without speaking, and then she said:

"Axel!"

"Dear Gräuben," I replied.

"This will be a great journey."

I gave a jump.

"Yes Axel, a journey worthy of the nephew of a *savant*. It is right for a man to distinguish himself by some great enterprise."

"What! Gräuben! Wouldn't you dissuade me from attempting such an undertaking?"

"No, dear Axel. I would gladly accompany you and your uncle, but a poor girl like me would only be an encumbrance."

"Is that the truth?"

"Perfect truth."

Ah, those women and young girls—female hearts—always incomprehensible. You are either the most timid or the bravest of beings. Reason has nothing to do with you. The idea of this child encouraging me in this expedition, and being willing to go herself, too; even urging me to it, though she loved me!

I was somewhat nettled, and why should I not own it—ashamed as well.

"Gräuben," I replied, "we'll see if you will say so to-morrow."

"To-morrow, dear Axel, I shall say the same as to-day."

"After all," thought I to myself, "the Kalends of July are a long way off yet, and many things may happen before that which may cure my uncle's craze for an underground journey."

It was late in the evening when we reached the house in Königstrasse. I expected to find everything quiet and my uncle gone to bed, as usual, and Martha in the dining-room with her dusting-brush, making all straight for the night.

But I had not allowed for my uncle's impatience.

I found him shouting and running about among a troop of porters, who were unloading sundry goods in the passage. The old servant was at her wits' end.

"Come along, Axel, pray!" he called out, as soon as I came in sight. "Unfortunate fellow! Here is your portmanteau not packed, and my papers not arranged, and the key of my traveling-bag not to be found, and my gaiters not come!"

I stood dumbfounded. Voice failed me. My lips could scarcely articulate the words:

"We are going, then?"

"Yes, unlucky boy, wandering about instead of being here!"

"We are really going?" I repeated feebly.

"Yes; the day after to-morrow, at dawn."

I could not bear to hear more, and flew to my own little room.

There could be no doubt about it. My uncle had been employing his afternoon in getting some of the articles and utensils necessary for the journey. The passage was full of rope-ladders, slip-nooses, torches, gourds, cramp-irons, pickaxes, alpenstocks, mattocks, enough articles to load ten men at least.

I spent a terrible night. Next morning, I heard myself called quite early. I determined not to open the door, but who could resist the soft voice which said:

"Axel, dear Axel!"

I came out of my room thinking to myself that Gräuben would change her mind when she saw my pale, haggard face and eyes, red with want of sleep.

But as she met me, she said:

"Ah! you are better to-day, dear Axel, I see. Your night's rest has quieted you."

"Quieted me!"

I rushed to my mirror, and looked at myself. Well, I must confess I did not look so bad as I supposed. It was incredible.

"Axel," said Gräuben, "I have been having a long talk with my guardian. He is a bold *savant*, a man of great courage, and you must not forget his blood runs in your veins. He has told me all his plans and hopes, and why and how he expects to gain his object. He will succeed, I have no fear of it. Ah! Axel, it is a grand thing to devote one's self to science. What glory awaits Mr. Lidenbrock, and will be reflected on his companion! When you come back, Axel, you will be a man, an equal, free to speak, free to act, free to—"

The girl blushed, and did not finish the sentence. Her words animated me, but I still refused to believe that we were really going away. I dragged Gräuben off with me to the professor's study.

"Uncle!" I said, "is it quite settled that we are to go?"

"What! Have you any doubt about it?"

"No," I said, afraid of vexing him. "Only I want to know what's to hurry us so?"

"Why, time, to be sure—time which is fast flying, and can never be overtaken."

"But this is only the 26th of May, and between this and the end of June—"

"And do you suppose, you ignoramus, that we can get to Iceland so easily? If you had not gone off like a fool, I would have taken you with me to the Copenhagen office at Liffender's & Co., where you would have learnt that there is only one service between Copenhagen and Reikiavik, and that is on the 22nd of every month."

"Very well?"

"Very well; why if we wait till the 22nd of June, we shall arrive too late to see the shadow of Scartaris touch the crater of Snäfell. We must, therefore, get to Copenhagen as quickly as we can, and find out some means of transport. Go and pack your portmanteau."

There was not a word to say, and I went upstairs again to my room. Gräuben followed me. She undertook to arrange and stow away in a little portmanteau everything I needed for the journey. She was as cool and collected as if I had been going on a mere pleasure-trip to Lubeck, or Heligoland. Her little hands went quickly to work without the least haste or fluster. She talked calmly, and gave me most sensible reasons in favor of our expedition. She enchanted me, and I felt furious at leaving her. Sometimes I was going to break out in a passion, but she took no notice, and went on methodically with her tranquil occupation.

At length the last strap was buckled. I went down to the ground-floor.

All this day philosophical instruments, arms, electrical machines were being brought to the house. Martha did not know what to make of it.

"Is the master mad?" she said.

I made an affirmative gesture.

"And he is going to take you with him?"

I repeated the affirmative gesture.

"Where to?" she asked.

I pointed with my finger towards the heart of the earth.

"Into the cellars?" cried the old domestic.

"No," I said, at last; "lower down than that."

Evening came. I didn't know how the time went now.

"To-morrow morning," said my uncle, "we start at six precisely."

At 10 P.M. I fell on my bed like a lump of inert matter.

During the night my fears returned in full force.

I dreamt of abysses. I was delirious. I felt myself in the iron grip of the professor, being dragged away and engulfed. I was falling down terrific precipices, always getting lower and lower, with the ever-increasing velocity of bodies falling in space, and yet I never reached the bottom. It was one interminable descent.

At five o'clock I awoke, exhausted with fatigue and emotion. I repaired to the dining-room, and found my uncle already at table, devouring all that came in his way. I almost shuddered when I looked at him. But Gräuben was there, and I said nothing. I could not. At half-past five I heard the rattling of a vehicle coming down the street. It was a big coach to take us to the railway station at Altona. It was soon packed with my uncle's luggage.

"And where is your portmanteau?" he said to me.

"It is ready," I replied, turning faint.

"Make haste and fetch it down then, or you will make us lose the train."

To struggle against my fate seemed impossible. I went up to my room, rolled my portmanteau down the stairs, and followed it immediately.

My uncle was just putting the reins of government solemnly into Gräuben's hands. My pretty Virlandaise retained her habitual composure and embraced her guardian passionately, but she could not keep back a tear, which dropped on my face when her sweet lips touched my cheek.

"Gräuben!" I cried.

"Go, dear Axel, go!" she said. "You are leaving your betrothed, but you will find your wife when you come back."

I clasped her once more in my arms and then took my place in the coach. Martha and the young girl stood at the door waving us a last adieu, and next minute we were dashing along at a gallop towards Altona.

VIII

At Altona, which, in fact, was only a suburb of Hamburg, commenced the line of rail to Kiel, by which we were to get to the shores of the Belt.

In less than twenty minutes we entered the territory of Holstein, and at half-past six the coach stopped before the railway station. The numerous packages of my uncle were unloaded, weighed, labeled, and deposited in the luggage van, and at seven we took our seats opposite each other in the same compartment. A shriek from the whistle and we were off.

Was I resigned? Not yet. However, the fresh morning air and the constant variety of scene, as the train bore us swiftly on, diverted my mind somewhat from its preoccupation.

As to the professor, the engine was evidently much too slow for his impatience, and his thoughts were far ahead of it. We were alone in the carriage, but neither of us spoke. My uncle was turning out his pockets and his traveling-bag, and investigating everything with the most minute attention. I soon saw that he had secured whatever was necessary for the execution of his projects.

Among others there was one sheet of paper, bearing the heading of the Danish Consulate, with the signature of M. Christiensen, the consul at Hamburg, and a friend of the professor. This would give us every facility for obtaining introductions at Copenhagen for the governor of Iceland.

I also perceived the famous document carefully stowed away in the most secret pocket of his portfolio. I anathematized it in my deepest heart, and turned away to look out again at the window. The country through which we were passing was a vast succession of uninteresting, monotonous, muddy plains, though tolerably fertile; a country very favorable for making railroads, as it would allow of the straight lines so prized by railway companies.

But this monotony had not time to grow wearisome, for in three hours from the time we started, the train stopped at Kiel, a few steps from the sea.

Our luggage was registered for Copenhagen, so we did not need to trouble ourselves about it. However, the professor looked anxiously after his property, as it was being carried on board the steamer, till it disappeared into the hold.

My uncle, in his haste, had calculated so well that we found a whole day would be lost here, as the steamer, the *Ellenore*, did not sail till night.

Nine hours' fever was the result, during which the irascible traveler stormed and swore at the managers of the railways and steamers, and the Government which allowed such abuses. I had to join in with him when he attacked the captain on the subject, insisting on the furnaces being lighted, and the vessel put in motion immediately. The captain merely sent him about his business.

But at Kiel, as everywhere else, a day must come to an end. By dint of walking along the verdant shores of the bay, in the heart of which the little town is situated, and roaming through the thick woods, which give it the appearance of a nest among the branches, and admiring the villas, and racing about and fuming, the time passed, and ten o'clock struck.

Clouds of smoke puffed out from the *Ellenore*, and the bridge shook with the vibration of the boiler when we came on board and took possession of our berths in the one solitary cabin of the steamer.

At a quarter past ten the cable was let go, and the steamer began to thread her way rapidly through the gloomy waters of the Great Belt.

The night was dark. There was a fine breeze and a strong sea. Here and there, on the coast, lights glimmered. Farther on—I don't know where—a lighthouse shone brilliantly over the waves, and this is all I recollect about this first stage of our journey.

At 7 A.M. we disembarked at Körsor, a little town on the eastern side of Zealand. Here we jumped into a fresh railway, which carried us over a country quite as flat as the plains of Holstein.

We had a three-hours' journey still before reaching the capital of Denmark. My uncle had not closed an eye. In his patience I do believe he was pushing the carriage along with his feet.

At last he caught sight of the sea in the distance.

"The Sound!" he cried.

On our left there was a huge building resembling a hospital.

"It is a mad-house," said one of our traveling companions.

"Well, now," I thought to myself, "that is an establishment we certainly ought to end our days in; and large as it is, it would still be too small to contain all the madness of Professor Lidenbrock."

At ten in the morning we set foot in Copenhagen. The luggage was put on a conveyance, and we drove to the "Phoenix Hotel," in Breda Gate. This occupied about half an hour, for the station was outside the town. There my uncle, after a brief toilette, dragged me out with him. The porter of the hotel spoke German and English, but the professor being a perfect polyglot, interrogated him in good Danish, and it was in good Danish that the man directed him to the Museum of Northern Antiquities.

The curator of the curious establishment, where a new history of the country might be compiled out of the old stone weapons, and bowls, and jewels, was Professor Thomson, a *savant*, and a friend of the consul in Hamburg.

My uncle had a warm letter of recommendation to him. As a rule, one *savant* is not very cordial to another, but here was an exception. M. Thomson, being an obliging man, gave Professor Lidenbrock a hearty welcome, and his nephew also. It is hardly necessary to say that we kept our secret from the worthy curator. We were simply visiting Iceland as disinterested amateurs.

M. Thomson placed himself entirely at our disposal, and ran about the quays for us, trying to find a vessel that was going there.

I fervently hoped his search would be unsuccessful. But it was nothing of the sort. A small Danish schooner, the *Valkyria*, was to sail on the 2nd of June for Reikiavik. The captain, M. Bjorne, was on board. His intending passenger almost crushed his hand by the hearty grip he gave it in his joy. The worthy man was a little astonished, for going to Iceland was an every-day occurrence to him. My uncle thought it sublime, and the brave captain took advantage of his enthusiasm to ask him double fare. But we did not look at matters too closely.

"Be on board on Sunday, at 7 A.M." said M. Bjorne, pocketing the dollars coolly, as the bargain was concluded.

We then returned to the "Phoenix," after giving our best thanks to M. Thomson for his trouble.

"This is capital! Most capital!" repeated my uncle. "What a fortunate chance to have found a ship ready to sail. Now we'll have breakfast, and then go and look at the town."

We went first to Kongens-Nye-Torw, an irregular square, where two harmless cannons were posted. Close by, at No. 5, there was a French "restauration," kept by a cook named Vincent. Here we breakfasted very well for the modest sum of four marks each.*

Then I wandered about the town with absolutely childish delight. My uncle walked along, but he saw nothing—neither the magnificent palace of the king, nor the pretty bridge built in the sixteenth century, which stretches across the canal in the front of the Museum, nor that immense cenotaph of Thorwaldsen adorned with horrible mural paintings outside, and containing in the interior the works of the sculptor, nor the Castle of Rosenberg, in a tolerably fine park, a miniature structure, looking like a *bon-bon* box; nor the Exchange, a handsome *renaissance* edifice, nor its tower, composed of the twisted tails of four dragons in bronze, nor the great windmills on the ramparts, the vast sails of which swelled out before the breeze like the canvas of a ship in a breeze.

What charming walks my pretty Gräuben and I would have had along the harbor where the two-deckers and the frigates sleep peacefully, below the red roof of the shed, and along the verdant banks of

---

* About 2s. 6d.

the strait, through the leafy shades of which the citadel peeps out, and its black line of cannon stretches along among the branches of the elders and willows.

But, alas! she was far away, and might I ever hope to see her again?

However, though my uncle noticed none of these enchanting views, he was much struck by the sight of a certain steeple in the island of Amack, which forms the south-west quarter of Copenhagen.

I was ordered to bend my steps towards it, and hailed a little steamer which ferried passengers over the canal. In a few minutes we landed on the quay of the dockyard.

After having traversed several narrow streets, where the galley-slaves, in their yellow and gray short trousers, were toiling under the baton of the sergeants, we came in front of the Vor-Frelsers Kirk. There was nothing remarkable in this church. But this was why the steeple had attracted the attention of the professor. It was of considerable height, and rising from the top of the tower there was a staircase outside which wound round the spire to the very top.

"Let us go up it," said my uncle.

"But it will make us giddy."

"All the more reason for going. We must accustom ourselves to it."

"But—"

"Come, I tell you; do not lose time." I was forced to obey. The man who kept the church lived on the other side of the street and I got the key from him and we commenced the ascent.

My uncle went first with a nimble foot. I followed him in some alarm, for I was desperately inclined to turn giddy. I had neither the steadiness nor the nerves of an eagle.

As long as we were inside the spiral I got on well enough, but after 150 steps I felt the wind in my face, and we reached the platform of the steeple where the outside stair commenced. It was protected by a frail balustrade, and the steps growing narrower and narrower seemed to climb up into space.

"I shall never do it!" I exclaimed.

"Would you be a coward? Go on!" replied the inexorable professor.

I was compelled to obey, clinging with all my might. The strong wind made me giddy, I felt the steeple oscillate at every gust. My legs gave way and I had to climb up soon on my knees and then on my stomach. I shut my eyes; I felt sick.

At last I reached the ball, my uncle dragging me by the collar.

"Look down," he said, "and look well. We must take *abyss lessons.*"

I opened my eyes. I saw the houses, looking flat and as if crushed by a fall, in the midst of thick smoke. Above my head scattered clouds were passing, and by an optical inversion they seemed to me motionless, while the steeple, and ball, and myself were whirling down with fantastic swiftness. In the distance, on one side lay the green plains, and on the other the sparkling sea. The Sound spread out before Elsinore, and sundry white sails, like the wings of sea birds, and in the mist, to the east, appeared the faint outlines of the Swedish coast. All the universe was swimming round before my eyes.

But for all that I was obliged to rise and stand up and gaze. My first lesson in *vertigo* lasted an hour, and when at last I was allowed to descend and my feet touched the solid pavement of the street, I was lame.

"We will begin again, to-morrow," said my master.

And so we did. For five days in succession this dizzy exercise was repeated, and in spite of myself I made sensible progress in the art of "high contemplation."

IX

The day of departure arrived. Our obliging friend, M. Thomson, brought us hearty letters of introduction to Baron Trampe, the governor of Iceland; to M. Pictursson, the suffragan of the Bishop; and M. Finsen, Mayor of Reikiavik, for which my uncle thanked him by the heartiest shake of the hand.

On the 2nd, at 6 A.M., our precious luggage was carried on board the *Valkyria*, and we were conducted to our narrow cabins by the captain.

"Have we a fair wind?" asked my uncle.

"Excellent!" replied Captain Bjorne; "a sou'wester. We shall go out of the Sound in full sail."

A few minutes later the schooner got under weigh, and with her mizzen, brigantine, and top-gallant sails spread, was running before the breeze through the Strait. An hour afterwards the capital of Denmark seemed to sink beneath the distant waves, and the *Valkyria* was coasting along by Elsinore. In my excited nervous state I expected to see the ghost of Hamlet wandering on the legendary terrace.

"Sublime madman!" I said to myself. "You would approve our proceedings, undoubtedly. Maybe you would follow us to the center of the globe, to seek there a solution of your eternal doubt!"

But nothing appeared on those ancient walls. The castle, moreover, is much younger than the heroic Prince of Denmark. It is used now as a sumptuous lodge for the toll-keeper of the Sound, through which 15,000 vessels of all nations pass every year.

The Castle of Kronsberg soon vanished in the mist, as also the town of Helsingborg, on the Swedish coast, and the schooner began to catch the breezes of the Cattegat.

The *Valkyria* was a good sailer, but one cannot reckon on a sailing vessel. She was loaded with coal for Reikiavik, and household utensils, earthenware, woolen clothing, and a cargo of wheat. Five men, all Danes, composed the crew.

"How long will the voyage take?" my uncle asked the captain.

"About ten days," was the reply, "if we don't get a taste of a 'nor'-wester' as we pass the Faroes."

"But, as a rule, are you liable to be much delayed?"

"No, M. Lidenbrock. Make your mind easy, we'll get there soon enough."

Towards evening the schooner doubled the Skagen, the northern point of Denmark, and during the night we passed through the Skager Rack, coasted along the extremity of Norway, by Cape Lindness, and out into the North Sea.

Two days afterwards we sighted the coast of Scotland off Peterhead, and the *Valkyria* began to steer straight towards the Faroe Islands, passing between the Orkneys and Shetlands.

The waves of the Atlantic were soon dashing against our schooner, and she had to tack to avoid the north wind, and had considerable difficulty in getting to the Faroes. On the 8th the captain sighted Myganness, the most easterly of the islands, and from that time steered a straight course for Portland Bay, situated on the southern coast of Iceland.

Nothing particular occurred during the passage.

I stood the sea pretty well, but my uncle, to his great vexation and still greater shame, was ill the whole time.

He was unable consequently to have any conversation with the captain about Snäfell and the means of communication with it or modes of transport. All these questions he was obliged to postpone till his arrival, and passed his time lying down in his cabin, the sides of which cracked and shivered with the pitching of the vessel. It must be owned he rather deserved his fate.

On the 11th we sighted Cape Portland. The weather happening to be clear just then allowed us a glimpse of Myrdals-Jokul, which rises above it. The cape is simply a low, broad hill, with very steep sides, standing alone on the shore.

The *Valkyria* kept a good way out from the coast in a westerly direction, sailing through numerous shoals of whales and sharks. Presently an immense rock was seen, pierced with holes, through which the foaming waves dashed furiously. The Westman islets seemed to rise out of the ocean like rocks strewed on the liquid plain. After this the schooner made a wide sweep to round Cape Reikianess, which forms the western angle of Iceland.

The stormy sea prevented my uncle from coming on deck to admire the broken, jagged shores, constantly beat upon by gales from the southwest.

Forty-eight hours later, just as we got out of a storm which obliged the schooner to take in every inch of canvas, we sighted, in the east, the beacon light of Cape Skagen, whose dangerous rocks extend a great distance below the waves. An Iceland pilot came on board, and three hours afterwards the *Valkyria* moored before Reikiavik in the Faxa Bay.

The professor emerged from his cabin at last, a little pale and exhausted, but as enthusiastic as ever, his eyes beaming with satisfaction.

The inhabitants of the town stood in a group on the quay, peculiarly interested in the arrival of a vessel which had brought everyone's commissions.

My uncle was all haste to leave his floating prison, or we might say hospital. But before leaving the deck of the schooner he dragged me away to the bow, and, pointing with his finger to the mouth of the bay, showed me a high mountain with two peaks, a double cone covered with eternal snows.

"Snäfell! Snäfell!" he exclaimed.

Thus reminding me by a gesture to keep silence, he took his seat in the boat which was waiting for us. I followed, and our feet soon touched the shores of Iceland.

Next minute a fine-looking man appeared in the uniform of a general. However, he was simply a magistrate, the governor of Iceland—Baron Trampe himself. The professor speedily discovered his rank, and presented him with his letters of introduction from Copenhagen. Then followed a brief conversation in Danish, which I did not understand a word of, and for a good reason. But the outcome of it all was that Baron Trampe placed himself entirely at the disposal of Professor Lidenbrock.

From the mayor, M. Finsen, no less military in costume than the governor, and equally pacific in temper and calling, my uncle received a most kindly welcome.

The bishop's suffragan, M. Pictursson, was making an episcopal visitation in the north, so we had to give up meantime the pleasure of being introduced to him. But there was one most fascinating man we met with, whose society became very precious to me; this was M. Fridrikson, professor of natural science in the school at Reikiavik. This modest *savant* only spoke Icelandic and Latin. It was in the soft tongue of Horace that he came to offer his services, and I felt at home with him at once. In fact he was the only person with whom I could exchange a word during my stay in Iceland.

Out of the three rooms which his house contained, this excellent man placed two at our disposal, and soon we were installed in them bag and baggage, the quantity of which rather astonished the good folks of Reildavik.

"Come now, Axel," said my uncle, "we are getting on famously. The worst part of the business is over."

"How do you make that out?" I exclaimed.

"Why, all we have to do now is to make the descent."

"Oh, if you look at it in that way you are right; but we have got to get up as well as to get down, I fancy."

"Oh, that does not trouble me at all. Come, there is no time to lose. I am going to the library. Perhaps there is some manuscript of Saknus-semm's to be found there; and I should like very much to consult it."

"And while you are there I will look over the town. Won't you do that much too?"

"Oh, that has but little interest for me. The most curious part of Iceland is not what is on the surface, but what is below."

I went out and wandered at haphazard. It would have been difficult to lose one's way in Reikiavik, seeing there are but two streets, so I was not obliged to ask my way by making signs, which exposes one to many mistakes.

The town lies between two hills, on a somewhat low and marshy soil. An immense layer of lava covers it on one side and slopes gently down to the sea. The wide bay of Faxa stretches out on the opposite side and is bounded by the enormous Snäfell glacier, and in this bay the *Valkyria* was the only vessel then at anchor. Generally the English and French fishery-keepers are moored in the offing, but just now they were wanted on the eastern coast of the island.

The longer of the two streets lies parallel with the shore. It is here that the merchants and traders live in wooden huts, made of red planks laid horizontally; the other street, more to the west, runs down to a little lake, between the houses of the bishop and others not connected with trade.

I had soon made my way through these dull, melancholy-looking streets, here and there catching a glimpse of a bit of faded turf, like an old threadbare carpet, or occasionally of a garden, the scanty produce of which, consisting of a few potatoes, cabbages, and lettuces, might have easily figured on a Lilliputian table. A few sickly gillyflowers were also trying to lift up their heads in the sunlight.

About the center of the non-commercial street I found the public cemetery, enclosed by a mud-wall, and apparently with plenty of room in it. A few steps farther brought me to the governor's house, a hut compared with the town hall of Hamburg, though a palace beside the huts of the Icelanders.

A church rose between the little lake and the town, built in the Protestant style and with calcined stones which the volcanoes brought up from the earth at their own expense. When strong gales blew from the south-west it was evident that the red tiles of the roofs would be scattered in all directions, to the great danger of the faithful worshipers.

On a neighboring eminence I perceived the national school where, as I was subsequently informed by our host, Hebrew, English, French, and Danish are taught; four languages of which, I am ashamed to say, I didn't know a single word. I should have stood at the bottom of the class in the little college numbering forty scholars, and been unworthy to sleep with them in one of those double closets where more delicate boys must have died of suffocation on the very first night.

In three hours I had gone over both the town and its environs. Its general aspect was singularly gloomy. No trees, no vegetation worth speaking of; everything bare volcanic rocks. The Icelandic huts are made of earth and turf, and the walls slope within. They resemble roofs laid on the ground; but these same roofs are meadows comparatively fertile. Thanks to the internal heat, tolerably good grass grows on them, which is carefully cut down in the hay season, for, if left, the domestic animals would come and graze on these green dwellings.

During my ramble I met but few of the inhabitants. In coming back, though, along the commercial street, I saw the greater part of the population engaged in drying, salting, and loading cod-fish—the principal article of exportation. The men looked robust, but heavy, a species of Germans, with fair hair and pensive eyes, feeling themselves a little outside the pale of humanity; poor exiles relegated to this land of ice, who should properly have been Esquimaux, since they were condemned by nature to live on the edge of the Arctic circle. I tried in vain to catch a smile on their features. Sometimes they laughed by a sort of involuntary contraction of the muscles, but they never smiled.

Their costumes consisted in a coarse jacket of black woolen stuff known as *vadmel* in Scandinavian countries, a wide-brimmed hat, trousers bordered with red, and a piece of leather wound round the feet for shoes.

The women had sad resigned faces, agreeable enough, but without expression, and were dressed in a gown and petticoat of dark *vadmel*. The girls wore their hair in plaits round their heads, and a little brown knitted cap over it; and the married women donned a colored handkerchief with a white peak of linen on the top.

When I returned to M. Fridrikson, after a good long walk, I found my uncle already in the company of his host.

X

Dinner was ready, and eagerly devoured by Professor Lidenbrock, whose compulsory abstinence on board had converted his stomach into a deep gulf. About the meal itself, which was more Danish than Icelandic, there was nothing remarkable, but our host, who was more Icelandic than Danish, reminded me of the hospitable heroes of ancient times. It was evident that he considered the house ours rather than his so long as we were his guests.

The conversation was carried on in the idiom of the country, though my uncle put in a little German now and then, and M. Fridrikson a little Latin for my especial benefit. It turned on scientific questions, as befitted *savants*, but Professor Lidenbrock displayed great reserve, and at every sentence warned me by a look to be careful not to breathe a word about our plans.

Almost the first question asked by M. Fridrikson was how my uncle had got on at the library.

"The library!" exclaimed my uncle. "Why, it only consists of a few odd volumes on a lot of empty shelves."

"What!" said M. Fridrikson, "we have 8,000 volumes, many of them very valuable and rare, and in addition to works in the old Scandinavian tongue, we have all the novelties every year that Copenhagen can furnish us."

"And where are these 8,000 volumes? For my part—"

"Ah, M. Lidenbrock, they are all over the country. In our ancient island of ice there is a taste for study. Not a farmer nor a fisherman could be found who cannot read, and who does not read. We are of opinion that instead of letting books grow moldy behind an iron grating, far from the vulgar gaze, it is better to let them wear out by being read. These volumes, therefore, circulate freely from hand to hand, and are turned over and read and re-read, and often only come back to their shelves after a year or two of absence."

"And, meantime," replied my uncle, a little snappishly, "strangers—"

"What would you have? Strangers have their own libraries at home, and our first business is to educate our countrymen. I say again the love of study is in the Icelandic blood. That is how, in 1816, we started a literary society which is now flourishing. Learned foreigners are proud to be members of it. It publishes books compiled for the instruction of our fellow-countrymen, and is a valuable boon to the island. If you will consent to be one of our corresponding members, M. Lidenbrock, you will confer on us the greatest pleasure."

My uncle belonged already to a hundred scientific societies, but he consented with so much grace that M. Fridrikson was quite touched by it.

"And now," he said, "if you will please to tell me what were the books you hoped to find, I may, perhaps, be able to give you some information about them."

I looked at my uncle. He had now to reply, for this was a question that immediately; affected his project. However, after a minute's reflection, he said:

"M. Fridrikson, I wanted to know whether there are any writings of Arne Saknussemm among the ancient works."

"Arne Saknussemm!" replied the Reikiavik professor. "You mean a *savant* of the sixteenth century, who was at once a great naturalist, a great alchemist, and a great traveler?"

"Precisely."

"One of the glories of Icelandic science and literature."

"Exactly so."

"An illustrious man everywhere."

"That's the very man."

"His daring equaled his genius."

"Ah! I see you know him thoroughly."

My uncle's eyes beamed at this eulogy of his hero, and he listened eagerly to every word.

"Well!" he said at last; "and what about his works?"

"Ah! his works; haven't one of them!"

"What? Not in Iceland!"

"They are neither to be found in Iceland nor anywhere else."

"And why?"

"Because Arne Saknussemm was persecuted for heresy, and in 1573 his books were burnt at Copenhagen by the hands of the common executioner."

"Very good! that's capital," exclaimed my uncle to the great scandal of the professor of natural science.

"Yes," continued my uncle, "all hangs together, all is clear now, and I can understand how it was that Saknussemm, when he found himself placed on the *Index Expurgatorius*, and obliged to conceal the discoveries of his genius, had to bury his secret in an incomprehensible cryptogram."

"What secret?" asked M. Fridrikson, sharply.

"A secret that—which—" stammered out my uncle.

"Is it some secret document that you have come into possession of?"

"No, no; a mere supposition that I was making."

"Oh! that was it," said M. Fridrikson, and kindly dropped the subject when he saw the embarrassment of his guest. "I hope," he added, "that you will not leave the island without having seen some of its mineralogical wealth."

"Certainly not; but I fear I am a little too late. The island has been already visited by learned men, I believe."

"Yes, M. Lidenbrock. The labors of MM. Olafsen and Povelson, undertaken by order of the king, the researches of Troil, the scientific mission of MM. Gaimard and Robert, in the French *La Recherche*,* and lastly the observations made by savants on the frigate *La Reine Hortense*, have largely contributed to our knowledge of Iceland. But believe me, there is plenty to do yet."

* The *Recherche* was sent out in 1835 by Admiral Duperré to find the traces of the lost expedition, that of M. de Blossville in the *Heloise*, which was never heard of.

"Do you think so?" said my uncle, carelessly, trying to look unconcerned.

"I do. How many mountains and glaciers and volcanoes there are about which little or nothing is known. Stop!—without going a step farther—look at that mountain on the horizon! That is Snäfell."

"Ah, indeed!" replied my uncle. "That is Snäfell?"

"Yes; one of the most curious volcanoes, and its crater has been seldom visited."

"Is it extinct?"

"Yes, for the last 500 years."

"Well, then," said my uncle, crossing his legs frantically, to keep himself from giving a great jump, "I should like to commence my geological explorations at this Seffel, or Fessel, did you call it?"

"Snäfell!" replied the worthy M. Fridrikson.

This part of the conversation was in Latin. I understood every word of it, and could scarcely keep grave to see my uncle trying to hide his satisfaction. He was brimful and bubbling over with delight, but wanted to put on an innocent, simple look. All he managed, however, was a sort of diabolical grin.

"Yes," he said, "what you tell me has decided me. We will attempt the ascent of Snäfells, and perhaps even study its crater."

"I greatly regret," replied M. Fridrikson, "that my occupations prevent me from accompanying you. It would have been most pleasant and profitable to me."

"Oh no, no," returned my uncle, quickly; "we should not like to disturb anybody, M. Fridrikson. I thank you most heartily. Your company would have been very useful to us, but the duties of your profession, of course—"

It pleases me to think that in the innocent guilelessness of his Icelandic nature, our host did not see through my uncle's clumsy maneuvers.

"I quite approve your plan, M. Lidenbrock, of beginning with Snäfell," he said. "You will reap a rich harvest there of curious observations. But now tell me," he continued, "how you think of getting there."

"By sea. The quickest way will be to go across the bay."

"No doubt; but it is impossible to do it."

"Why?"

"Because we have not a boat in Reikiavik."

"Hang it!"

"You'll have to go by land—keeping along the shore. It is a longer way, but more interesting."

"Very good then, I must find a guide."

"I just happen to know of one that will suit you, I think."

"A reliable, intelligent man?"

"Yes; and who lives on the peninsula. He is an eider-down hunter, a very clever fellow, that will please you. He speaks Danish perfectly."

"And when can I see him?"

"To-morrow, if you like."

"Why not to-day?"

"Because he won't be here till to-morrow."

"Well, it must be to-morrow, then," said my uncle with a sigh.

This important conversation ended a few minutes later with hearty acknowledgments from the German professor to the Icelandic professor for his great kindness. My uncle had gleaned much valuable information during dinner. He had learnt the history of Saknussemm, the reason of his mysterious document, and, moreover, that his host could not accompany him in his expedition, and that next day a guide would be waiting his orders.

XI

In the evening I took a short walk along the shore, and came back early. I retired to rest, and was soon sleeping soundly in my big bed, made of rough planks of wood.

When I awoke I heard my uncle talking at a great rate in the next room. I got up immediately, and hastened to join him.

He was talking in Danish to a very tall man, of strong, well-built frame. This strapping fellow was evidently endowed with unusual strength. He had a very large head, and an innocent, simple-looking face. His pale blue eyes, dreamy as they were, seemed to me full of intelligence. Long hair, which would have been called red even in England, hung down over his athletic shoulders. His movements were full of suppleness, but he scarcely stirred his arms, and seemed to be a man who either disdained, or was unacquainted with the language of gestures. Everything about him revealed a temperament of the most perfect calmness, not indolent, but placid. You felt that he was not one to ask favors, and that he worked when it suited him; and that his philosophy would never be disturbed or surprised by whatever might happen.

I could tell all this by the way the Icelander listened to the torrent of words poured out by his interlocutor. He stood with folded arms, motionless, in face of the multiplied gestures made by my uncle. His head turned from left to right if he wished to give a negative reply, and gently bowed for an affirmative one, but so gently that his long hair scarcely moved. It was economy of motion carried to extremes.

Certainly I should never have guessed the man was a hunter. He would never frighten the game away, it was true, but how could he so much as get near it?

All was explained when M. Fridrikson informed us he was only an eider-duck hunter, a bird whose down is the principal wealth of the island. The down is called "eider-down," and no great amount of movement is required to get it.

Early in the summer the female, a pretty species of duck, builds her nest among the rocks of the fiords which fringe the entire coast. This nest she lines with the downy feathers off her own breast. Immediately the hunter, or rather the trader, comes, and takes the nest away and the poor bird recommences her task only to be robbed again. This is repeated till her breast is stripped bare, when the male steps in and feathers it in his turn. This time she is allowed to lay her eggs in peace, as the coarse hard plumage of her mate has no commercial value; so the nest is completed, the eggs laid, the young ones hatched, and the birds left undisturbed till the following year, when the harvest begins again.

Now as the eider does not choose precipitous crags for her nest, but rather low-lying horizontal rocks which stretch out into the sea, the Iceland hunter might pursue his calling without disturbing himself much. He was a farmer who neither needed to sow nor to cut down his harvest. All he had to do was to gather it in. This grave, phlegmatic, silent personage was named Hans Bjilke. He came on the recommendation of M. Fridrikson. This was our future guide. His manner strangely contrasted with that of my uncle.

However, they soon came to a mutual understanding. Neither of them cared about terms; the one was ready to take whatever was offered, the other ready to give whatever was asked. Never was bargain more easily settled.

The result of the agreement was that Hans engaged to take us to the village of Stapi, lying on the southern side of the peninsula of Snäfell, at the very foot of the volcano. The distance by land was about twenty-two miles, a two days' journey, my uncle reckoned.

But when he found that in a Danish mile there are 24,000 feet he was obliged to alter his calculations, and taking into account the indifferent roads, allow seven or eight days.

Four horses were to be placed at our disposal, two to carry him and me, and two for our luggage; Hans, according to his habit, would go on foot. He knew this part of the coast perfectly, and promised to take us by the shortest route.

His engagement with my uncle was not to end with our arrival at Stapi. He was to remain in his service during the whole time of his scientific expeditions, for the sum of three rix-dollars a week.* It was also expressly agreed, and indeed was a *sine qua non* of the engagement, that this sum should be paid down every Saturday evening.

The departure was fixed for the 16th of June. My uncle wished to pay "earnest money" on the conclusion of the bargain, but the man refused by pronouncing the single word:

"*Efter.*"

"*After,*" explained the professor, for my edification.

"A first-rate fellow," said my uncle, as Hans withdrew, "but he has no idea of the marvelous part he has to play in the future."

"He will go with us then into—"

"Yes, Axel, into the center of the earth."

We had forty-eight hours still left before starting, but to my great regret they were obliged to be spent in preparations. We had to set all our wits to work to pack each article to the greatest advantage— instruments on one side, arms on the other: tools in this parcel, provisions in that; four sets in all.

The instruments comprised:—

---

*About 12s.

1. An Eigel's centigrade thermometer, graduated up to 150°, which seemed to me either too much or too little. Too much if the surrounding heat would rise to that, for we should be baked; too little if it was to be used for measuring the temperature of springs or any matter in a state of fusion.

2. A manometer for indicating higher atmospheric pressure than that at the level of the sea. An ordinary barometer would not have been enough, as the atmospheric pressure would increase in proportion to our descent below the surface of the earth.

3. A chronometer by Boisonas, jun., of Geneva, accurately regulated by the meridian of Hamburg.

4. Two compasses, for taking inclinations and declinations.

5. A night glass.

6. Two of Ruhmkorff's apparatus, which, by means of an electric current, give a very portable safe light.*

The arms consisted of two of Purdey-Moore's rifles and two of Colt's revolvers. What did we need arms for? It was not likely we should encounter savages or wild beasts, I thought. But my uncle seemed to consider his arsenal as necessary as his instruments, and took special care to lay in a stock of gun-cotton, which damp cannot affect, and the explosive force of which is superior to that of ordinary gunpowder.

---

* Ruhmkorff's apparatus consists of a Bunsen pile set in activity by means of bichromate of potash, which has no smell. An induction coil communicates the electricity produced by the pile to a lantern of peculiar shape. In this lantern there is a spiral tube where a vacuum has been made, and in which nothing remains but a residuum of carbonic-acid gas, or of azote. When the apparatus is put in motion this gas becomes luminous, producing a steady white light. The pile and the coil are placed in a leathern bag, which the traveler carries across his shoulder. The lantern placed outside gives sufficient light in deep darkness, and allows the adventurer, without fear of any explosion, to go through the most inflammable gases, and is not extinguished even in the deepest waters. M. Ruhmkorff is a savant and clever physician. His great discovery is this induction coil, by which electricity can be produced at high pressure. He obtained in 1864 the quinquennial prize of 50,000 francs, offered by the French Government for the most ingenious application of electricity.

The tools comprised two pickaxes, two spades, a silk rope-ladder, three iron-tipped sticks, a hatchet, a hammer, a dozen wedges and iron holdfasts, and long knotted ropes. A pretty sized package that made, for the ladder measured 300 feet.

Then there were provisions. But these did not take up much room, though it was comforting to know we had enough essence of beef and dry biscuits to last us six months. The only liquid we took was gin, and absolutely not a drop of water. But we had gourds, and my uncle reckoned on finding springs where we might refill them. Whatever objections to this I made, on the ground of their quality and temperature, or even their absence, was unsuccessful.

To complete the exact list of all we took with us, I must mention a portable medicine chest, containing blunt scissors, splints for broken limbs, a piece of unbleached linen tape, bandages and compressors, lint, a cupping glass, all terrible-looking things; and in addition to these a series of phials, containing dextrine, spirits of wine and liquid acetate of lead, ether, vinegar, and ammonia—all drugs suggesting painful possibilities. Lastly, all the necessary articles for Ruhmkorff's apparatus.

My uncle did not forget to take a supply of tobacco, powder for hunting, tinder, and a leathern belt, which he wore round his waist, and in which he carried a sufficient sum of money in gold, silver, and paper. Good boots, made waterproof by a solution of india-rubber and naphtha; six pairs in all were stowed away among the tools.

"With such an outfit and equipment as ours, there is no reason why we should not go far," said my uncle.

The 14th was entirely taken up with settling all our different articles. In the evening we dined at Baron Trampe's with the mayor of Reikiavik and Dr. Hyaltalin, the principal physician in the country. M. Fridrikson was not among the guests. I afterwards heard that he and the governor had differed in opinion on some question of administration, and were no longer on speaking terms. I had no opportunity, therefore, of understanding a word of the conversation during this semi-official dinner. I only noticed that my uncle was talking all the time.

Next day, the 15th, our preparations were completed. Our host afforded my uncle the liveliest pleasure by presenting him with a map of Iceland, far more perfect than that of Handersen. It was the map of Olaf Nikolas Olsen reduced to 1/480000 of the real size of the island, and published by the Iceland Literary Society. This was a precious document to a mineralogist.

The last evening was spent in close conversation with M. Fridrikson, for whom I felt a sympathetic attraction, and this was followed by a troubled sleepless night, as far, at least, as I was concerned.

At 5 A.M. the neighing of the four horses, as they stood pawing below the window, made me rise hastily and go down. I found Hans just finishing the loading of the horses, almost without stirring, one would say, but he did his work with uncommon cleverness. My uncle was making a great noise rather than helping, and the guide appeared to take no notice of his orders.

By 6 A.M. all was ready. We shook hands with M. Fridrikson, and my uncle thanked him most heartily for his great hospitality. As for myself, I launched out a cordial farewell in the best Latin I could find; then we jumped into our saddles, and M. Fridrikson repeated with his last adieux that line of Virgil which seemed to have been made for uncertain travelers on the road, like us:

Et quacumque viam dederit fortuna sequamur.

XII

The sky was gloomy when we started, but settled, so we had neither rain nor heat to fear. It was the very weather for tourists.

The pleasure of roaming over an unknown country on horseback easily reconciled me to this *début* of our enterprise. Indeed I felt quite in the mood of an excursionist rejoicing in his freedom, and, full of desires and expectations, I began to take my share in the business.

"Besides," I said to myself, "what risk is there? We are to travel through one of the most curious countries in the world, and to climb a most remarkable mountain, and, even at the worst, descend to the bottom of an extinct crater, for it is quite evident that is all that Saknussemm did. As to there being any passage out of it, right into the heart of the earth, that's a pure imagination, a sheer impossibility; so I shall make up my mind to get all the enjoyment I can out of this business, and not bother about the rest."

By the time I had reached this conclusion, we had quite got out of Reikiavik.

Hans was walking ahead at a rapid, even, continuous pace. The two baggage horses followed him without being led. My uncle and I brought up the rear, and really we did not cut a bad figure on our small but stout steeds.

Iceland is one of the largest islands in Europe. It is 14,000 miles in extent, and has only a population of 60,000. Geographers have divided it into four quarters, and we had crossed in a nearly diagonal direction the one called "Sudveste Fjordûnge" (the country of the south-west quarter).

After leaving Reikiavik, Hans kept straight along the coast. We went through scanty pastures, which tried their best to look green, and never succeeded in being anything but yellow. The rugged peaks of the trachyte rocks were faintly outlined on the misty eastern horizon. At times a few patches of snow, concentrating the scattered rays of light, glittered brilliantly on the tops of the distant mountains; certain peaks, bolder than the rest, pierced through the gray clouds, and reappeared above the moving matter like rocks out of the sea.

Often these chains of barren rocks made a sharp turn towards the sea, encroaching on the pasturage, but there was always room enough to pass. Our horses, moreover, instinctively chose the best footing, without once slackening speed. My uncle never even had the satisfaction of urging on his steed by voice or whip. He could not even get impatient with it. I could not help smiling, though, at seeing such a tall man on such a little horse. His long legs barely cleared the ground, and he looked like a Centaur with six legs.

"Good beast! good beast!" he said. "You will see, Axel, that a more intelligent animal does not exist than the Icelandic horse. Nothing stops him—neither snows, tempests, impassible roads, nor glaciers. He is brave, steady, and sure-footed. He never makes a false step—never shies. If we have to cross a river or fiord—and we shall be sure to meet with them—you will see him, without the least hesitation, plunge into the water as if he were some amphibious animal, and gain the opposite bank. But we must not be rough with him; leave him his liberty, and we shall get on at the rate of nearly thirty miles a day."

"I have no doubt *we* shall, but how about the guide?"

"Oh, I have no concern on that score. Men of his stamp get over the ground without perceiving it. He moves himself too little to get fatigued, and, besides, he shall have my horse at a pinch. I shall soon get the cramp if I have no exercise. I must study my legs as well as my arms."

We were getting on famously. The country was almost a desert already. Here and there a solitary farmhouse, called a *boër* in Icelandic, or a dwelling constructed of earth and wood and pieces of lava, stood up like a poor beggar by the roadside. These dilapidated-looking huts seemed as if asking alms from passers-by, and for two pins we would have given them a trifle. In this country there are neither roads nor paths, and, slow as vegetation is, travelers come so few and far between that their footsteps are soon overgrown.

And yet this part of the province, lying so near the capital, was reckoned among the inhabited and cultivated portions of Iceland. What would it be then in districts more deserted than this desert? We had gone half a mile without seeing as much as a farmer at the door of his hut, or a rude shepherd tending a flock less wild than himself. Nothing had come in sight but a few cows and sheep wandering about as they pleased. What, then, must those convulsed regions be, overturned by eruptions, themselves the offspring of volcanic explosions and subterranean commotions?

We were doomed to know that in good time. But on consulting Olsen's map I saw they would be avoided by keeping along the winding coast. In fact, the great plutonic action is specially concentrated in the interior of the island. Then the piled-up rocks, in horizontal layers, called *trapp* in Scandinavian, trachytes, basalt, tuff, and all the volcanic conglomerates, streams of lava and porphyry in a state of fusion, invest the country with supernatural horrors. I little imagined, however, the spectacle which awaited us on the peninsula of Snäfell, where these fiery materials make a very chaos.

Two hours after leaving Reikiavik we arrived at the burgh of Gufunus, called *aoalkirkja*, or principal church. There was nothing remarkable about it, in fact there was nothing in it but a few houses, scarcely enough to make a German hamlet.

Hans stopped here half an hour. He shared our frugal breakfast, and said "yes" or "no" to all my uncle's questions, except when he asked where we were to pass the night, and to this he replied:

"Gardär."

I consulted the map to see where Gardär was, and found a little town of that name on the banks of the Hvalfjörd, four miles from Reikiavik. I showed it to my uncle.

"Only four miles!" he said. "Four miles out of twenty-two! That's a pretty walk, certainly."

He began some remark to the guide about it, but Hans took no notice, and resumed his place ahead, so we had to set off again.

Three hours later, still treading the faded grass, we had to go round the Kollafiord, a shorter and easier route than across the inlet. We soon entered a "pingstan," or parish named Ejilburg, the clock of which would have struck twelve, if the Icelandic churches had been rich enough to possess clocks; but they are like the parishioners, they have no clocks, and manage to do without them.

The horses were baited here, and then we struck into a narrow path between a chain of hills and the sea, which brought us to our next stage, the "aoalkirkja" of Brantär, and a mile further on to Sarnböre "Annexia," a chapel-of-ease on the south shore of the Hvalfjörd.

It was then 4 P.M. We had gone four miles, equal to twenty-four English miles in this part.

The fiord was at least half-a-mile in breadth. The waves were dashing noisily over the sharp rocks. The inlet had rocky walls on either side, or rather steep precipices, and crowned with peaks 2,000 feet high, remarkable for their brown strata, separated by beds of reddish tuff. However intelligent our horses might be, I did not augur anything good from attempting to cross a regular arm of the sea on the back of a quadruped.

"If they are really as intelligent as they are said to be," I thought to myself, "they won't try to pass it. Anyway, I'll be intelligent for them."

But my uncle would not wait. He spurred right on to the shore. His horse snuffed the wind, and stopped short. My uncle, who had an instinct too, urged him forwards, and again the animal refused, and shook his head. Then came oaths and smart lashes with the whip, but the beast only kicked and tried to fling his rider. At last the little horse bent his knees, and managed to slip out from under the professor's legs, leaving him standing upright on two boulders, like the Colossus of Rhodes.

"The confounded brute!" exclaimed the horseman, suddenly transformed into a pedestrian, and as much ashamed as a cavalry officer would be if degraded to a foot soldier.

"*Färja!*" said the guide, touching his shoulder.

"What? A boat?"

"*Der!*" replied Hans, pointing to a boat.

"Yes," I exclaimed, "I see a boat yonder."

"Why didn't you say so before, then? Well, let us get to it."

"*Tidvatten!*" said the guide.

"What does he say?"

"The tide," replied my uncle, translating the Danish word.

"No doubt he means we must wait for the tide."

"*Förbida*," said my uncle.

"*Ja*," replied Hans.

My uncle stamped his foot and the horses went on to the boat.

I quite understood the necessity of waiting for a particular state of the tide to undertake the crossing of the fiord, viz., when the sea is at the flood; for then the flux and reflux are not sensibly felt, and there was no risk of the boat being dragged to the bottom, or out into the broad ocean.

The favorable moment did not arrive till six in the evening, then my uncle, myself, the guide, two ferrymen, and the four horses, took our places on a somewhat frail raft. Accustomed as I was to the steamers on the Elbe, the boatman's oars seemed to me a very miserable species of propeller. It took us more than an hour to get over, but the passage was made without any accident.

Half an hour afterwards, we reached the "aoalkirkja of Gardär."

XIII

I t should have been quite dark, for it was night, but under the 65th parallel the nocturnal light of the polar regions was not astonishing. During the months of June and July the sun never sets.

The temperature, however, had got much lower. I was cold, and worse still, very hungry. Welcome indeed was the *boër* which hospitably opened its door to receive us.

It was only a peasant's hut, but, in point of hospitality, equal to a king's palace. The master of it came to meet us with outstretched hand, and without further ceremony, beckoned us to follow him!

Literally to follow him, for to accompany him would have been impossible. A long narrow dark passage led into the dwelling, which was built of roughly squared planks. All the rooms opened into this passage. These were four in number; the kitchen, the weaving shop, the *badstofa* or sleeping room for the family, and best of all, a visitor's room. My uncle, whose height had not been considered in building the house, of course knocked his head three or four times against the projecting beams of the ceiling.

We were conducted to our room, a large room with an earth floor well beaten down, lighted by a window, the panes of which were formed of sheep's bladder, none too transparent. The bed consisted of dry fodder thrown into two wooden frames, painted red and ornamented with sentences in Icelandic. I did not expect such comfort, the only drawback was the unpleasant smell of dried fish, hung beef, and sour milk, which pervaded the house. When we had doffed our traveling attire, we heard the voice of our host inviting us into the kitchen, the only place where there was a fire, even in the coldest weather.

My uncle lost no time in obeying the friendly summons, and I followed.

The fire-place of the kitchen was in the ancient fashion—the hearth in the center of the room, and a hole in the roof above it, to let out the smoke. The kitchen also served for the dining-room.

On our entrance, the host, as if he had not yet seen us, greeted us with the word *sallvertu*, which means *be happy*, and kissed us on the cheek.

Then his wife pronounced the same words, followed by the same ceremonial, and afterwards, they both laid their right hand on their heart, and bowed profoundly.

I hasten to say that this Icelandic woman was the mother of nineteen children, big and little, buzzing about the room in the midst of the dense smoke which filled it. Every instant some little fair head, and rather melancholy face, would peep out of the clouds constantly curling up from the hearth. One would have said they were a band of angels, though their faces would have been the better for soap and water.

My uncle and I were very kind to this brood of youngsters, so before long we had three or four of the little monkeys on our shoulders, as many on our knees, and the rest among our legs. Those who could speak, repeated *"sallvertu"* in every imaginable tone, and those who could not, shrieked their loudest to make up for it.

This concert was interrupted by a summons to the repast. Our hunter just at this moment came back after seeing that the horses were provided with food, that is to say, he had, by way of economy, turned them out on the fields to find for themselves what moss they could on the rocks, and a few innutritious seaweeds, and they would return of their own accord in the morning to resume their labors.

"Salhertu!" said Hans.

Then quietly, automatically, and impartially, he kissed the host and hostess, and the nineteen children.

This performance over, we sat down to table, twenty-four in number, and consequently, we were literally one on the top of another. The most favored of us had at least two of the small fry on our knees.

But the appearance of the soup soon made silence in the little world, and the taciturnity which was natural, even among the *gamins* of Iceland, resumed its sway. The host assisted us to soup made of lichen, and not at all unpleasant. And this was followed by a huge piece of dried fish swimming in butter that had been kept twenty years, and was of course perfectly rancid—a qualification which made it greatly preferable to fresh butter, according to the gastronomical ideas of Iceland. With this we had *skyr*, a sort of clotted milk, and biscuits and the juice of juniper berries. Our beverage was whey mixed with water, called *blanda* in this country. I really am no judge of the merits of this singular diet, for I was enormously hungry, and at dessert I ate to the very last mouthful a plate of thick buckwheat porridge.

The moment the meal was over, the children disappeared and the grown-up folks gathered round the hearth, where not only peat was burning, but whins, cow-dung, and fish-bones. After this "pinch of heat" the different groups retired to their respective rooms. According to custom, our hostess offered to pull off our stockings and trousers, but after a most polite refusal on our part, she left us, and I was at last able to bury myself in my bed of moss.

At five next morning we bade the Icelandic peasant farewell, after persuading him with difficulty to take a fair remuneration, and Hans gave the signal to start.

About a hundred steps from Gardër the soil began to change its aspect. The ground became boggy and less favorable to our progress. On the right the chain of mountains extended indefinitely, like an immense system of natural fortifications, the counterscarp of which we were following. Often we came to streams, which we had to ford carefully, to prevent our baggage from getting wet, if possible.

The solitude deepened as we advanced. But now and again the shadow of a human being seemed to flee away in the distance as we approached. If a sudden turn brought us unexpectedly near one of these specters I fell back in disgust at the sight of a swollen head and shining scalp destitute of hair, and loathsome sores visible through the tattered rags that covered them.

The poor wretch would not approach us nor hold out his misshapen hand, but dart away as fast as his legs could carry him, though Hans would always manage to greet him with the usual salutation, *Sallvertu*.

"*Spetelsk*," he said.

"A leper," repeated my uncle.

The mere word had a repulsive effect. This dreadful disease of leprosy is pretty common in Iceland. It is not contagious but hereditary, and consequently marriage is forbidden the poor creatures.

Such apparitions as these were not calculated to enliven the landscape, which became more gloomy at every step. The last tufts of grass had disappeared. Not a tree was to be seen, unless a few dwarf birches, no higher than brushwood; not an animal, except a few horses, some which their owner could not feed, and had turned out to live as best they could.

Sometimes we could descry a hawk poising herself in the gray clouds and then flying away to the south. Such a dreary region made me melancholy, and my thoughts began to revert to my native country.

Before long we had to cross several small unimportant fiords and then a wide gulf. The tide being high just then, we got over without delay and reached the hamlet of Alftanas, about one mile beyond.

In the evening, after having forded two rivers, rich in trout and pike, the Alfa and the Heta, we were obliged to pass the night in a deserted building, worthy of being haunted by all the hobgoblins in Scandinavia. Jack Frost had certainly chosen it for his own abode, and he played us pranks all night.

Nothing unusual occurred next day. There was still the same boggy soil, the same uniformity and dreary outlook. By the evening we had gone half our journey, and we spent the night at the "annexia" of Krosolbt.

On the 19th of June, for about a mile, we walked over a stream of hardened lava. This ground is called *hraun* in the country. The furrowed surface of the lava presented the appearance of cables—sometimes stretched long, sometimes coiled up. An immense torrent of the same hardened material ran down the neighboring mountains, which were extinct volcanoes; but the ruins round attested their former power. Here and there jets of steam were still visible, issuing from hot springs beneath the surface.

We had no time to observe these phenomena; we had to go on steadily. Soon the boggy soil appeared afresh, intersected by little lakes. We were now pursuing a westerly direction. In fact we had gone round the great bay of Faxa, and the white peaks of Snäfell stood up against the clouds less than five miles off.

The horses held out well, undeterred by the difficulties of the soil. For my own part, I began to be very tired. My uncle was firm and upright as on the first day. I could not but admire him, even in comparison with the hunter, who looked on our journey as a mere promenade.

On the Saturday, June 20th, at 6 P.M., we reached Büdir, a village on the sea-shore. Here the guide claimed his promised wage and my uncle paid him. It was Hans' family, that is his uncle and cousins, who had offered us hospitality. We were kindly received by them, and without abusing the hospitality of those good people, I would willingly have stayed there a little to recruit myself after our fatigues. But my uncle, who had no need to recruit himself, would not hear of it, and next morning we had to remount our steeds.

The soil was plainly affected by the vicinity of the mountain, the granite foundations of which appeared above the ground, like the roots of an oak. We went round the immense base of the volcano, the professor devouring it all the time with his eyes, gesticulating, and apparently defying the giant, and saying, "There stands the giant I am going to conquer." At last, after four hours' walking, the horses stopped of their own will before the priest's house in Stapi.

XIV

Stapi is a village composed of about thirty huts, built of lava and lying in the sunlight reflected by the volcano. It extends along a small fiord, enclosed in a basaltic wall, which has the strangest effect.

Basalt, as is well known, is a brown rock of igneous origin. It affects regular forms, the disposition of which is often surprising. Here, nature proceeds geometrically, working after the manner of men with square and compass and plummet. Though everywhere else her art is seen in large masses thrown down in disorder, in unfinished cones, in perfect pyramids with the most fantastic succession of lines, here, as if to form an example of regularity and in advance of the very earliest architects, she has created a severe order which has never been surpassed by the splendors of Babylon and the marvels of Greece.

I had heard of the Giants' Causeway in Ireland, and Fingal's Cave in the Hebrides, but I had never before seen a basaltic formation.

This phenomenon I was to witness at Stapi in all its beauty.

The wall of the fiord, like all the coast of the peninsula, is composed of a succession of vertical columns thirty feet high. These straight shafts of perfect proportions supported an architrave, made of horizontal columns, the overhanging portion of which formed a semi-arch over the sea. At certain intervals under this natural shelter there were vaulted openings of admirable design, through which the waves came dashing and foaming. Fragments of basalt, torn away by the fury of the ocean, lay along the ground like the ruins of an ancient temple, ruins which never grew old, over which ages had passed without leaving an imprint behind them.

This was the last stage of our terrestrial journey. Hans had proved himself an intelligent guide, and it was a comfort to think he was not going to leave us here.

On arriving at the door of the rector's house, just a low cabin like his neighbor's, neither grander nor more comfortable, I saw a man engaged in shoeing a horse, hammer in hand, and a leather apron round him.

"*Sallvertu*" said the hunter.

"*God-dag*" replied the blacksmith in pure Danish.

"*Kyrkoherde*" said Hans, turning to my uncle.

"The rector!" said my uncle. "Axel, it appears this good man is the rector."

Meantime our guide was explaining about us to the *Kyrkoherde*, who left off his work, and gave a sort of cry, no doubt in common use among horses and jockeys. A tall vixenish-looking shrew instantly made her appearance. If she did not measure six feet high she certainly was not much less. I was afraid she would offer me the Icelandic kiss, but I need not have alarmed myself, for her manner was too ungracious for any such politeness.

The visitors' room to which she conducted us seemed to be the worst in the house, being close-smelling, dirty, and narrow. However, we were obliged to put up with it. The rector was clearly not given to ancient hospitality. Before the day was over, I saw we had to do with a blacksmith, a fisherman, a hunter, a carpenter, and not at all with a minister of Christ. True, we came on a week day. Perhaps he was a better man on Sundays.

I don't want to say anything bad of these poor priests, who, after all, are miserably off. The sum they receive from the Danish Government is ridiculously small, and all they have besides is a fourth part of the tithe, which does not amount to more than sixty marks (about £4). Consequently, they are obliged to work for a living. But fishing, and hunting, and shoeing horses gives a man at last the tone and habits and manners of fishermen and hunters and farriers and such-like people. I found at night that even sobriety could not be reckoned among his virtues.

My uncle quickly understood his man. Instead of a good and honorable man of learning, this was a coarse, lumpish peasant. He therefore resolved to commence his great expedition with the least possible delay, and to get out of this inhospitable parsonage. In utter disregard of his fatigues, he determined to go and spend a few days in the mountain.

The very next morning our preparations began. Hans hired three Icelanders to take the place of the horses and carry our luggage, but it was distinctly understood that as soon as they had deposited it in the crater they were to turn and go back, and leave us to do the best we could.

My uncle took this opportunity of apprising Hans of his intention to explore the volcano to its furthest limits.

Hans simply nodded. To go there or anywhere else, into the bowels of the earth, or on the surface, was all alike to him. For myself, hitherto I had been amused by the incidents of the journey, and been somewhat forgetful of the future, but now my terrors returned in full force. But what was to be done? If I wished to resist Professor Lidenbrock, it was at Hamburg I should have done it, and not at Snäfell.

One thought especially tormented me—one which might apall stouter nerves than mine.

I said to myself, "We are going to ascend Snäfell. That's well enough. We are going to visit the crater. Well enough too. Others have done that, and they came up alive. But that is not all. If there should actually be a passage into the bowels of the earth, and that unlucky Saknussemm spoke truth, we shall go and lose ourselves in the subterranean windings of the volcano. But what is there to prove that Snäfell is extinct? Who will guarantee that an eruption is not preparing to break out? Because the monster has been sleeping since 1229, does it follow that he will never wake up again? And if he does wake up what will become of us?" This was worth thinking about, and I did think about it. I could not sleep without dreaming of eruptions, and I must say I did not feel inclined to play the part of scoria.

At last I could not bear myself any longer and resolved to submit the case to my uncle with as much tact as possible and under the form of an impossible hypothesis.

I went in quest of him, and told him my fears, and then drew back to let his first outburst of passion pass over.

But all he said was:

"I have been thinking of it."

What could he mean? Was he really going to listen to the voice of reason? Could he be going to suspend his project? It was too good to be true.

After a few minutes' silence, which I did not venture to interrupt, he repeated again:

"I was thinking of it. Ever since we arrived here at Stapi my mind has been occupied with the grave question you have just submitted to me, for it would not do for us to be imprudent."

"No, indeed," I said emphatically.

"For 600 years Snäfell has been silent, but he may speak. Still, eruptions are always preceded by well-known phenomena. I have been therefore interrogating the inhabitants of this district on the subject. I have examined the ground and I am in a position to say there will be no eruption."

I was amazed at this declaration, and could make no reply.

"Do you doubt what I tell you?" resumed my uncle, "Well, come with me!"

I obeyed mechanically. The professor took a direct course away from the sun by going through an opening in the basaltic wall. Soon we were in the open country, if the word can apply to an immense heap of volcanic matter. The whole region seemed to have been overwhelmed with a flood of enormous fragments of trap, basalt, granite, and all the pyroxene rocks.

Here and there I could see puffs of white vapor rising in the air. These are called by the Icelanders "reykir," and issue from the thermal springs, which, by their violence, indicate the volcanic activity of the soil. This seemed to justify my fears. But I fell from the clouds when my uncle went on to say:

"You see all this smoke, Axel. Well, they prove that we have nothing to fear from the fury of the volcano."

"What an idea!" I exclaimed.

"Remember this," continued the professor; "at the approach of an eruption these vapors redouble their activity, but disappear entirely while the phenomenon lasts, for the electric fluids being relieved from pressure, escape by the crater instead of finding their way out through the cracks in the ground. Since, then, these vapors are now in the usual state, and there is no increase of energy, and also that the wind and rain have not given way to a heavy dead calm, you may be sure no eruption is at hand."

"But—"

"Enough. When science has spoken, it is for us to hold our peace."

I went back to the parsonage, very crestfallen. My uncle had vanquished me by scientific arguments. One hope, however, still remained; and this was that, on our reaching the bottom of the crater, we should find no passage, in spite of all the Saknussemms in the world.

I passed the night in all the miseries of nightmare. I was in the midst of a volcano, in the depths of the earth; I felt myself hurled into the planetary spaces, in the form of ejected rock.

The next day, the 22nd of June, Hans was ready, waiting us, with his companions bearing the provisions, tools, and instruments. Two stout sticks, tipped with iron, and two rifles and two shot-belts were reserved for my uncle and myself. Hans, like a wise man, had added to our baggage a leathern bottle filled with water, which, with our gourds, would be a sufficient supply for a week.

It was 9 A.M. The rector and his tall shrew stood at the door of the parsonage, doubtless to bid us farewell. But their adieux took the shape of a tremendous bill! They charged us for everything, even to the air we breathed, and that was polluted enough, I can vouch for it. This worthy couple fleeced us like any Swiss hotel-keeper, and made us pay a good price for their make-believe hospitality.

My uncle settled the account, however, without any higgling. A man who is just about to start for the center of the earth does not care about a few rix-dollars.

This matter arranged, Hans gave the signal for starting, and a few minutes afterwards we left Stapi.

XV

Snäffel is 5,000 feet high. Its double cone terminates in a trachytic belt, which stands out from the mountain system of the island. From our starting-point we could not see its two peaks outlined against the gray clouds. I could only see an enormous cap of snow coming down low over the giant's forehead.

We walked in file, preceded by the hunter, who was climbing by such narrow paths, that two could not go abreast. All conversation was therefore nearly impossible.

Beyond the basaltic wall of the fiord at Stapi the ground was herbaceous, fibrous peat, the remains of the ancient vegetation of the bogs on the peninsula. The quantity of this unworked combustible was enough to warm all the people in Iceland for a century. This vast turf-pit measured in certain ravines seventy feet deep, and presented successive layers of carbonized detritus separated by sheets of tufaceous pumice.

As a true nephew of Professor Lidenbrock, and notwithstanding my mental preoccupation, I was interested in observing the mineralogical curiosities displayed in this vast cabinet of natural history, and, at the same time, was going over in my mind the whole geological history of Iceland.

This most curious island has evidently risen from the depths of the sea at a comparatively recent epoch. Perhaps it may be even still rising by an insensible motion. If that be so, its origin can only be attributed to the action of subterranean fires, and, in this case, Humphry Davy's theory, and Saknussemm's document, and my uncle's speculations, too, all vanish in smoke. This hypothesis made me carefully examine the nature of the soil. I could soon account for the successive phenomena which attended its formation.

Iceland being wholly destitute of alluvial soil, is entirely composed of volcanic tufa, that is, a conglomeration of stones and rocks of a porous texture. Prior to the existence of volcanoes it was composed of trappean rock, slowly upheaved from the sea by the central forces. The interior fires had not yet burst forth.

But at a subsequent period a large fissure appeared running in a diagonal direction from south-west to north-east, by which all the trachyte gradually forced its way out. This phenomenon was not attended with any violence, but the issue was enormous, and the fused matter thrown up from the bowels of the earth spread slowly in vast sheets or rounded protuberances. To this epoch the felspars, syenites, and porphyries belong.

But thanks to this outflow, the thickness of the island increased considerably, and in consequence its powers of resistance. It can be imagined what quantities of electric fluids had accumulated within its bosom when no channel of escape presented itself after the trachytic crust had cooled and hardened. There came then a time when the mechanical force of these gases became such that they upheaved the heavy crust, and made for themselves tall chimneys. The upheaval of the crust first formed the volcanoes, and then a crater suddenly opened at the summit.

To the eruptive phenomena succeeded the volcanic. By the newly-created openings the basaltic ejections first escaped, of which the plain we were just crossing presented the most wonderful specimens. We were walking over gray rocks, which had cooled into hexagonal prisms. In the distance a great number of truncated cones were visible, each of which had formerly been a mouth of fire.

After the basaltic eruption, the volcano, which increased in force by the extinction of other craters, made a passage for lavas and for tufa, viz., ashes and scoria, long streams of which I could see on the mountain sides, hanging down like flowing hair.

Such was the succession of phenomena which produced Iceland, all proceeding from the internal fire, and to suppose that the mass within was not still in a state of fusion was folly. And, surely, to pretend to try and reach the center of the globe was the very climax of folly.

I reassured myself, therefore, about the issue of this enterprise, even while we were on our way to the assault of Snäfell.

The route became more and more difficult—the ground was rising. The loose masses of rock trembled, and the utmost care was needed to prevent dangerous falls.

Hans walked on as quietly as if he were on level ground. At times he would disappear behind great blocks, and for a moment we lost sight of him, then a sharp whistle told us the direction in which to follow him. Often, too, he stopped, picked up some fragments of rock, and arranged them in a recognizable manner, making landmarks in this way all along the road, to show us the route back—a good precaution on his part, though future events rendered it useless.

Three hours of fatiguing walking had only brought us to the base of the mountain. There Hans made a signal to stop, and a hasty breakfast was shared among us. My uncle took two mouthfuls at a time, to dispatch it the quicker. But this halt was not only for breakfast, but for rest, and Hans did not make a start till one hour had elapsed. The three Icelanders, as taciturn as their comrade, never uttered a syllable, and munched away with solemn gravity.

Now the steep ascent of Snäfell commenced. His snowy summit, by an optical illusion, common enough in the mountains, seemed very near, and yet what long hours it took to reach it. Above all, what toil! The stones not being cemented by any earth, nor adhering together by any roots of herbage, rolled away under our feet, and rushed down the plain with the speed of an avalanche.

In certain places the sides of the mountain formed an angle of 36° at least with the horizon. It was impossible to climb them; and these stony cliffs had to be rounded, which was no easy matter. We had to assist each other with our sticks.

I must say that my uncle kept as close to me as possible. He never let me out of his sight, and many a time his arm was my powerful support. He himself certainly had some inner sense of equilibrium, for he never stumbled. The Icelanders, in spite of their loads, climbed with the agility of mountaineers. To look at the height of Snäfell it seemed impossible to reach the summit. But after an hour's fatigue and athletic exercise, a sort of staircase suddenly appeared in the midst of the vast carpet of snow lying on the croup of the volcano, and this greatly simplified our ascent. It was formed of one of those torrents of stones ejected by the eruption, and which the Icelanders called *stinâ*. If this torrent had not been arrested in its fall by the formation of the mountain sides, it would have dashed down into the sea, and new islands would have been the result.

As it was, it did us good service. The steepness increased, but these stone steps helped us to climb up easily, and indeed so rapidly, that when I stopped for a moment behind the rest, I perceived them already so diminished in size by distance that their appearance was microscopic.

At seven in the evening we had gone up the 2,000 steps of the stair, and risen above an extinct cone of the mountain, a sort of bed on which the actual cone of the crater rested.

The sea stretched below us 3,200 feet. We had passed the limit of perpetual snow, which, on account of the humidity of the climate, is rather lower in Iceland. It was bitterly cold. The wind blew violently. I was exhausted. The professor saw that my legs refused to carry me, and, in spite of his impatience, he determined to stop. He made a sign to the hunter to that effect, but Hans shook his head, and said:

"Ofvanför."

"We must go higher it seems," said my uncle, and asked the reason.

"*Mistour*" replied the guide.

"*Ja, mistour,*" repeated one of the Icelanders, in a terrified tone.

"What does the man mean?" I asked, uneasily.

"Look!" replied my uncle.

I gazed down below. An immense column of pulverized pumice, sand, and dust was rising, whirling round like a waterspout. The wind was driving it on to the side of Snäfell, to which we were clinging. The thick curtain across the sun projected a great shadow on the mountain. Should this waterspout-like column bend over it would inevitably catch us in its whirl. This phenomenon, not uncommon when the wind blows from the glaciers, is called in Icelandic *mistour.*

"*Hastigt, hastigt!*" cried our guide. Though I was unacquainted with Danish, I understood we were to follow Hans as quickly as possible. He began to go round the cone of the crater, but diagonally, to make the task easier. Before long the huge column fell on the mountain, which trembled at the shock. The loose stones caught up in its circling eddies flew off in a shower as during an eruption. Fortunately, we had gained the opposite side and were in safety. But without this precaution on the part of our guide, our mangled bodies, reduced to dust, would have been carried away far into the distance, and considered as the product of some unknown meteor.

Hans did not think it prudent though to pass the night on the sides of the cone. We had to continue our zigzag ascent. The 1,500 feet remaining took us nearly five hours to climb; the circuitous windings, the diagonal and counter-marches measured three leagues I am sure. I was "dead beat," sinking with cold and hunger. The somewhat rarefied atmosphere, scarcely allowed my lungs full play; but at length, at 11 P.M., in the dead of the night, the summit of Snäfell was reached, and before seeking shelter in the crater, I had time to see the midnight sun at his lowest point gilding the sleeping island at my feet with his pale rays.

XVI

The supper was quickly dispatched, and the little company housed themselves as best they could. The couch was hard, the shelter rather insufficient, and the situation trying, for we were 5,000 feet above the level of the sea. But in spite of everything my slumbers this night were particularly peaceful. It was the best sleep I had had for a long time. I did not even dream.

Next morning, we awoke half frozen by the keen air. The sun was shining gloriously, when I rose from my granite bed, and went out to enjoy the magnificent panorama that awaited my gaze.

I was on the summit of one of the twin peaks of Snäfell, the south-ernmost. I commanded a view of almost the whole island. By an optical effect common to all great elevations, the shores looked raised and the center depressed. I could have said that one of Helbesmer's relievo maps lay before me. I saw deep valleys intersecting each other in all directions, precipices seemed mere walls, lakes changed into ponds, and rivers into little streams. On my right there were glaciers without number, and innumerable peaks, over some of which there was a plume-like cloud of white smoke. The undulating lines of these endless mountains, on which the snow lay like foam, reminded me of a stormy sea. If I turned to the west, there lay old Ocean in all his majesty, like a continuation of these foamy summits. I could scarcely tell where the earth ended and the waters began.

I was reveling in the magical delight which is awakened in the mind by all great elevations, and this time without giddiness, for at last I had become accustomed to "sublime contemplations." My dazzled eyes were bathed in a flood of radiant sunshine. I forgot who I was, and where I was, to live the life of elves and sylphs, imaginary beings of the Scandinavian mythology. I gave myself to the luxury of the heights, without a thought of the depths into which I must shortly plunge.

But I was recalled to reality by the appearance of the professor and Hans, who rejoined us on the summit.

My uncle turned westward and pointed out to me a light vapor, a sort of mist, an appearance of land just above the waves, and said:

"That's Greenland."

"Greenland?" I cried.

"Yes; we are only thirty-five leagues from it, and when thaws come the white bears find their way to Iceland on the ice-floes from the north. But that's no matter. We are on the top of Snäfell, and here are two peaks, the one to the south, the other to the north. Hans will tell us what the Icelanders call the one we are on at this moment."

The question was put, and Hans replied:

"Scartaris."

My uncle glanced at me triumphantly, and said:

"To the crater, then!"

The crater of Snäfell resembled an inverted cone, the orifice of which was perhaps half a league in diameter. Its depth I estimated was about 2,000 feet. Imagine such a reservoir full of thunders and flame. The bottom of the shaft could not measure more than 500 feet in circumference, so that the gentle slope permitted us to get down easily. I involuntarily thought of an enormous wide-mouthed mortar, and the comparison made me shudder.

"To go down into a mortar," I thought, "when it is perhaps loaded, and may go off at any moment, is to act like fools!"

But I could not draw back. Hans, with an air of perfect indifference, took his place at the head of the party. I followed without saying a word.

In order to facilitate the descent, Hans pursued a winding track down. He was obliged to go through eruptive rocks, some of which, shaken out of their beds, rushed bounding down the abyss. Their fall awoke echoes of wonderful clearness.

Certain parts of the cone form glaciers. Hans would then walk with extreme precaution, sounding the ground at every step with his iron-tipped stick, to discover any *crevasses*. At doubtful parts we were fastened together by a long rope, so that any one who missed his footing would be supported by his companions. This arrangement was prudent, but it did not exclude all danger.

However, notwithstanding all the difficulties of the descent, down steeps unknown to the guide, the journey was accomplished without any accident, except the loss of a coil of rope, which fell from the hand of one of the Icelanders, and took the quickest road to the bottom of the gulf.

At mid-day we reached it. I looked up and saw the upper orifice of the cone framing a bit of sky, much reduced in size, but almost perfectly round. Just on the edge appeared the sunny peak of Scartaris, which lost itself in immensity.

At the bottom of the crater were three chimneys, out of which, in its eruptions, the central fire of Snäfell had belched out smoke and lava. Each of these chimneys had a diameter of about 100 feet. They gaped at us with wide-open mouths. I had not the courage to look at them. But Professor Lidenbrock had made a rapid survey of all three. He was quite panting, rushing from one to another gesticulating, and talking incoherently. Hans and his companions, seated on blocks of lava, looked wonderingly at this procedure, and evidently thought him mad.

All at once my uncle gave a cry. I thought he had lost his footing, and was falling into one of the holes. But no, there he was with outstretched arms, and legs wide apart, standing in front of a granite rock, laid in the center of the crater like an enormous pedestal ready to receive a statue of Pluto. He was in the posture of a man who is stupefied, but whose stupefaction will soon give place to the wildest delights.

"Axel, Axel!" he cried; "come, come!" I ran to him. Neither Hans nor his companions moved.

"Look!" said the professor.

And sharing at least his stupefaction, if not his joy, I read on the western face of the block, in Runic characters half eaten away by time, this thrice-accursed name:

$$\text{ᛝᛅᚾᛏ   ᛋᛁᚱᚾᛐᛋᛋᛏᛪ}$$

"Arne Saknussemm!" cried my uncle. "Do you still doubt?"

I made no reply, but went back to my seat in consternation. This evidence crushed me. How long I sat lost in my own reflections, I cannot say. All I know is that when I looked up again only Hans and my uncle were in the crater. The Icelanders had taken their leave and were now on their way down the side of Snäfell back to Stapi.

Hans was sleeping quietly at the foot of a rock in a stream of lava, where he had improvised a bed for himself. My uncle was pacing about like a wild beast in a trapper's pit. I had neither the wish nor the power to rise, and, following the guide's example, I fell into a troubled sleep, fancying I could hear the noises and feel the tremblings of the mountain.

Thus passed the first night in the bottom of the crater.

Next day a gray, gloomy, heavy sky overshadowed the mouth of the cone. I did not know it so much by the obscurity of the gulf as by my uncle's rage over it.

I understood the reason, and a ray of hope dawned on me. This was why:

Of the three routes open to us, only one had been followed by Saknussemm; and, according to the learned Icelander, it was to be recognized by the particular fact mentioned in the cryptogram, that the shadow of Scartaris would come and fall softly over the edge of it during the last days of June. That sharp peak might, in fact, be considered as the gnomon, or pin, of an immense sundial, whose shadow on a given day would point out the road to the earth's center.

Now, no sun, no shadow, and consequently no indication. It was the 25th of June now, and, should the sky remain overcast four days longer, our observations would have to be deferred till another year.

I cannot attempt to depict the wrath of Professor Lidenbrock. The day passed and no shadow appeared. Hans never stirred, though he must have asked himself what we were waiting for, if, indeed, he could ask himself anything at all. My uncle never once addressed me, but kept his eyes fixed on the gloomy sky.

On the 26th there was still nothing. Rain mingled with snow kept falling all day long. Hans made a hut of pieces of lava. I rather enjoyed watching the thousands of cascades that came rushing down the sides of the cone, the deafening noise increasing at every stone they came against.

My uncle was beside himself with passion. And certainly it was enough to irritate a far more patient man than he. It was like foundering within sight of the harbor.

But Heaven never sends great sorrow without great joy, and there was satisfaction in store for Professor Lidenbrock to compensate for his agonizing suspense.

The next day was again overcast, but on Sunday, the 28th of June, the last day but two of the month, with the change of moon came the change of weather. The sun poured a flood of rays into the crater. Every hillock, each rock and stone, every projection had its share in this affluence of light, and threw its shadow forthwith on the ground. Amongst the others was the shadow of Scartaris, which lay like a sharp peak, and it began to move round insensibly with the radiant orb. My uncle moved with it. At noon, when it was at its least, it fell softly on the edge of the middle chimney.

"It is there! it is there!" exclaimed the professor, adding in Danish: "Now let's away to the center of the globe!"

I looked at Hans.

"Forüt!" was his quiet reply.

"Forward!" returned my uncle.

It was nineteen minutes past one.

XVII

The real journey now commenced. Hitherto our fatigues had been more than our difficulties, but now the latter would multiply at every step. I had not yet even looked down the bottomless well, in which I was about to be engulfed. The moment had come. I must now take my part in the enterprise, or refuse the risk. But I was ashamed to draw back before the hunter, and Hans accepted the adventure so coolly, with such indifference, and such a perfect disregard of danger, that I blushed at the idea of being less brave than he. Had we been alone I should have renewed my arguments, but in the presence of the guide I kept silent. Memory recalled for an instant my pretty Virlandaise, and I approached the central chimney.

I have already said that it measured 100 feet in diameter and 300 feet in circumference. Holding on by a jutting rock I looked down into it. My hair stood on end. The feeling of vacuity took possession of my being. I felt my center of gravity becoming displaced, and my head began to reel as if I were intoxicated. There is nothing stranger than this abyss attraction. I was about to fall in when a powerful hand held me back. It was that of Hans. Evidently I had not taken enough *abyss* lessons at the Frelsers-Kirk in Copenhagen.

But short as my survey had been of this well I had a good idea of its conformation. Its walls, which were nearly perpendicular, were thick with sharp projections, which would greatly facilitate descent. But if the staircase was there, the rail was wanting. A rope fastened to the edge of the orifice would have been sufficient support, but how could we unfasten it when we reached the lower extremity?

My uncle employed a very simple method to obviate this great difficulty. He undid a coil of rope, about the thickness of a finger and

400 feet long. He let half of it slip down first, then he rolled it round a block of lava, which jutted out, and threw down the other half. Each of us could then descend by holding both lines of rope in his hand, which could not get loose. When he had gone 200 feet nothing could be easier than to haul the rope in by pulling one end. Then the exercise would begin again and go on *ad infinitum*.

"Now," said my uncle, after these preparations were completed, "let's see about the luggage. We will divide it into three parts, and each of us will strap one on his back. Of course I mean only fragile articles."

The daring man evidently did not include us in the category.

"Hans," he said, "will take charge of the tools and a portion of the provisions. You, Axel, will take another third of the provisions and the arms, and I will take the rest of the provisions and the delicate instruments."

"But who is to take the clothes?" said I, "and that heap of ropes and ladders?"

"They will take care of themselves."

"How?"

"You'll see."

My uncle liked to employ grand means. He ordered Hans to make a bundle of all the non-fragile articles, which was then firmly roped and thrown right down into the abyss. I could hear the loud roaring noise it made in whizzing through the air, and my uncle stooped down and watched its progress till it was out of sight. Then my uncle said:

"That's all right. Now it is our turn."

I ask any sane man if it was possible to hear these words without a shudder.

The professor forthwith fastened the package of instruments on his back, and Hans took the tools, and I the arms. The descent commenced in the following order:—Hans first, then my uncle, then myself. It was made in complete silence, only broken by the fall of fragments of rock into the abyss.

I let myself drop, as it were, frantically clutching the double cord in one hand, and propping myself with my stick with the other. One idea possessed me. I was afraid the support would give way. The cord seemed to me so frail to bear the weight of three persons. I hung upon it as little as possible, performing wonderful feats of equilibrium upon the projections of lava which my feet sought to catch hold of like a hand.

Whenever one of these slipping steps shook beneath Hans' foot, he said in his quiet voice:

"*Gif akt!*"

"Attention!" repeated my uncle.

In about half an hour we found ourselves on the slab of a rock that was firmly embedded in the wall of the chimney.

Hans pulled the rope by one end and the other rose in the air. After passing the upper rock it fell down again, and a shower of stones and lava came rattling after it like rain, or dangerous hail rather.

Leaning down over the edge of our narrow plateau, I noticed that the bottom of the hole was still invisible.

Then the rope maneuver began again, and half-an-hour afterwards we had gone another 200 feet.

I don't know whether the maddest geologist would have attempted to study, during his descent, the nature of the rocks through which he passed. For my own part, I didn't trouble myself about it. I didn't care whether they were pliocene, miocene, eocene, cretaceous, jurassic, triassic, permian, carboniferous, devonian, silurian, or primitive. But, no doubt the professor was taking observations or making notes, for he said to me:

"The farther I go the more confident I feel. The disposition of these volcanic formations strongly supports the theory of Humphry Davy. We are now among the primitive rocks, on which the chemical operation took place produced by the contact of metals with air and water. I reject absolutely the theory of a central heat. However, we shall soon see."

Always the same conclusion. I was not inclined to amuse myself by arguing, and he took my silence for agreement.

The descent began afresh, but at the end of three hours, I could not yet catch a glimpse of the bottom. When I looked up, I perceived the orifice narrowing sensibly. The sides seemed to approach each other, and it was gradually getting dark.

Still we went on; down, down. I fancied the loosened stones fell quicker to the bottom, and with more noise.

I had taken care to keep an exact account of our maneuver with the ropes, so that I knew exactly the depth attained and the time elapsed.

Each descent occupied half an hour, and we had made fourteen. I calculated then that we had been seven hours, and three hours and a half extra for rest and meals, as we had allowed us a quarter of an hour between each maneuver. Altogether ten hours and a half. We had started at one. It must therefore now be eleven.

As to the depth—fourteen times 200 feet gave a depth of 2,800 feet. At this moment, I heard the voice of Hans, calling:

"Halt!"

I stopped instantly, just in time to keep my feet from knocking my uncle's head.

"We are there!" he cried.

"Where?" said I, slipping down beside him.

"At the bottom of the perpendicular shaft."

"Then there is no outlet?"

"Yes, there is a passage, I think, to the right. I only caught a glimpse of it, but we shall see to-morrow. We'll sup now, and then go to sleep." The darkness was not yet complete. We opened the bag of provisions and took some food, and then we all three settled ourselves for the night, as comfortably as we could on the stones and fragments of lava.

As I lay on my back, I chanced to open my eyes and perceived a bright spot at the extremity of the tube, 3,000 feet long, transformed now into a gigantic telescope.

It was a star, but deprived of all scintillation by the distance. By my reckoning, it was β Ursa Minor.

Then I fell fast asleep.

XVIII

At eight next morning, a ray of daylight came to awaken us. The myriad facets on the lava walls received it and threw it back in a shower of sparks.

This light was strong enough to enable us to discern surrounding objects.

"Well now, Axel, what do you say to it?" cried my uncle, rubbing his hands. "Did you ever pass a quieter night in the old house in König-strasse? No noise of carts, or street cries, no boatman's vociferations."

"Certainly, we are quiet enough, but the very calm has something terrifying about it."

"Now, now!" cried my uncle, "if you are frightened already, how will you get on by-and-by. We haven't gone one inch yet into the bowels of the earth."

"What do you mean?"

"I mean that we have only reached the level of the island. This long vertical tube which opens in the crater of Snäfell ends almost at the level of the sea."

"Are you sure of that?"

"Quite sure. Consult the barometer."

I found the mercury, which had risen gradually in the instrument, in proportion as we descended, had stopped at twenty-nine inches.

"You see," continued the professor, "we have only yet the pressure of the atmosphere, and I am impatient for the manometer to replace the barometer."

The barometer, in fact, would become useless, from the moment the weight of the air should exceed the pressure at the level of the sea.

"But," said I, "isn't there reason to fear that this always-increasing pressure will be very painful?"

"No. We shall descend slowly, and our lungs will get accustomed to the denser air. Aeronauts end by having too little air, as they rise constantly higher, and we shall have too much perhaps. But I prefer that. Don't let us lose an instant. Where is the bundle we rolled down before us?"

This reminded me that we had looked for it the night before and could not find it.

My uncle asked Hans about it, who, after gazing round with the keen eye of a hunter, replied:

"*Der huppe.*"

"Up there."

Sure enough there was the bundle hanging on a rocky projection 100 feet above our head. The agile Icelander climbed up after it like a cat, and in a few minutes the bundle was in our possession again.

"Now," said my uncle, "let us breakfast, and eat like men who are likely to have a long day's walk before them."

The biscuit and extract of beef were washed down with a drink of water mixed with a little gin.

After breakfast my uncle drew a note-book out of his pocket for observations. Then he took up his different instruments and wrote down the following result:

"*Monday, June 29th.*

"Chronometer, 8h. 17m. A.M.

"Barometer, 29' 7 in.

"Thermometer, 6°.

"Direction, E.S.E."

This last observation applied to the dim passage, and was indicated by the compass.

"Now, Axel!" exclaimed the professor, enthusiastically, "we are actually going to push our way into the heart of the earth. This is the exact time when our journey commences."

So saying my uncle took up the apparatus of Ruhmkorff suspended from his neck, with one hand, and with the other placed it in communication with the electric coil in the lantern, and immediately a light was produced, bright enough to illumine the dark passage.

Hans carried the other apparatus, which was also set in action. This ingenious application of electricity would enable us to go on for a long time, creating an artificial day, safe even in the midst of the most inflammable gases.

"Forward!" said my uncle.

Each one resumed his load; Hans undertook to push the bundle of ropes and clothing before him along the ground, and I came behind him into the gallery.

Just as I was about to enter the gloomy passage, I looked up through the distant aperture and saw once more the sky of Iceland, which I should never gaze upon again.

At the time of the last eruption, in 1229, the lava had forced this passage for itself, and the sides of it were covered with a thick shiny coating of it, which reflected and intensified the electric light. The great difficulty of the route was to avoid slipping too rapidly down an incline of forty-five degrees. Happily, certain erosions and protuberances served for steps, which we descended, letting our luggage slip before us from the end of a long rope.

But what were steps under our feet became stalactites in every other part. The lava, which was porous in certain places, was covered with small rounded blisters—crystals of opaque quartz adorned with clear drops of glass, and suspended from the roof like chandeliers, which seemed to light up as we passed. It looked as if the genii of the abyss were illuminating their palace for the reception of their terrestrial visitants.

"It is magnificent!" I exclaimed, involuntarily. "What a sight, uncle! Don't you admire all those shades of lava, from reddish brown to bright yellow? And those crystals looking like luminous globes?"

"Ah, you like that, Axel!" replied my uncle. "You call that splendid, my boy; you will see many of those, I hope. Let us walk on."

He would have been more correct if he had said slide, for we let ourselves slip, without effort, down the steep inclines. It was the *facilis descensus Averni* of Virgil. The compass, which I consulted frequently, indicated the south-east with undeviating regularity. This stream of lava neither turned aside to the east nor west. It had the inflexibility of the straight line.

However, there was no sensible increase of heat. This supported the theories of Davy, and more than once I was astonished when I consulted the thermometer. Two hours after it only marked 10°, that is to say, an increase of 4°. This authorized me to suppose that our descent was more horizontal than vertical. The depth reached might have been easily ascertained, as the professor measured with exactitude the angles of deviation and inclination on the road, but he kept his observations to himself.

About 8 P.M. he gave the signal to stop; Hans sat down immediately. The lamps were hung up to a jutting piece of lava. We were in a sort of cavern, but the air was not deficient. Quite the contrary. Certain puffs of it even reached us. What had produced them? To what atmospheric disturbance must we attribute their origin? I did not care just now to pursue the subject, however. I was too hungry and tired to argue the question. A seven hours' descent involves considerable expenditure of strength. I was exhausted, and rejoiced to hear the word, "Halt!" Hans spread provisions for us upon a block of lava, and we all ate heartily. One thing, however, made me uneasy. Our supply of water was half consumed. My uncle reckoned on replenishing it from subterranean springs, but hitherto not even one had appeared. I could not help drawing his attention to this fact.

"And are you surprised at seeing no springs?" he replied.

"Most certainly, and what's more, I am very uneasy; we only have water enough for five days."

"Don't worry yourself, Axel. I'll answer for it. We shall find water, and more than we want."

"And when?"

"When we get out of this lava that envelops us. How can you think springs could burst through such walls as these!"

"But perhaps this passage runs to a great depth. It seems to me that we have not made great progress vertically."

"What makes you think that?"

"Because the heat would be much greater if we had penetrated very far through the crust."

"According to your system," replied my uncle. "What is the thermometer?"

"Scarcely 15°, which shows only an increase of 9° since we started."

"Well, and what is your conclusion?"

"This is my conclusion. According to the most exact observations the increase of heat in the interior of the globe is 1° in 100 feet. But certain localities may modify this figure. For instance, at Yakoust, in Siberia, the increase is 1° in 36 feet. This difference evidently depends on the conducting power of rocks. I may add, too, that in the neighborhood of an extinct volcano and through gneiss it has been observed that the elevation of the temperature was only 1° in 125 feet. Let us adopt this last hypothesis and calculate."

"Do so, my boy."

"Nothing is easier," I said, writing down the figures in my notebook. "Nine times 125 feet make 1,125 feet of depth."

"That's it exactly. Well, then?"

"Well, according to my observations, we are 10,000 feet below the level of the sea."

"Is it possible!"

"Yes; or figures are no longer figures."

The professor's calculations were exact. We had already exceeded by 6,000 feet the greatest depth ever reached by man, such as the mines of Kitz-Bahl in the Tyrol, and those of Wuttembourg in Bohemia.

The temperature, which ought to have been 81°, was scarcely 15°.

This was certainly well worth thinking over.

XIX

Next day, Tuesday, June the 30th, at 6 A.M., the descent was resumed.

We still followed the gallery of lava, a real natural staircase, sloping as gently as those inclined planes which are found in place of stairs even yet m some old houses. We went on till 12.17, the exact time when we overtook Hans, who had just stopped short.

"Ah!" cried my uncle, "then we have come to the end of the gallery!"

I looked round me. We were in cross roads. Two paths lay before us, both dark and narrow. Which should we take? Here was a difficulty.

However, my uncle would not allow himself to show any hesitation before me or the guide. He pointed to the eastern tunnel, and soon we were all three treading it.

Besides, we might have stood hesitating for ever, for there was nothing to determine the choice. We were absolutely forced to trust to chance.

The slope of this fresh gallery was scarcely perceptible, and its sections very unequal. Sometimes a succession of arches would be disclosed, like the nave of a gothic cathedral. The architect of the middle ages might have studied here all the forms of church architecture which start from the ogive. A mile farther and we had to stoop our heads beneath elliptic arches in the Roman style, and massive pillars in the wall bent beneath the abutments of the arches. In other places this arrangement gave place to low substructures, like beavers' huts, and we had to crawl along narrow tube-like passages.

The heat was always bearable. But involuntary thoughts came over me of its intensity when the lava, ejected by Snäfell, rushed along by the route which was now so quiet. I imagined the torrents of fire dashing against the angles of the gallery, and the accumulation of heated vapors in this narrow channel.

"It is to be hoped," thought I, "that the old volcano may not take it into his head to play his old pranks again!"

These reflections I did not communicate to my uncle Lidenbrock. He would not have understood them. His one thought was to get forward. He walked, he slid, he even tumbled over with a resolution that, after all, was worth admiring.

At 6 P.M., after a not very fatiguing walk, we had made two leagues south, but were scarcely a quarter of a mile deeper. My uncle gave the signal to rest. We ate without talking much, and went to sleep without thinking much.

Our preparations for night were very simple. A railway rug, in which we each rolled ourselves, composed our bedding. There was neither cold to fear nor nocturnal intruders. Travelers in the heart of Africa, among the Saharas, in the old world, or in the bosoms of forests in the new, are obliged to take turns at watching each other during the hours of sleep, but here there was absolute solitude and complete security; neither savages nor wild beasts were to be feared.

We woke up next morning fresh and bright. The route was resumed. We followed the passage of lava as on the preceding day. It was impossible to tell the nature of the rocks. The tunnel, instead of going down, seemed gradually becoming absolutely horizontal. I thought even it seemed rising to the surface. This upward inclination became more evident about 10 A.M., and consequently so fatiguing that I was obliged to slacken pace.

"Come on, Axel, what's keeping you?" said the professor, impatiently.

"I must stop; I can't keep up with you," I replied.

"What! after only three hours' walking on such an easy road!"

"Easy, it may be, but most certainly very tiring."

"What! when it is all down-hill?"

"All up-hill, if you please."

"Up-hill!" exclaimed my uncle, shrugging his shoulders.

"Undoubtedly. For the last half hour the slope has changed, and if we continue this way we shall certainly get back to Iceland in time."

The professor shook his head like a man determined not to be convinced. I tried to resume the conversation, but he would not answer me, and gave the signal to go on. I saw quite well that his silence was mere temper.

However, I shouldered my load bravely and went quickly after Hans, who was following my uncle. I was always afraid of letting them out of sight, for the idea of losing myself in the depths of this labyrinth made me shudder.

Besides, though the upward route was more fatiguing, I had the comfort of thinking it was bringing us always nearer to the surface of the earth again. Each step confirmed me in this, and I rejoiced in the idea of seeing my little Gräuben once more.

At noon I noticed a change in the appearance of the walls of the tunnel. I was first aware of it by the reflection of the electric light becoming fainter, when l discovered that solid rock had displaced the lava coating. This rock was composed of sloping layers, often disposed vertically. We were among strata of the transition or Silurian period.*

"It is plain enough!" I exclaimed. "There are the sedimentary deposits of the waters, these shales, limestones, and grits. We are leaving the granitic rock behind us. It is just as if Hamburg people should take the train to Hanover to go to Lubeck!"

---

* So called, because rocks of this period are extensively found in England in districts once peopled by the Silures, a Celtic race.

I had better have kept my observations to myself. But my geological temperament got the better of my prudence and my uncle heard my exclamation.

"What's all that about?" he asked.

"Look!" I replied, pointing to the varied succession of grits and limestones, and the first indications of the slaty cleavage.

"Well?"

"We have reached the period when the first plants and first animals appeared."

"Ah! so that's what you think?"

"Look for yourself and examine carefully."

And I made him turn his lamp so as to throw the light on the wall. I expected some outburst, but he did not make the slightest remark and walked on.

Had he understood me or not? Or was it that the *amour-propre* of uncle and *savant* was too great to allow himself to admit that he had chosen the wrong tunnel? Or had he determined to explore it to the very end? It was so evident that we had left the lava route, and that this road would never take us to the heart of Snäfell.

However, I began to wonder whether, after all, I was not attaching too much importance to this change of strata. Perhaps I myself might be mistaken. Were we really going through the layers of rock above the granite base?

"If I am right," I said to myself, "I ought to find some remains of primitive vegetation. I will look round and see."

I had not gone a hundred steps before incontestable proof met my eyes. And necessarily, for at the Silurian period the seas contained upwards of 1,500 species of vegetables and animals. My feet, accustomed to treading on the hard lava, suddenly came in contact with the dust, the *débris* of plants and shells. On the walls were distinct impressions of fucoids and lycopodiaceae. Professor Lidenbrock could not be deceived. I fancy he first shut his eyes, and walked straight on.

It was obstinacy in the extreme, and at last I could not stand it longer. I picked up a shell in a complete state of preservation, which had belonged to an animal nearly resembling a woodlouse; and I turned to my uncle and said:

"Look!"

"Well," he replied calmly, "it is the shell of a crustacean of the trilobite species, now extinct That's all."

"But does it not bring you to the conclusion that—"

"To the same conclusion as yours? Yes. Perfectly so. We have left the granite rock and the lava passage. It is possible I have made a mistake, but I shall not be sure of it till we have reached the very end of this gallery."

"You are quite right, uncle; and I should approve your intention, if we were not threatened with a danger which becomes each moment more imminent."

"And what is it?"

"The want of water."

"Well, we must put ourselves on rations, Axel."

XX

And this, indeed, we were forced to do. Our provisions would not last three days longer. I saw that when supper-time came; and, unhappily, we had little hope of meeting with a spring in the transition system.

All next day we continued our course through an interminable succession of arcades. We walked on without saying a word. The taciturnity of Hans seemed to have infected us.

The path was not rising now, at least hot sensibly. Sometimes even it appeared to slope. But this tendency, besides being very slight, could not reassure the professor, for the nature of the layers remained unmodified, and the transition period became more distinct.

The electric light made the schists and limestone and old red sandstone sparkle magnificently. We might have thought ourselves examining some excavations in Devonshire, a county which gives its name to this series. Specimens of magnificent marbles clothed the walls, some of a gray agate, fantastically streaked with white; others of rich crimson or yellow, with red patches. Then came specimens of speckled marbles in dark colors, relieved by the light shades of the limestone.

The greater part of these marbles bore the imprint of primitive animals. Since the day before, creation had made evident progress. Instead of the rudimentary trilobites, I noticed the *débris* of a more perfect order: amongst others of fishes, the Ganoids and the Sauropterygia, in which palaeontologists have sought to discover the earliest forms of reptiles. The Devonian seas were peopled with a large number of animals of this species, and they deposited them by thousands in the rocks of the new formation.

It became evident that we were ascending the scale of animal creation of which man is at the top. But Professor Lidenbrock seemed not to notice it.

He was expecting one of two things, either that a vertical well would open below his feet, and allow him to resume his descent, or that some obstacle would prevent him from continuing this route. But evening came, and neither hope was realized.

On Friday, after a night during which I began to feel the torments of thirst, our little company again plunged into the windings of the gallery.

After ten hours' walking, I noticed that the reflection of our lamps on the walls had strangely become fainter. The marble, the schist, the limestone, and the sandstone of the walls gave way to a dark dull lining. Just then we came to a very narrow part, and I leaned my left hand against the wall. When I removed it, I saw it was quite black. I looked closer. We were in a coal mine!

"A coal mine!" I exclaimed.

"A mine without miners!"

"Indeed, who knows that?"

"I know it," said the professor curtly; "and I am certain that this gallery through coalpits has not been bored by the hand of man. But whether it is Nature's work or not, is nothing to me. It is supper-time. Let us sup."

Hans prepared the meal. I scarcely ate anything, and drank the few drops of water that fell to my share. Our guide's gourd, and that only half full, was all that remained to quench the thirst of three men.

After the repast, my companions lay down on their rugs, and found the remedy for all their fatigues in sleep. But I could not close my eyes, and counted the hours till morning.

On Saturday, at 6 A.M., we set off again. Twenty minutes later, we arrived at a vast excavation. I owned then that human hands could never have dug out such a pit; the vaults would have been shored up, and certainly they must have been supported by some miracle of equilibrium.

The cavern we were in was 100 feet wide, and 150 feet high. It was evidently a hole, made in the coal formation by some violent subterranean commotion.

The whole history of the coal period was written on these gloomy walls, and a geologist could have easily made out the different phases. The beds of coal were separated by strata of sandstone or compact clay, and appeared crushed by the upper layer.

In that age of the world which preceded the secondary period, immense types of vegetation clothed the earth, owing to the double action of tropical heat and continued moisture. An atmosphere of vapors enveloped the earth completely, depriving it still of the sun's rays.

Thence arises the conclusion that the high temperatures were not caused by this new fire. Perhaps even the orb of day was not yet prepared for his glorious mission. Climates did not yet exist, and a torrid heat overspread the entire surface of the globe, alike at the equator and the poles. From whence did it come? From its interior.

In spite of the theories of Professor Lidenbrock, a fierce fire brooded then within the spheroid; its action was felt to the last layers of the earth's crust. The plants, deprived of the beneficent influences of the sun, yielded neither flowers nor perfumes; but the roots drew a vigorous life from the burning soil of those primeval days.

There were but few trees, nothing but herbaceous plants, immense grasses, ferns, lycopods, sigillaria, asterophyllites, rare orders now, but then numbering thousands of different species.

Now it is from this very period of exuberant vegetation that the coal formation dates. The crust of the globe, still in an elastic state, obeyed the movements of the liquid mass it covered. Hence arose numerous fissures and depressions. The plants, dragged down by the waters in great numbers, formed gradually considerable heaps below.

Natural chemical action then ensued. The vegetable masses beneath the waters first changed into peat, then, owing to the influence of the gases, and the heat of fermentation, they underwent complete mineralization. Thus were formed those immense coal fields, which excessive consumption must exhaust, however, in less than three centuries, if the industrial world does not see to it.

These reflections occupied my mind while I was gazing at the wealth of combustibles stored up in this portion of the earth. They will doubtless never be discovered. The working of such deep mines would involve too great sacrifices. Besides, what would be the use when coal deposits are lying, one might say, on the surface of the globe in a great many countries! None but I saw these untouched mines, so they would remain till the last day of the world.

Meantime we were walking on, and I alone of the little company forgot the length of the way in geological contemplations. The temperature remained as it was during our passage through the lava and schists. Only my sense of smell was affected by the exceedingly strong odor of protocarburet of hydrogen. I recognized immediately the presence in this gallery of a large quantity of that dangerous fluid known among miners as fire-damp, the explosion of which has often caused such frightful catastrophes.

Happily we were illumined by Ruhmkorff's apparatus. If we had unfortunately been so imprudent as to have ventured to explore the gallery with torches in our hands, a terrible explosion would have made an end of the journey and the travelers.

This excursion in the mine continued till evening. My uncle could scarcely contain his impatience at this horizontal route. The darkness, quite deep twenty steps distant, prevented the length of the gallery from being reckoned, and I began to think it was positively interminable, when at six o'clock a wall appeared suddenly in front of us. There was no opening right or left, above or below. We had reached the end of a blind alley.

"Well, so much the better!" exclaimed my uncle. "I know at least what I'm about now. We are not on Saknussemm's route, and must just turn and go back to where the road forks."

"Yes," said I, "if our strength holds out."

"And why shouldn't it?"

"Because to-morrow, every drop of water will be gone."

"And of courage too, it seems," said the professor, looking sternly at me. I did not dare to reply.

XXI

The departure was fixed for an early hour next morning. No time was to be lost, for it would take us five days to reach the crossroads.

I need not dwell on the sufferings of our return. My uncle bore them like a man who is angry with himself for yielding to weakness: Hans, with the resignation of his placid nature; and I, to speak the truth, complaining and despairing the whole time. I could not bear up against this stroke of ill-fortune.

As I had foreseen, the water came to an end the very first day of our journey back. Our only store of liquid now was gin, but this horrible drink burnt the throat, and I could not even endure the sight of it. I felt the temperature stifling. Fatigue paralyzed me. More than once I fell motionless. Then we had to come to a halt and my uncle or the Icelander did their best to revive me. But I saw already that the former was struggling painfully against the extreme fatigue and the tortures of thirst.

At last, on Tuesday, the 7th of July, dragging ourselves along on our knees and hands, we arrived half dead at the junction of the two passages. There I lay like an inert lump, stretched full length on the lava floor. It was 10 A.M.

Hans and my uncle, clinging to the wall, tried to nibble a few bits of biscuit. Long moans escaped my swollen lips. I fell into a profound stupor.

After a little, my uncle came to me, and, lifting me in his arms, said in a tone of genuine pity:

"Poor child!"

His words touched me, for I was not accustomed to tenderness from the austere professor. I seized his trembling hands in mine. He let me do it and looked at me. Tears stood in his eyes.

I saw him lift the gourd slung at his side, and, to my great bewilderment, he put it to my lips, and said:

"Drink!"

Had I heard him right? Was my uncle mad? I looked at him stupidly. I could not understand him.

"Drink!" he repeated.

And lifting up his gourd, he drained the contents into my mouth.

Oh! infinite boon! A gulp of water moistened my burning mouth, one only, but it sufficed to call back my ebbing life.

I thanked my uncle with clasped hands.

"Yes," he said, "a mouthful of water! The last, do you hear, the last? I kept it on purpose for you. Twenty times, aye, a hundred times, I have had to fight with my fearful longing to drink it; but no, Axel, I kept it for you."

"Oh, uncle!" I murmured, and big tears started to my eyes.

"Yes, poor child, I knew, when you reached these cross roads, you would drop down half dead, and I kept my last few drops of water to revive you."

"Thanks, thanks!" I cried.

Slightly as my thirst was quenched, I had somewhat recovered my strength. The muscles of my throat, which had become contracted, now relaxed, and the inflammation of my lips subsided. I could speak.

"Well, come," said I, "there is only one course open to us now; our water is done, and we must go right back."

While I was speaking, my uncle avoided looking at me, and hung down his head, unwilling to meet my eyes.

"We must go back," I cried, "and find our way to Snäfell. May God give us strength to climb to the summit of the crater."

"Go back!" said my uncle, speaking to himself, it seemed, more than to me.

"Yes, go back, and without losing an instant."

A pretty long silence ensued.

Then, in an odd tone, the professor went on to say:

"Well then, Axel, those few drops of water have not restored your strength and courage?"

"Courage!"

"I see you are as down-hearted as ever, and still speak despairingly."

"What sort of man was this I had to do with, and what projects was his bold spirit still entertaining?"

"What! you are unwilling?"

"Shall I give up this expedition at the very moment when everything promises success?"

"Never!"

"Then we must make up our minds to perish!"

"No, Axel, no! Start off! Let Hans go with you. Leave me alone!"

"Leave you behind?"

"Yes, I tell you; leave me here. I have commenced the journey, and I will complete it or never return. Go, Axel, go!"

My uncle was violently excited. His voice, which had softened for an instant, sounded harsh and threatening. He was struggling with gloomy energy against impossibilities. I was unwilling to leave him at the bottom of this abyss, and yet the instinct of self-preservation urged me to fly from it.

The guide watched this scene with his accustomed indifference. He understood what was going on, however. Our gestures showed him that each was trying to drag the other a different road; but Hans evidenced no interest in the question, though his own life was involved in it. He was ready to go if the signal to start was given, and ready to stay in obedience to the slightest wish of his master.

What would I not have given that minute to have been able to make him understand me! My words and groans and accent would have moved his cold nature. I would have pointed out dangers which he never seemed to suspect. I would have made him fully alive to them, and together we might, perhaps, have succeeded in convincing the obstinate professor. Nay, if all other means failed, we might have compelled him to regain the summit of Snäfell.

I went up to Hans and laid my hand on his. He did not stir. I pointed to the way out of the crater. He still remained motionless. My gasping breath showed my sufferings. The Icelander gently shook his head, and quietly pointing to my uncle, said:

"Master!"

"The master!" I cried. "Madman! He is not the master of your life. We must fly, we must drag him along. Do you understand?"

I had grasped Hans by the arm, and was trying to make him get up. I struggled with him, but my uncle interposed and said:

"Be calm, Axel, you will get nothing out of that impassible servant. Listen, therefore, to what I propose."

I crossed my arms and looked my uncle firm in the face.

"The want of water," said he, "is the only obstacle in our path. In this tunnel to the east, composed of lavas, schists, and coal, we have not found a single drop of liquid. It is possible we may be more fortunate if we explore the one to the west."

I shook my head with profound incredulity.

"Hear me to the end," said the professor, in a constrained voice. "While you were lying motionless, I went to examine the conformation of the passage. It leads straight into the heart of the globe, and in a few hours we shall reach the granite foundation. There we must meet with springs in abundance. The nature of the rock favors this, and instinct agrees with logic in support of my conviction. Now, this is what I propose to you. When Columbus asked his ships' crews for three days longer to let him discover new countries, the men, sick and dismayed as they were, allowed the justice of his demand, and he discovered the New World. I am the Columbus of these subterranean regions, and I ask you to give me one day more. If I have not found water before the time expires, I swear to you we will return to the surface of the earth."

In spite of my irritation, I was moved by my uncle's words and by the violent restraint he was putting on himself.

"Very well," I said. "It shall be as you wish, and may God reward your superhuman energy. You have only a few hours to try your fortune, so let us start at once."

XXII

The descent commenced this time by the new gallery. Hans walked first as usual. We had not gone a hundred steps, when the professor, throwing the light of his lantern on the wall, exclaimed:

"Here are the primitive rocks. We are in the right track. Forward! forward!"

When the earth's surface gradually cooled in the first stages of its formation, the diminution of its bulk produced disruptions, rents, contractions, and chasms. The passage itself was a fissure of this kind, through which the eruptive granite had forced a passage at some time. Its myriad windings formed an inextricable labyrinth through the primordial rock.

The deeper we went, the more clearly defined became the successive layers of the primitive period. Geological science considers this primitive rock as the basis of the mineral crust, and she recognizes in it three distinct layers—the schist, the gneiss, and the mica-schist, resting on the immovable rock called granite.

Never before were mineralogists in such wondrously favorable circumstances for studying their science. What the boring machine, an insensible inert instrument, could not bring to the surface, we could examine with our eyes, and touch with our hands.

Through the beds of schist, colored with beautiful shades of green, metallic threads of copper and manganese, mixed with traces of platinum and gold, were twisted and intertwined. I could not but think what riches are hid in the depths of the earth, which covetous humanity will never appropriate. These treasures have been buried so deep by the convulsions of primeval times, that neither mattock nor pickax will ever disinter them.

To the schists succeeded the gneiss, of a stratiform structure, and remarkable for the regularity and parallelism of its laminae. Then the mica schists disposed in great flakes, which are revealed to the eye by the sparkles of the white mica.

The light of our lanterns, caught by the little facets of the rocky mass, flashed up by brilliant jets at every angle, and I could have fancied myself traveling through a hollow diamond, in which the rays crossed and mingled and shot out in a thousand brilliant coruscations.

About six o'clock this illumination began to lose its splendor and almost ceased. The walls assumed a crystallized but somber appearance, the mica became more closely mingled with the feldspath and quartz, to form the rock *par excellence*, the hardest of all stones, that bears, without being crushed by it, the weight of the four systems. We were shut up in a prison of granite.

It was 8 P.M., and no sign yet of water. My sufferings were terrible. My uncle still pushed forward. He would not stop, and kept listening for the murmur of some spring. But there was not a sound.

However, I could not hold out long, for my legs refused to carry me. I struggled against my tortures as long as I could, for I did not want to make him stop. This would be to him the death-knell of all his hopes, for the day was fast drawing to an end, and it was his last.

At length my strength failed completely. I screamed out, "I'm dying! Come to me." And then I fell flat on the ground. My uncle turned back, folded his arms, and looked at me attentively. Then I heard him mutter in a hollow tone:

"This finishes it." A frightful gesture of rage met my glance, and I closed my eyes.

When I opened them again, I saw my two companions lying motionless, wrapped in their rugs. Were they asleep? For my part, I could not get a moment's sleep. I was in too much suffering, aggravated, too, by the thought that there was no remedy for it. My uncle's words echoed in my ears, for in such a feeble state the idea of regaining the surface of the globe was out of the question.

A league and a half of terrestrial crust lay above us. The whole weight of it seemed to lie upon my shoulders. I felt crushed, and exhausted myself in frantic efforts to turn round on my granite couch.

Some hours elapsed. Deep silence reigned—the silence of a tomb. Nothing could reach us through these walls, the thinnest of which was five miles thick.

However, in the midst of my stupor, I thought I heard a noise. It was dark in the tunnel, but looking closely, I fancied I could see the Icelander disappearing, lamp in hand.

Why was he going? Was Hans really forsaking us? My uncle was asleep. I tried to call out, but my voice could not make itself heard through my parched lips. The gloom had deepened into blackness, and the faint echo of the sound had died away.

"Hans has abandoned us!" I cried. "Hans, Hans!"

But these words were spoken within me. They never left my lips. However, after the first moment of fear, I was ashamed of suspecting a man who had given us no ground of suspicion. His departure could not be a flight. Instead of going up the passage he was going down farther in it. A bad intention would have dragged him upwards, not downwards. This reasoning calmed me a little, and I came back to another train of ideas. Hans was so tranquil that only some grave motive could have induced him to give up his rest. Had he gone on a voyage of discovery? Had he heard some distant murmur break on the silent night, though I had not?

XXIII

For a whole hour I was imagining in my delirious brain all the reasons which might have actuated the quiet Icelander. A perfect tangle of absurd ideas got into my head. I thought I was going mad.

But at last, a noise of footsteps was heard in the depths of the abyss. Hans was coming up again. The faint light began to glimmer on the walls, and then shone fully at the opening of the passage. Hans appeared.

He went up to my uncle, put his hand on his shoulder, and gently awoke him. My uncle sat up and asked what was the matter.

"*Vatten,*" replied the hunter.

Violent pain certainly seems to make one become a polyglot, for though I did not know a single word of Danish, I instinctively understood what the guide meant.

"Water! water!" I cried, and clapped my hands, and gesticulated as if I were crazy.

"Water!" repeated my uncle. "*Hvar?*" he asked, addressing the Icelander.

"*Nedat!*" replied Hans.

"*Where? Down below?*" I understood every word. I seized the hunter's hands and grasped them in mine, but he looked at me with perfect calmness.

We were soon ready, and set out along a passage that made a slope of two feet in the fathom.

In about an hour we had gone 1,000 fathoms and made a descent of 2,000 feet.

That very moment I heard an unusual sound of something running within the granite wall, a sort of dull roar, like distant thunder. I had been beginning to give way again to despair when we had walked half an hour, and still no spring had come in sight, but my uncle apprised me that Hans was not mistaken in his announcement, for that noise I heard now was the roaring of a torrent.

"A torrent?" I exclaimed.

"There is not a doubt of it. A subterranean river is flowing round us."

We hastened our steps, spurred on by hope. The sound of the murmuring water refreshed me already. It increased sensibly. The torrent which was running above us at first was now taking its course along the left wall, roaring and leaping. I passed my hands frequently over the rock, hoping to find some traces of moisture. But in vain.

Another half hour passed, and another half league.

It was evident that the hunter could not have gone farther than this while he was away. Guided by an instinct, peculiar to mountaineers, he felt this torrent through the rock, but certainly he had not seen the precious liquid at all, nor drank of it.

It soon became evident too, that if we went farther, we should be going away from the stream, for the rush was growing fainter.

We turned back. Hans stopped at the precise spot where the torrent seemed nearest.

I sat down beside the wall, the waters dashing within two feet of me with extreme violence, but still the granite wall between.

Instead of thinking over the likeliest means of getting over this barrier, I yielded once more to despair.

Hans looked at me, and I fancied I caught a smile on his lips.

He rose, and took the lamp. I followed him. He went to the wall, and I saw him lay his ear against the dry stone, slowly moving his place, and always listening intently. He was plainly trying to find out the exact part where the current made most noise. This point he discovered in the side wall to the left, about three feet from the ground.

How excited I felt! I could not venture to guess what he was going to do. But I soon understood and applauded, and loaded him with caresses when he lifted his pickax to attack the solid rock.

"Saved!" I shouted.

"Yes!" cried my uncle, in rapture. "Hans is right! Ah! the brave fellow! We should never have hit upon that!"

I quite believe it. Such an expedient, simple enough as it was, would never have entered our heads. Nothing seemed more dangerous than to give a blow with a pickax in this part of the earth's frame. Suppose some dislodgement should occur which would crush us? And what if this torrent should burst through the opening and engulf us! There was nothing chimerical in these dangers, but they could not hinder us. Our thirst was so intense, that we would have risked being crushed or drowned, and dug in the very bed of the ocean to relieve it.

Hans did the work, for neither my uncle nor myself could have done it. Our impatient hands would have made the rock fly off in fragments under our hasty blows. The guide, on the contrary, was calm and collected, and gradually wore away the rock by little but continuous strokes, till he had dug an opening about six inches wide. I could hear the torrent getting louder, and I seemed already to feel the beneficent water touch my lips.

Soon the pick had buried itself two feet in the granite. The operation had already lasted an hour.

I waited with impatience, and my uncle wished to employ stronger measures, though I did all I could to dissuade him. He had already seized his pickax, when suddenly there came a hissing noise, and then a jet of water spouted out violently, and dashed against the opposite wall.

Hans, who was almost upset by the force of the shock, gave a cry of pain, the cause of which I soon understood, and cried out in my turn when I found, on plunging my hands into the water, that it was boiling.

"Water at 200°!" I exclaimed.

"Well, it will cool," replied my uncle.

The passage was filled with steam, and a stream formed, which began to run away and lose itself in the subterranean windings. Soon we were able to indulge in our first draft.

Oh, how delicious! What a priceless luxury this was. It mattered not what the water was or whence it had come. It was water, and though still warm, it brought back the ebbing life. I drank without stopping, without even tasting.

But after my first moment's delectation I exclaimed, "Why it is mineral water! It tastes of iron!"

"Capital for the stomach," said my uncle, "and highly mineralized! This journey is as good as going to Spa or Töplitz!"

"Oh, isn't it good?"

"I should think so, water obtained two leagues below the ground. There is an inky taste about it, but it is not disagreeable. No, it is really a famous tonic Hans has procured us, so I propose this health-giving stream shall receive his name."

"By all means," said I. And the river was called "Hansbach" forthwith.

Hans was not the least proud of the honor. After he had refreshed himself moderately, he sat down in a corner with his accustomed placidity.

"Now," said I, "we must not let this water run away."

"Why not?" replied my uncle. "I suspect the spring is unfailing."

"Never mind, let us fill our gourds and the leather bottle, and then try and stop up the hole." My advice was followed. Hans made a bung of granite and tow, and did his best to drive it in. But it was not so easily done. We scalded our hands over the business, and our efforts were fruitless after all. The pressure was too great.

"It is evident," I said, "that the source of this river is at a great height, to judge by the force of the jet."

"There is no doubt of it," replied my uncle. "If this column of water is 32,000 feet high, it has the weight of 1,000 atmospheres. But an idea has just struck me."

"What is it?"

"Why should we be so bent on bunging up this hole?"

"Why, because—"

Here I stopped, for it was not easy to find a reason.

"When our gourds are empty again, how do we know for certain that we shall be able to fill them?"

"That's true."

"Well, then, let the water run. It will flow down naturally, and be both our guide and refreshment on the route."

"That's a capital idea," I exclaimed, "and with this river for our companion, there is no reason now why our projects should not succeed."

"Ah! you are coming round to my way of thinking, my boy," said the professor, smiling.

"I am doing better than coming, I have come."

"Not quite yet. We must have a few hours' rest." I actually forgot it was night. But the chronometer reminded me of the fact, and before long. After we had recruited our strength with food, we lay down, and were soon all three sleeping soundly.

XXIV

Next day we had already forgotten our past sufferings. I was amazed at first when I awoke, not to feel thirsty, and asked myself what could be the reason. The stream running at my feet gave me sufficient answer.

We breakfasted and drank of this excellent chalybeate water. I felt quite merry, and decided to go on. Why should not a man so thoroughly confident as my uncle succeed, when he had a zealous guide like Hans, and a determined nephew like me? Such were the grand ideas that came into my head.

If any one had proposed my going back to Snäfell I should have refused indignantly.

But, fortunately, we had only to continue our descent.

"Come, let us start!" I shouted, awakening the old echoes of the globe by my enthusiastic tones.

We set out again on Thursday at 8 A.M. The granite passage, with its varied windings and unexpected bends, seemed almost like a labyrinthine maze; but, on the whole, the direction was uniformly S.E. My uncle consulted his compass constantly, that he might know exactly how much ground we had gone over.

The gallery extended almost horizontally, not sloping more than two inches in a fathom at most. The stream ran murmuring softly at our feet. I compared it to some kindly genius, who was guiding us underground, and I caressed with my hand the warm Naiad whose songs accompanied our steps. My gay mood involuntarily took a mythological turn.

As for my uncle, he kept fuming at the path for being so horizontal. He loved vertical lines, and it put him out of patience to be always going by an hypotenuse to the center, instead of sliding along the radius, to use his own expression. But we had no choice, and so long as we were going towards the center, however indirectly, we had no right to complain. Moreover, from time to time we came to steep slopes, down which the Naiad ran rushing and roaring, and we went with her.

On the whole, that day and the next we went over a great distance horizontally, though comparatively little vertically.

On Friday, July 10th, we reckoned we were thirty leagues to the south-east of Reikiavik, and two and a half leagues deep.

We were in front of a yawning abyss, and frightful enough it looked, though my uncle clapped his hands when he reckoned its depth.

"Famous!" he exclaimed. "This will take us a long way, and without any trouble, for the projections all the way down make a regular staircase."

The ropes were arranged, to avoid any risk of accident, and we commenced the descent. I dare not call it perilous, for I was already accustomed to that kind of exercise.

This abyss was a narrow chasm in the rock, called a "fault," in scientific language. It had been evidently caused by the unequal cooling of the earth's surface. If it had ever served as a passage for the eruptive matter ejected by Snäfell, I could not understand how there was no trace left of it whatever. We were going down a sort of spiral staircase, which one might have thought had been constructed by the hand of man.

We halted every quarter of an hour, to take needful rest, and to stretch our legs. Then we sat down on some projection, with our legs hanging down, eating and talking, and refreshing ourselves with a draft from the stream.

The Hansbach, of course, made a cascade down this fault, to the loss of its volume necessarily, but enough remained to quench our thirst, and we knew it must resume its quiet course when it reached more level ground.

In its present foaming, angry state, it made me think of my uncle in some of his passions, while its calm continuous flow hitherto reminded me of the tranquil Icelander.

On the 6th and 7th of July we were constantly following the windings of the stairs, and had attained a further depth of two leagues. We were altogether nearly five leagues below the level of the sea. But on the 8th, at noon, the "fault," though still going S.E., began to get less vertical, only making an incline of 45°.

The road now became easier, though intensely monotonous. It could hardly be otherwise, for there was no scenery to enliven it.

On Wednesday, the 15th, we were seven leagues below the earth, and fifty from Snäfell. Though somewhat fatigued, we were in perfect health, and our medicine-chest remained untouched.

My uncle noted down, every hour, the indications of the compass, the chronometer, manometer, and the thermometer, those which he has published in the scientific account of his journey. By this means he could always ascertain our exact position. When he apprised me that we had gone fifty leagues horizontally, I could not forbear an exclamation.

"What's the matter?" asked my uncle.

"Nothing; I was only making a reflection."

"What is it, my boy?"

"Just this: that if your calculations are correct, we are no longer below Iceland."

"Do you think so?"

"We can make sure at once."

I took my measurements, with the compasses, on my map, and found I was quite right.

"We have passed Cape Portland," I said, "and fifty leagues S.E. bring us to the open sea."

"Below mid-ocean!" cried my uncle, rubbing his hands.

"Then the ocean is really above our heads?"

"Of course, Axel. That's not so wonderful. Are there not coal mines at Newcastle extending far along under the sea?"

The professor saw nothing extraordinary in the fact, but my mind was quite excited with the idea of walking below the depths of the ocean. And yet what difference did it make whether the plains and mountains of Iceland were over our heads, or the waves of the Atlantic.

It was all one, since the solid granite overarched us. I soon got used to the thought, for the passage, whether straight or winding, fantastic alike in its slopes and in its turns, but always running S.E., was rapidly leading us towards the heart of the globe.

Four days later, on Saturday, July 18th, in the evening, we reached a sort of grotto, of considerable size. Here my uncle came to a halt and paid Hans his weekly wage, and it was agreed that the morrow should be a day of rest.

XXV

I awoke consequently on Sunday morning without the usual impression on my mind, that I must be up and off immediately. And though we were in the deepest depths, it was not disagreeable. We were quite fit for this existence of troglodytes. I scarcely thought of sun, or stars, or moon, or trees, or houses, or towns, or any of those terrestrial superfluities which are necessaries to sublunary beings. We were fossils now, and thought such useless marvels absurd.

The grotto was an immense hill. The faithful stream ran over the granite floor. At this distance from its source, the water was hardly lukewarm, and could be drank comfortably.

After breakfast, the professor determined to devote an hour or two to the arrangement of his daily notes.

"First," he said, "I am going to make calculations, that I may ascertain our situation exactly. I wish to be able on my return to draw a map of our journey, a sort of vertical section of the globe, giving a profile of our expedition."

"That would be a curiosity, uncle; but would your observations be sufficiently exact?"

"Yes. I have carefully noted the angles and inclines. I am certain there has been no mistake. Let us see first where we are. Take the compass, and observe its direction."

I looked at the instrument, and after watching it carefully, I replied: "S.E. by E."

"Very good," said the professor, marking it down, and making some hasty calculations. "Well then, my conclusion is, that we have made eighty-five leagues from our starting-point."

"Then we are walking under the Atlantic now?"

"Just so."

"And perhaps, at this moment, a tempest is raging above our heads; and ships are being wrecked amid the wild hurricanes?"

"Likely enough."

"And whales are lashing the walls of our prison with their tails?"

"Don't be frightened, Axel, they can't shake them. But to return to our calculations; we are in the S.E., eighty-five leagues from the base of Snäfell, and according to my preceding notes, I reckon we have reached a depth of sixteen leagues."

"Sixteen leagues!" I exclaimed.

"Undoubtedly."

"But that is the extreme limit of the earth's crust, according to science."

"I don't say it is not."

"And if there is any law of increase in temperature, the heat here ought to be 1,500°."

"Ought to be, my boy."

"And all this granite would be in a state of fusion, as it could not possibly remain in a solid state."

"You see, however, that it is nothing of the sort, and that facts, as usual, give the lie to theories."

"I am obliged to own it, but still I am very much astonished at it."

"How does the thermometer stand?"

"27 6/10."

"Then philosophers are out in their reckoning by 1,474 4/10. Then the proportional increase of temperature is a mistake, and Humphry Davy was right, and so was I to listen to him. What do you say to it now?"

"Nothing."

I could have found plenty to say if I chose. I could not admit Humphry Davy's theory in the least, and still believed in the central heat, though I did not feel the effect of it. I would really rather have admitted that this chimney of an extinct volcano, being covered with nonconducting lava, did not allow the heat to pass through it.

But, without stopping to seek for new arguments, I confined myself to the consideration of our actual situation.

"Uncle," I said, "I have no doubt all your calculations are right, but they bring me to a rigorous conclusion."

"And what is it, my boy? Speak your mind."

"At the point where we are, under the latitude of Iceland, the radius of the earth is scarcely 1,583 leagues."

"It is 1,583 1/3."

"Put down 1,600 leagues in round figures. Out of a journey of 1,600 leagues, we have gone twelve."

"That's just it."

"And at the cost of eighty-five degrees diagonally?"

"Perfectly so."

"In about twenty days?"

"In twenty days."

"Now sixteen leagues are $\frac{1}{100}$ of the earth's radius. If we go on at this rate, we should take 2,000 days, or nearly five and a half years to descend."

The professor made no reply.

"Without reckoning that if a depth of sixteen leagues is obtained by going eighty horizontally, that would make 8,000 leagues S.E.; and it would be a long time before we reached the center, if we did not chance first to emerge at some point of the circumference."

"Hang your calculations!" cried my uncle, passionately; "and hang your hypothesis, too! On what ground do they rest? Who told you, pray, that this passage did not lead direct to the center? Besides, I have a precedent. What I am doing, another has already done; and where he has succeeded I can succeed too."

"I hope so; but at least I may be allowed—"

"To hold your tongue, Axel, if you wish to argue in that senseless fashion."

I saw plainly the terrible professor was about to leap out of my uncle's skin, and I thought I had better be silent.

"Now," he said, "consult the manometer. What does it indicate?"

"Considerable pressure?"

"Well, then, you see in descending gradually we get accustomed to the density of the atmosphere, and are not the least affected by it."

"Not in the least, except a little pain in the ears."

"That is nothing, and you can get rid of it at once by breathing very quickly for a minute."

"Quite so," said I, determined not to contradict him again. "There is a positive pleasure even in feeling one's self getting into a denser atmosphere. Have you noticed the wonderful clearness of sound here?"

"Yes, indeed. A deaf man would soon get his hearing again."

"But this density will of course increase?"

"Yes, according to a somewhat indefinite law. It is true that the intensity of the weight will diminish in proportion as we descend. You know that it is on the surface that its action is most felt, and at the center of the globe objects have no longer any weight?"

"I know that; but tell me, in the end will not the air acquire the density of water?"

"Undoubtedly, under the pressure of 710 atmospheres."

"And lower still?"

"Lower still of course the density will increase still more."

"How shall we descend, then?"

"Well, we must put stones in our pockets."

"I declare, uncle, you have an answer for everything."

I did not dare to go any farther into the field of hypothesis, for I should have been sure to have stumbled against some possibility, which would have made the professor start out again.

But it was quite evident that the air, under a pressure of possibly a thousand atmospheres, would pass at last into a solid state; and in that case, even supposing that our bodies might have held out, we should be forced to stop in spite of all the reasonings in the world.

But it was no use advancing this argument. My uncle would have met me with that everlasting Saknussemm, a precedent of not the slightest value, for even quoting the truth of the learned Icelander's narrative, this simple answer might be made to it: "In the sixteenth century neither barometers nor manometers were invented, consequently how could Saknussemm know that he had reached the center of the earth?"

But I kept this objection to myself and waited the course of events.

The rest of the day passed in talking and making calculations. I always sided with Professor Lidenbrock, and envied the perfect indifference of Hans, who went blindly wherever destiny led him, without troubling himself about cause and effect.

XXVI

I must own that up till now things had not gone so very badly with us, and I should have been graceless to complain. If the average of difficulties did not increase, we must accomplish our purpose in the end. And what glory we should win! I began positively to reason like Lidenbrock himself. Seriously I did. I wonder if it was owing to my strange surroundings at present. Maybe it was.

For some days we came to a succession of steep inclines. Some of them almost frightfully perpendicular, which brought us a long way towards the interior. On some days we advanced a league and a half to two leagues. But these were perilous descents, in which we were greatly helped by the adroitness of Hans, and his marvelous *sangfroid*. Thanks to him we got over many a bad place that we could never have scrambled through by ourselves.

His absolute silence, however, increased every day. I even think it grew upon us also. External objects have an actual influence on the brain. Any one shut up within four walls loses the faculty at last of associating words and ideas. Look at prisoners in solitary cells. How they become imbeciles, if not insane, by the disuse of their thinking faculties!

During the fortnight which followed our last conversation, nothing occurred worth mentioning.

I can only recall to mind one event of any importance, and that I can never forget. I have reason to remember every particular of it, even the smallest detail.

On the 7th of August our successive descents had brought us to a depth of thirty leagues, that is to say, we had over our heads thirty leagues of rocks, ocean, continents, and cities. We must have been then 200 leagues from Iceland.

That day the tunnel was but very slightly slanting. I was ahead of the others. My uncle was carrying one of Ruhmkorff's apparatus, and I had the other examining the beds of granite.

All at once, on turning round, I found myself alone.

"All right!" I thought. "I have been going too fast, or Hans and uncle may have stopped for a minute on the road. Come, I must get back to them. Fortunately, the path is not steep."

I retraced my steps, and, after walking for a quarter of an hour, looked round me. Nobody was in sight. I called out. No answer. My voice was drowned in the midst of the hollow echoes awakened by the sound.

I began to be uneasy, and a shudder crept over me.

"Be calm," I said to myself, aloud. "I am sure of finding them again. There are not two roads. I was walking in front, so I must just keep going back."

I went back for half an hour longer, and then I listened to hear if any one called me, for in so dense an atmosphere I should hear a long way off. There was not a sound. A strange silence reigned throughout the gallery.

I stopped. I could not believe in my isolation. I had lost my way; I was not lost; I should get right again presently.

"There is only the one passage," I kept saying to myself, "and as they are in it, I must come up to them soon. I have only to keep ascending. Unless, not seeing me, and forgetting I was in front, they had gone back to look for me. But even then, by hurrying, I shall overtake them, that's evident."

I repeated these last words like a man who is not very certain, and moreover it took me a long time to put my ideas together at all in the shape of a conclusive argument, simple enough as they were.

Then a doubt crossed my mind. Was I really ahead of my companions when I got parted from them? Certainly I was. Hans was following me, and my uncle came after him. He had even stopped for a minute to fasten his packages on his shoulder. I remembered this circumstance distinctly. It was at this very moment I must have gone on too far.

"Besides," thought I, "it is impossible I could have gone far wrong, for I have a guide to lead me through this labyrinth; one that will never fail me—my faithful stream. I have only to follow it back and I cannot help finding my companions."

This conclusion reanimated me, and I resolved to set out immediately, without losing an instant.

How I blessed the foresight of my uncle now, in not allowing the hunter to stop up the hole in the granite. This beneficent spring, after having refreshed us on the road, was now to be my guide through the winding mazes of the earth's crust.

Before starting I thought I should be the better of sundry ablutions. I dipped my face into the Hansbach; but judge of my stupefaction! I touched dry, rough granite! The stream no longer ran at my feet.

XXVII

I cannot describe my despair. No human tongue could tell what I felt. I was buried alive, with the prospect before me of dying of cold and hunger.

I passed my burning hands mechanically over the ground. How dry the rock seemed!

But could I have forsaken the course of the stream? For here it certainly was not. Now I understood the cause of this strange silence, when I listened for the last time expecting to hear a call from my companions. I had not, till this moment, noticed the absence of the stream. It is evident that just as I took the first wrong step the gallery must have forked, and I had followed the new opening, while the Hansbach, obeying the caprice of another incline, had gone away with my companions towards unknown depths. How could I get back? There was not a track. My feet left no imprint on the granite. I racked my brain to discover the solution of this problem. One single word expressed all the misery of my situation—Lost!

Yes, lost at, what seemed to me, an immeasurable depth. These thirty leagues of the earth's crust were weighing down my shoulders terribly. I felt crushed.

I tried to bring my thoughts back to the upper world. But I scarcely succeeded. Hamburg, the house in Königstrasse, my poor Gräuben— all the living world, beneath which I was lost, passed rapidly before my terrified memory. I saw, as if in some hallucination, all the incidents of the journey—the voyage, Iceland, M. Fridrikson, Snäfell! I said to myself that to have the faintest shadow of hope in my position would be madness, and that I had far better despair.

What human power, indeed, could bring me back again to the surface of the globe, or tear down these enormous arches supporting each other above my head? Who could set me in the right track one more, and take me to rejoin my companions?

"Oh, uncle!" I cried in accents of despair.

This was the only word of reproach that came to my lips, for I knew how much the poor man would suffer while he was vainly searching for me.

When I saw myself thus wholly cut off from human succor, incapable of attempting anything for my deliverance, I thought of heavenly succor. Memories of my childhood, of my mother, whom I had only known in the sweet days of my infancy, came back to me. I began to pray, little as I deserved that God should know me when I had forgotten Him so long; and I prayed fervently.

This cry for help to heaven made me calm, and I was able to bring all my mind to the survey of my actual position.

I had provisions enough for three days, and my gourd was full. However, I could not stay where I was any longer, but what course should I take? Should I ascend or descend?

Ascend, evidently—always keep ascending. I must then inevitably come to the part where the gallery had forked, and, could I but regain the stream, I could at any rate get back to the crater of Snäfell.

How hadn't I thought of this sooner? There was clearly some chance of deliverance here. My very first business was to find the Hansbach again.

I rose up, and leaning on my iron-tipped staff, began to climb the gallery. The incline was pretty steep, but I walked on hopefully and unconcerned, like a man who has not the choice of roads before him.

For half-an-hour I met with no obstacles. I tried to recognize the way by the form of the tunnel, and by the projections of certain rocks, and the disposition of the fractures. But no particular appearance recurred to me, and I soon saw that this gallery would not bring me to the point of demarcation. It was a blind alley. I struck against an impenetrable wall and fell on the rock.

What terror and despair took hold of me then I have no power to depict. I was completely prostrated! My last hope was shattered against the granite wall!

Lost in a labyrinth amidst a perfect maze of windings, it was useless to attempt an impossible flight. The most terrible of all deaths stared me in the face! And, strangely enough, the thought crossed me that if some day my fossilized body should see the light, what grave scientific questions would be raised by its discovery thirty leagues below the earth's surface.

I tried to speak aloud, but hoarse accents alone issued from my parched lips. I was gasping for breath.

In the midst of my anguish, a new terror seized me. My lamp had gone wrong when I fell. I could not rectify it, and its light was paling and would soon go out.

I saw the luminous current always diminishing in the coil of the apparatus. A procession of moving shadows appeared on the gloomy walls. I did not dare to close my eyes, dreading to lose the least atom of this fainting light. Every instant it threatened to go out and enwrap me in the blackness of night.

At last there was only a faint glimmer in the lamp. I watched it with trembling eagerness, concentrating all my gaze on it as on the last ray of light that my eyes would ever see before total darkness should fall on me.

What a terrible cry escaped me! On the earth, even in the darkest night, the light never wholly abandons his rule. It is diffused and subtle, but little as may remain, the retina of the eye is sensible of it. Here there was nothing. Absolute darkness made me blind in the literal acceptation of the word.

Then I lost my senses. I got up with outspread arms, endeavoring to feel my way, but the attempt was most painful. I rein along wildly through inextricable labyrinths, always going down deeper into the heart of the earth, like a denizen of the subterranean regions; calling, shouting, howling, striking myself against projecting rocks, falling down and getting up again, feeling the blood trickling from me, and trying to drink it as it dropped from my face, and always expecting to come to some wall to dash my head against.

Whither did the said course lead me? That I am ignorant of to this day.

After several hours, no doubt, when all my powers were exhausted, I fell against the wall like a lifeless mass, and lost all consciousness of existence.

XXVIII

When I revived my face was wet—wet with tears. How long this state of insensibility had lasted I cannot say, I had no longer any means of reckoning time. Never was solitude like mine, never was abandonment so absolute.

After my fall I lost a quantity of blood—I felt myself deluged with it.

Oh! how sorry I was that death had still to come! That it was not over already. I refused to think, I banished every suggestion, and, overcome by grief, I rolled myself towards the opposite wall.

I could feel myself ready to swoon again, and I thought with satisfaction that with it would come the final unconsciousness, when a violent noise struck my ear. It was like a long rolling peal of thunder, and I heard the waves of sound lose themselves, and die away in the distant depths of the abyss.

Whence came the noise? Doubtless from some physical source in the bosom of the terrestrial mass. The explosion of some gas, or the fall of some of the vast beds of the earth's crust.

I listened again. I wanted to know if that noise would be repeated. A quarter of an hour passed. Silence reigned in the gallery. Nothing was audible but the beating of my heart.

Suddenly my ear, which happened to touch the wall, was startled by a sound like distant, indistinguishable, inarticulate words. I trembled.

"Is it a hallucination?" thought I.

But no! On listening more attentively, I could plainly hear a murmur of voices, but I was too weak to make out what was said; but that some one was speaking, I was certain.

I feared for a moment that it might be the sound of my own words brought back by an echo. Perhaps I might unconsciously have cried out. I closed my lips tightly, and again applied my ear to the wall.

Yes! yes! voices undoubtedly!

I dragged myself to some distance along the wall, and then heard the sounds more distinctly. I could catch an indistinct murmur of distorted and unmeaning words. They sounded as if some one was humming them in a low voice. Once or twice I caught the word "forlorad" repeated with an accent of sorrow.

What did it mean? Who was speaking? Clearly either my uncle or Hans. But if I could hear them, surely they might hear me!

"Here!" I called with all my strength. "Here!"

I listened, and watched in the darkness for an answer, a cry, a sigh. Not a sound. A crowd of ideas ran through my brain. I fancied my enfeebled voice could not reach my companions.

"For it is certainly they," said I. "What other mortals would there be here, ninety miles underground?"

I listened again. In trying backwards and forwards along the wall I found a point where the voices appeared to attain their maximum of sound. The word "forlorad" again reached my ear, and the thundersound which had at first arrested my attention.

"No!" I exclaimed; "it is not through this rock that I hear the voices. The wall is of granite, and the loudest sound would not penetrate it.

The sound comes by way of the gallery itself. There must be a very peculiar acoustic effect!"

I listened once more. Yes! this time I heard my own name distinctly echoed through the gloom!

It was my uncle who uttered it! He was doubtless talking to the guide, and the word "forlorad" was a Danish word.

Then I understood it all. To make them hear me, all I had to do was to speak with my mouth close to the wall, which would serve to conduct my voice, as the wire conducts the electric fluid.

But I had no time to lose. If my companions happened to change their position, even by a few paces, the acoustic phenomenon would have been destroyed. I went close to the wall, and I said, slowly and distinctly:

"Uncle Lidenbrock!"

And I waited with painful anxiety. Sound does not travel quickly here. The density of the atmosphere increases its intensity but not its velocity. A few seconds, which seemed ages, passed, and at last I heard these words:

"Axel! Axel! is that you?"

. . . . .

"Yes! yes!" I answered. "My child, where are you?"

. . . . .

"Lost in the most intense darkness."

. . . . .

"Where is your lamp?"

. . . . .

"Out!"

. . . . .

"And the brook?"

. . . . .

"Disappeared."

· · · · ·

"Axel, my poor lad: take courage!"

· · · · ·

"Wait a little; I am exhausted. I have not got strength to answer. But talk to me!"

"Have courage," said my uncle. "Don't try to speak, just listen to me. We searched up and down the gallery, looking for you. We failed to find you. I wept for you, my child! Then we came down again, firing as we came, always supposing you still on the channel of the Hansbach. Now that our voices meet it is by a purely acoustic phenomenon, and we cannot touch hands. But do not despair, Axel! To hear one another is something!"

· · · · ·

During this time I had been thinking. A ray of hope, slight indeed, raised my spirits. First of all it was necessary to know one thing. I put my lips to the wall and said:

"Uncle?"

· · · · ·

"My child!" he replied, after the lapse of several seconds.

· · · · ·

"We must first ascertain what distance separates us."

· · · · ·

"That is easy."

· · · · ·

"You have your chronometer."

· · · · ·

"Yes."

· · · · ·

"Well, take it! Call my name, and note the exact moment. I will repeat it the instant I hear it, and you will again note the precise moment."

. . . . .

"Yes! and half the interval between the question and the answer will be the time required for my voice to reach you."

. . . . .

"Just so, uncle!"

. . . . .

"Are you ready?"

. . . . .

"Yes!"

. . . . .

"Well, listen now; I am going to call out your name!"

. . . . .

I put my ear to the wall, and as soon as the word "Axel!" reached me I instantly answered "Axel," and then waited.

. . . . .

"Forty seconds!" said my uncle. "Therefore the sound took twenty seconds to ascend. Now, at the rate of 1,020 feet per second, that makes 20,400 feet, or nearly four miles."

. . . . .

"Nearly four miles," I murmured.

. . . . .

"Well, that is a practicable distance, Axel!"

. . . . .

"But must I go up or down?"

. . . . .

"Down, and for this reason—we have come upon a vast hollow space, into which several galleries open. The one you have got into must lead here, for I feel certain that all these earth fractures radiate from the immense cavern in which we stand. Rouse yourself and go on. Walk, crawl, slide down steep inclines, if necessary, and you will find our strong arms waiting to support you at the end. Forward, my child, forward!"

· · · ·

These words filled me with new life.

"Good-bye, uncle," I cried; "I go. When I leave this spot we can speak to each other no more, so adieu!"

· · · ·

"Till we meet again, Axel!"

· · · ·

I heard nothing more.

This singular colloquy, uttered in the bowels of the earth, exchanged at a distance of nearly four miles, ended with words of hope. I thanked God for having led me through the labyrinth of darkness to the only point at which the voices of my companions could reach me.

This astonishing acoustic effect was easily accounted for by physical laws alone; it was produced by the form of the gallery and the conducting power of the rock. There are many instances of imperceptible sounds being conveyed to a distance. I have experienced the phenomenon myself more than once, among others in the gallery of St. Paul's Cathedral in London, and notably in those curious caves in Sicily, and in the labyrinths near Syracuse, of which the most wonderful is known as Dionysius' Ear.

These recollections occur to me, and it seemed obvious that, as my uncle's voice reached me, there could be no solid barrier between us. If I traveled the road by which the sound came, I need not despair to reach him unless my strength failed me.

I rose—I dragged myself rather than walked. The slope was very great, and I let myself slide. After a little the rapidity of my descent was alarmingly increased, and threatened to turn into a falling motion. I had no strength to stop myself.

Suddenly my feet lost their hold. I felt myself rolling, and now and then striking the rough projections of what seemed to be a well, a sort of vertical gallery. My head struck a sharp point of rock, and I lost consciousness.

XXIX

When I came to myself I was in semi-darkness, lying on thick rugs. My uncle was watching me, hoping for a sign of life in my face. At my first sigh he took my hand; when I opened my eyes he uttered a joyful cry.

"He lives! he lives!" he exclaimed.

"Yes," I answered, with a feeble effort.

"My child!" said my uncle, pressing me to his heart, "thank heaven you are saved!"

I was deeply touched by the tone in which these words were spoken, and more deeply still by the attentions which accompanied them.

But it required such dangers to excite the professor to such demonstrations.

Then Hans arrived. He saw my hand in that of my uncle. I may say at least that his eyes expressed great satisfaction.

"God-dag," said he.

"Good day, Hans," I whispered. "Good day. And now, uncle, tell me where we are."

"To-morrow, Axel, to-morrow; to-day you are too weak. I have bound up your head with bandages, which must not be disturbed;

therefore, try to sleep now, and to-morrow you shall hear all I have to tell."

"Well," said I, "at least tell me what hour—what day is it?"

"Eleven o'clock in the evening, and to-day is Sunday, August 9th; and I will answer no more questions till the 10th of this month."

I was really very weak, and my eyes closed involuntarily. I was in want of a night's rest, so I went to sleep, with the knowledge that I had been four long days in my state of isolation.

Next day, when I awoke, I looked round me. My bed, composed of all the traveling rugs, was situated in a lovely grotto, adorned with magnificent stalactites, and the ground was covered with fine sand. Twilight reigned. No torch nor lamp was lighted, and yet gleams of light seemed to penetrate by a narrow opening in the grotto. I could hear, too, a gentle undefined murmur, like the moan of the waves breaking on the sands, and now and again the whisper of a breeze.

I wondered whether I was really awake, or if I was dreaming still; or if my brain, injured in my fall, was suggesting imaginary sounds. Still, neither my ears nor my eyes could be so far mistaken.

"It is really a gleam of daylight," thought I, "that peeps in at that crevice in the rock! And I am sure that what I hear is the murmur of the waves. There is the whistling of the wind. Can I be deceived? Or are we once more on the surface of the earth? Has my uncle abandoned his expedition, or has he brought it to a satisfactory close?" I was asking myself these questions, to which I could find no answer, when my uncle came in.

"Good morning, Axel," said he, joyously. "I would wager a good deal that you are better."

"Yes, indeed!" said I, sitting up under my blankets.

"That is right. You slept quietly. Hans and I sat beside you in turns, and we have seen you get better step by step."

"In fact, uncle, I feel quite a man again; and you will say so when you see the breakfast I shall make if you give me the chance."

"Certainly, my boy; you shall eat. The fever has left you. Hans has rubbed your wounds with some Icelandic nostrum, of which he knows the secret; and they have cicatrized with wonderful rapidity. Our hunter is very proud, I can tell you."

As he spoke, my uncle prepared some nourishment, which I ate greedily, in spite of his advice, while at the same time I overwhelmed him with questions, which he did his best to answer.

I then learnt that my providential fall had brought me to the end of an almost perpendicular gallery. As I arrived in the midst of an avalanche of stones, the smallest of which would have been sufficient to crush me, it was to be judged that part of the mass had fallen with me.

This fearful mode of locomotion had landed me in the arms of my uncle, where I fell bleeding and inanimate.

"I am truly astonished," said he, "that you were not killed a thousand times over. But, for God's sake, never let us part, for the chances are that we should never meet again."

"Let us never part again!" Then the voyage was not over? I opened my eyes with astonishment, which provoked the question:

"What ails you, Axel?"

"A question that I want to ask. You say I am safe and sound?"

"Beyond a doubt."

"All my limbs uninjured?"

"Certainly."

"And my head?"

"With the exception of some contusions, your head is safe on your shoulders."

"Well, I am afraid my brain is affected."

"Your brain?"

"Yes; we are not on the surface of the earth again?"

"No, indeed!"

"Well—then I am crazy; for I see the light of day, I hear the wind blowing, and the sea breaking."

"Oh! is that all?"

"Well, but explain to me—"

"I will explain nothing, for it is inexplicable; but you will see for yourself, and you will understand that geological knowledge is far from final."

"Let us go out, then," said I, rising suddenly.

"No, Axel, no; the open air might be injurious to you."

"The open air?"

"Yes; the wind is rather strong, and I forbid you to expose yourself."

"But I assure you I am perfectly well."

"A little patience, my boy! If you had a relapse it would be a serious matter for us all, and we cannot afford to lose time, for it may be a long distance across."

"Across?"

"Yes; take another day's rest, and we will embark to-morrow."

"Embark?"

The word made me jump!

What—embark? Had we a river, a lake, a sea at our disposal? Was there a ship anchored in some subterranean port?

My curiosity was strongly excited. My uncle tried in vain to quiet me, and when he at length saw that to deny me would do me more harm than to yield, he gave up the point.

I dressed quickly, and as a precaution wrapped one of the rugs round me and went out of the grotto.

XXX

At first I could discern nothing. My unaccustomed eyes closed against the light When I was able to open them I was stunned rather than astonished.

"The sea!" I exclaimed.

"Yes " said my uncle. "The sea of Lidenbrock; and it pleases me to think that no navigator is likely to contest the honor of having discovered it, or deny my right to call it by my name!"

A great sheet of water, the commencement of a lake or ocean, stretched farther than the eye could reach. The shore, sloping gradually, presented to the waves a beach of fine golden sand, strewn with the small shells in which the first created things had lived. The waves broke there with the echoing murmur peculiar to vast hollow spaces. A light spray was blown by the breeze, which sprinkled a few drops on my face. On this gently shelving shore, about 300 yards from the fringe of foam, curved gradually the last undulations of the steep of the rocky counterscarp, which rose with a widening sweep to an immeasurable height. Some of these had their edges torn into capes and promontories by the beating of the surf, and, farther still, the eye could follow their outlines sharply defined on the cloudy background of the horizon.

It was a real ocean, with the varying contour of terrestrial shores, but lonely and fearfully wild in aspect.

That I could see to a distance along this sea was owing to a "special" light, which radiated the smallest details. It was not the light of the sun, with his glorious glittering darts, nor the pale, uncertain radiance of the star of night, which is only a cold reflection. No! The illuminating power of this light, its quivering diffusion, its clear, sharp whiteness, the low degree of its temperature, its more than moonlight brightness, all proclaimed its electric origin. It was like a continuous aurora borealis which filled this cavern, so vast in extent as to contain an ocean.

The arch, or sky, suspended over my head seemed composed of great clouds, moving bodies of vapor, which some day would certainly fall, by condensation, in torrents of rain. I should have thought that under such a heavy atmospheric pressure water could not evaporate, and yet, from some physical reason which I was unacquainted with, large clouds were spread above us. But it was then "fine weather." The electric masses produced a wonderful play of light on the very high clouds. Well-defined shadows were thrown on their lower folds, and often between two disjoined layers a gleam of singular brightness was thrown on us. In short, it was not the sun, for there was no heat. The effect was mournful—intensely melancholy. Instead of a sky, bright with stars, I felt that above these clouds was the granite vault crushing me with its weight; and this space, immense though it was, was not large enough for the orbit of the humblest satellite.

I then recalled the theory of an English captain who likened the earth to a vast hollow sphere, in whose interior air maintained its luminosity by reason of its compression; and that two stars, Pluto and Proserpine, described within this sphere their mysterious orbits. Perhaps he was right, after all. We were really imprisoned in a vast hollow, of whose breadth we could form no estimate, as the shore widened as far as we could see; nor of its length, as the eye was soon stopped by an irregular horizon line. Its height must be eight or nine miles. Where this vault meets the granite buttresses the eye cannot decide, but a cloud was suspended in the air, whose height must have been at least 2,000 fathoms, a greater height than is attained by terrestrial vapors, owing, no doubt, to the greater density of the air.

The word "cavern" does not convey any impression of this vast space. But the language of human speech is inadequate to picture what may exist in the subterranean abysses.

Nor could I conjecture what geological cause could have produced this great excavation. Could the cooling process have induced it? I knew, from the narratives of travelers, of the existence of celebrated caves, but none of them had such dimensions as this.

If the Guacharo Cave in Colombia, which Von Humboldt visited, was not exactly ascertained to be 2,500 feet deep, it was measured with sufficient precision to warrant the assumption that it was not much beyond that depth. The immense Mammoth Cave in Kentucky boasts of giant proportions, for its arch rises 500 feet above an unfathomable lake, which has been followed for thirty miles without coming to the opposite shore. But what were these compared with the one I was contemplating, with its sky of clouds, its electric irradiation, and its vast ocean.

I thought silently over all these wonders. I had no words to express my sensations. I felt as if I had been transported to a distant planet, Uranus or Saturn, and was gazing on phenomena of which my Earth-nature had no cognizance. To express such novel impressions, I wanted new words, and my imagination was unable to supply them. I looked, I thought, I wondered with amazement, not unmixed with fear.

The unexpectedness of the spectacle had brought back the hue of health to my face; astonishment was called to my aid, and cured me by a new system of therapeutics; and, in addition, the dense air was a source of invigoration, by furnishing an abundant supply of oxygen to my lungs.

It will be easy to understand that, after forty-seven days spent in a narrow gallery, there was infinite enjoyment in breathing this moist salt-laden atmosphere.

I had indeed no reason to regret having quitted my dark grotto. My uncle, already accustomed to these wonders, betrayed no surprise.

"Are you able to take a little walk?" he asked.

"Yes, certainly," said I; "and I should like nothing better."

"Well, take my arm, Axel, and let us follow the bend of the shore."

I eagerly consented, and we began to coast along this new sea. On the left, the abrupt rocks, piled one on the other, formed a Titanic group of imposing grandeur; down the sides poured countless waterfalls, which flowed away in clear gurgling streams. Light wreaths of vapor, curling here and there among the rocks, indicated the place of hot springs, and brooks ran down the declivities with a delicious murmur, and lost themselves in the common basin.

Among these rivulets I perceived our faithful traveling companion, the Hansbach, which here merged quietly into the sea, as if it had been doing nothing else since the world began.

"We shall miss it, now," said I, with a sigh.

"Bah!" said the professor, "what matters whether we have that or another?"

I thought him ungrateful. But at this moment my eye was attracted to an unexpected sight. Five hundred paces off, round a high promontory, rose a lofty forest, thick and close. It consisted of trees of medium height, shaped like parasols, with clear geometrical outlines; the wind did not seem to have clipped their leaves, and in the midst of gusts they remained motionless, like a forest of petrified cedars.

I quickened my steps. I could find no name for these singular growths. Did they belong to any of our already known 200,000 species, and were they to have a special place in the flora of lacustrine vegetation? No; when we arrived under their shade, my surprise was not greater than my admiration.

I found myself gazing on terrestrial products, cut on a gigantic pattern. My uncle named them instantly.

"It is nothing but a forest of mushrooms," said he.

He was right. Fancy the development of these cherished plants in a warm damp atmosphere. I knew that the "Lycoperdon giganteum" attains, according to Bulliard, a circumference of nine feet; but these were white mushrooms, thirty or forty feet high, with a head in proportion. They were in millions. The light could not pierce their dense shades, and complete darkness reigned beneath these domes, which lay side by side, like the domed roofs of an African city.

But I was anxious to go farther in. A deathly chill was reflected from these fleshy arches. For half an hour we wandered among the dusky shades, and I felt it quite a relief when we regained the seashore.

But the vegetation of this subterranean region did not stop at mushrooms. Farther on rose groups of other trees with discolored foliage. They were easy to recognize—the humble arbutus of the upper earth, but of gigantic proportions; lycopods, 100 feet high; monster sigillarias, tree-ferns as tall as the northern pines; lepidoden-drons, with cylindrical forked stems, terminating in long leaves and bristling with rough hairs.

"Astounding, magnificent, splendid!" cried my uncle. "Here is the whole flora of the second epoch—the transition epoch—the humble plants of our gardens which grew as trees in the early ages of the world! Look, Axel, and admire! No botanist in the world ever was at such a show."

"You are right, uncle. Providence seems to have preserved in this great hot-house the antediluvian plants, which scientific men have so successfully reconstructed."

"It is, as you express it, Axel, a vast hothouse; but you might with equal justice call it a menagerie."

"A menagerie?"

"Yes, indeed! Look at the dust beneath our feet—the bones scattered on the ground."

"Bones!" I exclaimed. "Bones of the antediluvian animals?"

I eagerly examined this primeval dust, formed of an indestructible mineral (phosphate of lime), and had no hesitation in naming these immense bones, which only resembled dried-up tree-trunks.

"There," said I, "is the lower jaw of the mastodon; here, the molars of the dinotherium; there is a femur, which can only have belonged to a megatherium. Yes, truly, it is a menagerie, for the bones cannot have been brought here by a convulsion of nature. The animals to which they belonged must have lived on the shore of this subterranean sea, under the shade of the arborescent plants. Look! there are even whole skeletons. And yet—"

"Yet what?" said my uncle.

"I cannot understand the existence of animals in this granite cavern."

"Why not?"

"Because there was no animal life on the earth, except during the secondary period, when the sedimentary formation was produced by the alluvial forces, and replaced the igneous rocks of the primitive epoch."

"Well, Axel! there is a very simple answer to your objection, and that is, that this is a sedimentary formation."

"What, at such a depth below the surface of the earth?"

"Beyond a doubt! and the fact can be geologically explained. At a certain period the earth's crust was elastic, subject to alternate upward and downward movements, by reason of the law of attraction. It is probable that depressions were produced, and that portions of the sedimentary strata were engulfed in abysses opened suddenly."

"That may be so. But if antediluvian animals have lived in these subterranean regions, who can say that some of these monsters are not still wandering in the midst of these gloomy forests, or behind these inaccessible rocks?"

At the bare idea I involuntarily scanned the various points of the horizon, but no living being appeared on the desert shores.

I was a little tired. I went and sat down on the point of a promontory at whose feet the waves dashed with a hoarse noise. Thence I could see the whole of the bay formed by a bend in the coast. At the bottom a little harbor nestled between the pyramidal rocks. Its calm waters were sheltered from the wind. A brig and two or three schooners could have lain at anchor easily. I almost expected to see some ship come out in full sail and put to sea before the southerly wind.

But this illusion was soon dissipated. We were but too surely the only living creatures in this lower world. In a sudden hush of the wind, a stillness more intense than that of the desert fell upon these barren rocks, and hung over the ocean. I tried to see through the distant mists, to pierce the curtain that veiled the mysterious horizon. What questions crowded to my lips? Where did this sea end? Whither did it lead? Should we ever behold the other shore?

My uncle, at any rate, had no misgiving. As for me, I hoped and feared at the same moment.

After an hour passed in gazing on the wondrous panorama, we took the beach road once more to regain the grotto.

XXXI

I awoke next day quite recovered. I thought a bath would be of service to me, and I went and took a dip in the waters of the Mediterranean Sea. Of all seas, surely this best deserved the name.

I came back to breakfast with a sharpened appetite. Hans was busy cooking our meal, and having fire and water at his disposal this time, he was able to vary our bill of fare. He supplied us with several cups of coffee, and that delicious beverage never seemed to me so palatable.

"Now," said my uncle, "it is nearly high water, and we must not lose the opportunity of observing the phenomenon."

"What, the tide?" exclaimed I.

"Undoubtedly."

"Do you think the influence of sun and moon is felt in this region?"

"Why not? Every particle of a solid body is governed by the force of attraction. This mass of water cannot escape the universal law, and, therefore, notwithstanding the atmospheric pressure on its surface, you will see it rise just like the Atlantic."

At this moment we reached the sandy shore, and the waves were gradually gaining ground.

"The tide is certainly coming in," said I.

"Yes, Axel, and you may see by these foam streaks that it rises at least ten feet."

"It is wonderful!"

"Not at all; it is in the natural order of things."

"You may say as you will, uncle. I cannot but think it extraordinary; in fact, I can hardly believe my senses. Who would have imagined that beneath the earth's crust there is a real ocean, with its ebb and flow, its breezes and its storms!"

"Why not? Is there any physical reason against it?"

"I know of none, if you abandon the central fire theory."

"Then, so far, Davy's theory is supported?"

"So it would seem; and if that is so, there may be seas and countries in the interior of the globe?"

"Yes, but uninhabited."

"Why so? Why may not these waters contain fish of some unknown species?"

"At any rate, we have met with none, so far."

"Well, we can make some line, and see if the fishhook will be as successful here as in our sublunary waters."

"We will try, Axel; for we must do our utmost to find out all the secrets of these unexplored regions."

"But where are we, uncle? For I have not yet asked you that question. Your instruments will have told you our whereabouts."

"Our position is, horizontally, 1,050 miles from Iceland."

"So far?"

"I am certain within 500 fathoms."

"And the compass still pointing north-east?"

"Yes, with a western declination of 19° 40', just as on the surface. As to the inclination, there is a curious fact, which I have observed very carefully: the needle, instead of dipping towards the pole, as it does in the northern hemisphere, has an upward direction."

"Then we may conclude that the magnetic pole is a point contained between the surface of the globe and the depth we have reached?"

"Exactly; and I think it very likely that, if we arrived in the polar regions towards that 70th degree, where Sir James Ross discovered the magnetic pole, we should see the needle take a vertical position; therefore, this mysterious point is at no great depth."

"That is a fact which science has never guessed."

"Science, my boy, is made up of mistakes; but of mistakes which lead to the discovery of truth."

"And how far down are we?"

"About 100 miles."

"Well then," said I, after consulting the map, "the mountainous part of Scotland is above us, where the lofty Grampians raise their snowy summits."

"Yes," said the professor, smiling. "There is some weight to carry, but the arch is strong; the great architect of the Universe has used good materials, and no human builder could have given it such a span! What are the great arches of bridges and cathedrals beside this great nave, whose radius is nine miles, and under which there is space for an ocean and its storms?"

"Oh! I am not afraid of the roof falling over my head. But now, uncle, what are your plans? Do you not intend returning to the surface?"

"Returning! What a notion! On the contrary, we will go on, as we have had such luck so far!"

"Still, I do not see how we are to get below this watery plain."

"I do not intend to plunge into it head first; but as oceans are, properly speaking, nothing more than lakes, as they are surrounded by land, no doubt this interior sea is bounded by granitic masses."

"That is probable enough."

"Well then, on the opposite shore I am sure of finding new outlets."

"How long do you guess this ocean to be?"

"From 100 to 120 miles."

"Hem!" said I to myself, thinking that a very wild calculation.

"So you see we have no time to spare; we must put to sea to-morrow." I involuntarily looked round for the wherewithal.

"Ah!" said I, "we are to embark to-morrow. On what vessel shall we take passage?"

"Not on a vessel, my lad, but on a strong safe raft."

"A raft!" said I, "but we can no more build a raft than a ship, and I don't see—"

"You don't see, Axel, but if you listened, you could hear. Those sounds of hammering might tell you that Hans is already at the work."

"Do you mean that he is making a raft?"

"I do."

"What? Has he felled trees with his axe?"

"Oh! the trees were all ready to his hand. Come and look at him at work."

After a quarter of an hour's walking, and on the farther side of the promontory which enclosed the little port, I could see Hans at work. A few more steps, and I was at his side. To my great surprise, a raft already half-completed lay on the sand! It was made of logs of a peculiar-looking wood, and a vast number of planks, knees, ties, strewed the ground. There was material for a fleet.

"Uncle," said I, "what kind of wood is that?"

"It is pine, fir, birch, all the northern conifers, mineralized by the action of sea-water."

"Is it possible?"

"It is called 'surtur-brand,' or fossil wood."

"But, then, like lignite, it must be as hard as stone, and cannot float?"

"Occasionally, that is so. There are woods which become true anthracites; but others, like this, are only partially fossilized. But, look for yourself," said my uncle, throwing into the water one of these precious fragments.

The log first disappeared, then rose to the surface of the waves and followed their undulations.

"Are you satisfied?" said my uncle.

"I am convinced that it is incredible."

The next evening, thanks to the skill of our guide, the raft was ready. It was ten feet long by five feet wide; the logs of surtur-brand, bound each to each with strong rope, offered a solid floor, and once launched, this impromptu vessel floated quietly on the waters of the "Sea of Lidenbrock."

XXXII

On the morning of August 13 we were early astir.

We were to commence our new kind of locomotion—a rapid and easy one.

A mast, made of two logs mortised together; a yard formed by a third, a sail made of one of our rugs, was all our rigging. We had plenty of ropes, and the whole affair was strongly put together.

At six o clock the professor gave the signal to embark. Our provisions, baggage, instruments, firearms, and a good stock of fresh water collected among the rocks, were arranged on board.

Hans had set up a rudder, so as to be able to guide his vessel. He took the helm. I cast off the rope that moored us to the shore. The sail was set, and we rapidly left the land.

As we quitted the little harbor, my uncle, who made a great point of his geographical nomenclature, wished to fix on a name for it, suggesting mine, among others.

"Uncle," said I, "I beg to propose the name of Gräuben. Port Gräuben would look very well on a map."

"Well, Port Gräuben be it."

And thus it was that the name of my beloved Virlandaise came to be connected with our daring adventure.

A light breeze blew from the north-east. We made rapid way, with the wind aft. The density of the atmospheric strata gave great force, and the wind acted on the sail like an immense ventilator.

An hour enabled my uncle to estimate our speed.

"If this rate continues," said he, "we shall do about ninety miles in twenty-four hours, and shall soon gain the other shore."

I made no reply, but went and stationed myself in the fore-part of the raft. Already the northern shore was sinking below the horizon. The projecting arms of the land opened wide to let us go. A vast extent of ocean was spread before my gaze. Great clouds moved rapidly over its surface, casting gray shadows, which seemed to weigh down the melancholy waste of waters. The silvery rays of the electric light, reflected here and there by the spray, dotted our wake with luminous points. Soon we lost sight of land, and of every point of observation, and but for our track of foam, I could have believed that we were motionless.

Towards noon immense algae were seen floating on the waves. I was aware of the powerful vitality of their growth, which enables them to exist at a depth of over 12,000 feet, at the bottom of the sea, and to fructify under a pressure of 400 atmospheres; I also knew that they sometimes form beds compact enough to impede the motion of a ship; but I think there can be no algae so gigantic as those of the "Sea of Lidenbrock."

Our raft passed along by *fuci* 3,000 or 4,000 feet long, great serpentine bands twisting away far out of sight; I tried to follow their endless ribbons and never came to an end, and hour after hour increased my astonishment if not my patience.

What power of nature produces such growths, and what must have been the aspect of the earth in the first ages of its formation, when under the combined action of heat and moisture the vegetable kingdom alone developed on its surface!

Evening came, and, as I remarked the day before, the luminous state of the air seemed to suffer no diminution. It was a constant phenomenon on whose stability we could reckon.

After supper I lay down at the foot of the mast, and soon lost myself in sleep mingled with idle reveries.

Hans, motionless at the helm, had only to leave the raft to itself—the wind being astern we hardly needed steering.

Since leaving Port Gräuben, Professor Lidenbrock had appointed me to keep the "journal on board;" to note every observation; to record all interesting phenomena; the direction of the wind; the speed attained; the distance accomplished; in a word, all the incidents of this novel voyage.

I shall confine myself, therefore, to reproducing these daily notes, written, so to speak, from the dictation of events, so as to give a perfectly exact account of our voyage across this ocean.

Friday, August 14.—Steady breeze from the N.W. The raft goes fast, and in a straight line. We have left the coast ninety miles behind us in the direction of the wind. Nothing on the horizon. The intensity of the light is unvarying. Weather fine, that is, the clouds are high, not dense, and bathed in a white atmosphere like molten silver. Thermometer 58°.

At mid-day, Hans fastened a fish-hook to the end of a rope; he baited it with a morsel of meat and threw it into the sea. After two hours he had taken nothing. Then these waters are uninhabited? No! There is a bite. Hans draws in his line, and behold a fish which resisted violently.

"A sturgeon!" I exclaimed. "A small sturgeon!"

The professor looks, and does not agree with me. This fish has a round, flat head, the back of its body covered with bony plates, teeth wanting, pectoral fins large, no tail. The creature belongs to the order where naturalists have placed the sturgeon, but it differs from the sturgeon in very essential points.

My uncle, after a short examination, pronounced that this animal belongs to a family which has been extinct for centuries, and of which the Devonian beds alone show fossil remains.

"How," said I, "can we have taken a living specimen of an inhabitant of primeval seas?"

"Yes," said the professor, "and you see these fossil fishes have no identity with present species. To have obtained a living specimen is a glad era for a naturalist."

"But to what family does it belong?"

"It is a ganoid, one of the Cephalaspidæ, species Pterichthys, I am sure! But this individual offers a peculiarity common to the fish of all subterranean waters—it is blind! It not only does not see, but the organ of sight is wanting."

I looked closely and saw that this was really the case, but perhaps an exceptional one.

The line is baited again and thrown into the sea. This sea must be well stocked with fish, for in two hours we took a great number of Pterichthys, as well as some others belonging to another extinct family, the Dipteridæ—of what species, however, my uncle was unable to pronounce. All were deficient in organs of vision.

This unexpected take of fish was a welcome addition to our stock of provisions.

Thus much seems certain, that this sea is inhabited only by fossil species, of which the fish and the reptiles are more perfect as their date is more remote. Perhaps we shall meet some of the saurians which science has recreated from a fragment of bone or cartilage!

I take the glass and scan the sea. It is a desert. Perhaps we are still too near the shore. I turn to the air. Why do we see none of the birds reconstructed by the immortal Cuvier, flapping their great wings in this dense atmosphere: these fish would supply them with stores of food. I gaze into space, but the air is as lonely as the waters.

My fancy ran riot among the marvelous hypotheses of palæontology. I dream with my eyes open. I fancy this sea covered with chelonia, those antediluvian turtles that resembled floating islands. I peopled its gloomy strand with the giant mammifers of ancient times, the leptotherium, found in Brazilian caves, the mericotherium, from the icy region of Siberia. And, farther on, the pachydermatous lophiodon (the gigantic tapir) hides itself behind the rocks, ready to tear the prey from the anoplotherium, a strange animal akin to the rhinoceros, the horse, the hippopotamus, and the camel, as if in the hurry of creation one animal had been made up of several. The giant mastodon writhed his trunk and ground his tusks on the rocky shore, while the megatherium, propped on his mighty paws, turns up the earth, and roars till the granite echoes to the sound.

The whole fossil world lives again in my imagination. I go back in fancy to the biblical epoch of creation, long before the advent of man, when the imperfect earth was not fitted to sustain him. Then still farther back, to the time when no life existed. The mammifers disappeared, then the birds, then the reptiles of the secondary epoch, and then the fishes, crustaceans, molluscæ, articulata. The zoophytes of the transition period returned to oblivion. All life was concentrated in me, my heart alone beat in a depopulated world. Seasons were no more; climates were unknown; the heat of the earth increased till it neutralized that of our radiant star. Vegetation was gigantic. I passed under the shade of tree-ferns, trampling with uncertain step iridescent clay and particolored sand: I leaned against the trunks of immense conifers; I lay down in the shade of sphenophylles, asterophylles, and lycopods 100 feet high.

Ages seemed to pass like days! I followed step by step the transformation of the earth. Plants disappeared; granite rocks lost their hardness: the fluid replaced the solid under the influence of growing heat; water flowed over the earth's surface; it boiled, it volatilized; gradually the globe became a gaseous mass, white hot, as large and as luminous as the sun.

In the center of the nebulous mass, 14,000 times larger than the earth it was one day to form, I felt myself carried into planetary space. My body became ethereal in its turn and mingled like an imponderable atom with the vast body of vapor which described its flaming orbit in infinite space!

What a dream! Where is it carrying me? My feverish hand tries to note a few of the wild details. I was unconscious of all around—professor, guide, raft—everything. My mind was under a hallucination.

"What ails you?" said my uncle.

My staring eyes were fixed on him without seeing.

"Take care, Axel, you will fall into the sea!"

At this moment I felt Hans' strong grip on my arm. But for him, the delirium of my dream would have made me jump overboard.

"Has he lost his senses?" cried the professor.

"What is it?" said I at last, regaining consciousness.

"Are you ill?"

"No; I had a moment of hallucination, but it is over now. Is all going well?"

"Yes; a good breeze and a calm sea; and if my calculation is correct we shall not be long before we touch land."

As he spoke I rose and carefully scrutinized the horizon, but, as before, the line of sea is lost in the clouds.

XXXIII

Saturday, August 15.—The sea preserves its dreary monotony! No land in sight. The horizon looks very distant.

My head is heavy from the excitement of my dream. My uncle had no dream, but he is out of humor. He sweeps the horizon with his glass, and crosses his arms with an air of vexation.

I remark in Professor Lidenbrock a tendency to become, as of old, a man impatient of the past, and I record the fact in my journal. My danger and my sufferings barely sufficed to draw from him a spark of humanity; but since my recovery his nature has got the upper hand again. And yet what has he to complain of? Our voyage has been most favorable, and the raft sails with wondrous rapidity.

"You seem uneasy, uncle?" said I, seeing him constantly using his glass.

"Uneasy? Oh no!"

"Impatient, then?"

"One might be impatient with less reason."

"And yet our speed?"

"What is the speed to me? The speed is well enough, but the sea is too vast."

I remembered that the professor, before our departure, estimated the length of this subterranean sea at about 100 miles. We had sailed three times that distance, and the southern shore was not yet in view.

"We are not descending," said the professor. "All this is lost time, and in fact I did not come so far to make one of a boating party on a pond."

"But," said I, "if we have followed the route pointed out by Saknussemm—"

"That is the very question. Have we followed his route? Did he meet with this ocean? Did he cross it? Did the stream we followed mislead us utterly?"

"At any rate, we have no reason to regret having come so far. The scene is grand. . . ."

"The question is not of scenery. I have an object in view, and I wish to attain it. Don't talk to me of scenery."

I took the hint, and left the professor to bite his lips in silence. At six o'clock Hans claimed his wages, and his three rix-dollars were counted out to him.

Sunday, August 16.—Nothing new. Weather continues the same. Wind tends slightly to freshen. When I awake, my first thought is to observe the intensity of the light. I always fear the electric phenomenon may decrease, and die away. But there is no diminution. The shadow of the raft is sharply defined on the waves.

This sea seems boundless. It must be as large as the Mediterranean, or even the Atlantic. Why not?

My uncle has repeatedly taken soundings. He fastened one of our heaviest pickaxes to a long rope, and let out 200 fathoms. No bottom! We had great difficulty in hauling in the line. When the ax came up, Hans called my attention to some strongly-defined marks on its surface. It had the appearance of having been strongly compressed between two hard surfaces. I looked at the hunter.

"*Täuder!*" said he.

I did not understand. I turned to my uncle, but he was absorbed. I did not care to disturb him. I came back to my Icelander, who opened and closed his mouth, and I at last understood him.

"Teeth!" said I, with amazement, and looking more closely at the iron bar.

Yes! it was certainly teeth that made that impression. What prodigious power of jaw! Are some of those extinct monsters lying at the bottom of this deep ocean—monsters more voracious than the shark, more formidable than the whale? My eyes were fascinated to that half-gnawed bar. Is my dream of last night to be realized?

These thoughts agitated my mind all day, and my imagination only calmed down after a sleep of several hours' duration.

Monday, August 17.—I am trying to recollect the peculiar instincts of the antediluvian animals of the secondary period which, following the mollusca, the crustaceans, and the fish, preceded the appearance of the mammifers on the globe. These monsters were the monarchs of the Jurassic seas.*

Nature furnishes them with the most complete organization. What giant forms! What enormous power! The saurians of our day, alligators or crocodiles, the largest and most formidable, are only feeble miniatures of their primeval ancestors!

I shudder at the phantoms I have evoked. No human eye has seen their living forms. They appeared on earth countless ages before man, but their fossil skeletons found in the calcareous clays known as *Lias* have allowed us to reconstruct them anatomically, and to become acquainted with their colossal figures.

I have seen, in the Hamburg Museum, the skeleton of one of these saurians, that measured thirty feet in length. Am I destined to behold face to face these representatives of an antediluvian family? No, it is impossible. And yet the mark of mighty teeth is stamped on that iron bar, and their impress shows that the teeth are conical like those of the crocodile.

I gazed nervously at the sea. I feared to see one of these inhabitants of submarine caves.

I suppose Professor Lidenbrock was struck with the same idea, though not by the same fears, for when he had examined the pickax, he threw a glance round on the ocean.

---

* Seas of the secondary period, which formed the strata of which the Jura Mountains are composed.

"What possessed him to take soundings," thought I; "he has disturbed some animal in its retreat, and if we are not attacked—"

I looked over our firearms to satisfy myself that they were in good order. My uncle observed me, and nodded approbation.

Already long swells on the surface of the sea indicated disturbances in the depths. The danger is at hand! We must be watchful!

Tuesday, August 18.—Evening came, or rather there came the moment when sleep weighed down our eyelids, for there is no night on this ocean, and the unvarying light fatigues our eyes, as if we were voyaging on the Arctic Seas. Hans was at the helm. During his watch I went to sleep.

Two hours after, I was awakened by a fearful shock. The raft was lifted off the water with indescribable force, and thrown on the waves again forty yards off.

"What is the matter?" cried my uncle. "Have we struck?"

Hans pointed to a dusky mass about 400 yards off, which rose and fell alternately I looked, and then exclaimed:

"It is a colossal porpoise!"

"Yes," said my uncle, "and there is a sea-lizard of uncommon size."

"And beyond that a monstrous crocodile! See the great jaws and the rows of teeth! Ah! he is gone."

"A whale! a whale!" exclaimed the professor. "I see his enormous fins! And see the jets of air and water he expels from his blowholes."

I saw two liquid columns rising to a considerable height in the air. We stood, amazed, helpless, terrified in the presence of these monsters of the sea. They were of supernatural size, and the smelliest of them could have crushed our raft with a snap of his teeth. Hans wanted to turn up into the wind to escape this dangerous neighborhood; but on that side, new enemies, no less formidable, came into view; a turtle, forty feet long, a serpent, thirty feet, who moved his enormous head with a darting motion above the waves.

Flight was impossible. The reptiles were drawing nearer, they circled round the raft with a rapidity unequaled by an express train, they described concentric circles round us. I took my carbine. But what effect would a ball have on the scale-armor of these creatures?

We were dumb with fear. They came nearer! The crocodile on one side, the serpent on the other. The rest disappeared. I was about to fire. Hans stopped me by a sign. The monsters passed within 100 yards of the raft, fell on one another, and in their fury they overlooked us. The battle was fought 200 yards away from us. We could distinctly see the struggles of these monsters. But as I watched, it appeared to me that other creatures came and took part in the contest—the porpoise, the whale, the lizard, the turtle. I had momentary glimpses of them all. I pointed them out to Hans. He shook his head.

"*Tva!*" said he.

"What! two? He says there are only two."

"He is right," said my uncle, whose glass had never left his eyes.

"You are jesting, uncle."

"No! the one has the muzzle of a porpoise, the head of a lizard, the teeth of a crocodile, and that deceived us. It is the most formidable of all the antediluvian reptiles—the ichthyosaurus!"

"And the other?"

"The other is his great antagonist, a serpent hidden in the carapace of a turtle, whom we know as the plesiosaurus."

Hans was right. Two monsters only made all this commotion in the sea, and I really beheld two reptiles of the primitive age. I saw the bloodshot eye of the ichthyosaurus, as big as a man's head. Nature has provided him with an optic apparatus of great power, and capable of resisting the pressure of the water at the depth he inhabits. He has been justly named the whale of the saurians, for he has the shape and the speed. His jaw is enormous, and naturalists tell us he has no less than 182 teeth.

The plesiosaurus is a serpent with a cylindrical trunk, short tail, and claws arranged like oars; his body is entirely covered by the carapace, and his neck, as flexible as that of the swan, stretches to a height of thirty feet above the waves.

These animals fought with incredible fury, they raised mountainous waves, which flowed back towards the raft; hissing sounds of great force were heard. The two brutes had closed with each other. I could not distinguish one from the other. We had still to fear the fury of the victor.

An hour, two hours passed: the battle still raged with unabated vehemence. The combatants sometimes veered towards us, and sometimes away from us. We remained motionless, ready to fire.

Suddenly the two monsters disappeared, creating a maelstrom in the waters. Some minutes elapsed. Were they fighting it out down below?

All at once an enormous head darted up—the head of the plesiosaurus. The great creature is mortally wounded. I could see nothing of his gigantic carapace, only his long neck, which rose and fell, curved and lashed the waters like a mighty whip, and writhed like a divided worm. The water was dashed to a considerable distance. It blinded us. But soon the struggles of the enormous body drew to an end; his motions diminished, his contortions became fewer, and his long serpent neck lay an inert mass on the calm waves.

As to the ichthyosaurus, we asked ourselves whether he had reached his submarine cavern, or whether he would again show himself on the surface.

XXXIV

Wednesday, August 19.—Fortunately the wind, which is blowing pretty fresh, has enabled us to make a rapid flight from the scene of the conflict. Hans is still at the helm. My uncle, who had been aroused from his absorbing reflections by the incidents of the struggle, relapsed into his impatient watching of the sea.

The voyage is as monotonous as ever, but I should not care to have the dreariness varied at the price of yesterday's dangers.

Thursday, August 20.—Breeze N.N.E. unsteady. Temperature hot. We are going about nine miles and a half per hour.

Towards mid-day we heard a very distant sound. I note the fact here without being able to account for it. It is like a continuous roar.

"There must be in the distance," said the professor, "some rock or island on which the sea breaks." Hans crawled up the mast but could see no breakers. The ocean is undisturbed as far as the eye can reach.

Three hours pass, the noise assumes the sound of a far-off fall of water. I remark this to my uncle, who shakes his head, but I am convinced I am right. Are we running towards some cataract which will precipitate us into an abyss? Such a descent may suit the professor, as it approaches the vertical, but as for me—

Whatever it is, there must be a few miles off a phenomenon of a noisy kind, for now we can hear a violent roaring sound. Does it come from sky or sea?

I look towards the vapor suspended in the atmosphere and try to estimate its depth. The sky is tranquil. The clouds, which have risen to the roof of the vault, seem motionless, and are lost in intensity of light. Not there can I find the cause of the phenomenon.

Then I turn to the horizon, now clear and free from mist. Its aspect is quite normal. But if this noise comes from a fall or a cataract, or if the waters of this sea fall into a lower basin, if these roarings are produced by a falling mass of water, the current ought to increase, and its rate of acceleration may give us the measure of our danger. I try the experiment. There is no current; a bottle thrown into the water remains unaffected by aught but the wind.

About four o'clock Hans rises, takes a grip of the mast, and goes to the top. Thence his eyes wander over the circle of the ocean; at a certain point they stop. No surprise is visible on his face, but his eye is riveted.

"He sees something," said my uncle.

"I think so."

Hans came down. Then he extended his arm to the south and said: "*Der nere.*"

"Down there?" said my uncle.

And seizing his glass he gazed attentively for a minute, which seemed to me an age.

"Yes, yes!" cried he.

"What do you see?"

"An enormous jet of water rising above the waves."

"Another marine animal?"

"Perhaps."

"Well, then, let us keep her head more to the west, for we have had experience enough of the danger of meeting the antediluvian monsters."

"No," said my uncle; "let her go."

I turned towards Hans—he kept the tiller with inflexible steadiness. But I cannot conceal from myself that if, at this distance, which must be thirty-six miles at the very least, we can discern the column of water he ejects, the creature must be of preternatural size. To fly would only be to obey the dictates of vulgar prudence. But we did not come here to be prudent.

So on we went. The nearer we approached, the higher the jet of water became.

What monster could imbibe and expel without cessation such a mass of water?

At eight o'clock in the evening we were not six miles from him. His enormous body, a dark mountainous mass, lay along the sea like an island. Am I under an illusion? Has fear got the better of me? His length seems to be over 2,000 yards. What great cetacean can it be, never predicated by Cuvier or Blumenbach. It is motionless, perhaps asleep; the sea cannot lift it, for the waves break on its flanks. The jet of water rising 500 feet high, falls again in rain with a deafening noise. And we are running madly on towards this mighty mass, which 100 whales would not suffice to feed for a day.

Terror seized me. I would go no farther. I resolved to cut the halyard, if necessary. I attacked my uncle, who made no answer.

All at once Hans rose, and pointing with his finger to the spot where the danger lay:

"*Holm!*" said he.

"An island!" cried my uncle.

"An island," I repeated, shrugging my shoulders.

"To be sure it is," said the professor, bursting into a laugh.

"But the column of water?"

"*Geyser,*" said Hans.

"Undoubtedly a 'geyser,' like those in Iceland."

At first I was annoyed at having mistaken an island for a marine monster. But I cannot help myself, and must own my error. It is nothing but a natural phenomenon.

As we drew near, the dimensions of the liquid shaft became really grand. The island bears a wonderful resemblance to an immense cetacean, whose head rises sixty feet out of the water. The "geyser," which in Icelandic signifies "fury," rises majestically at its extremity. Muffled sounds of explosion occurred every moment, and the enormous jet rose with greater force, convulsed its canopy of vapor, and leaped up to the lower clouds. It was a solitary geyser. Neither fumerolles nor hot springs surround it. All the volcanic force is centered in itself. The rays of the electric light mingled with this dazzling fountain, investing every drop with the hues of the rainbow.

"Let us go round the island," said the professor.

But we had to be very careful to avoid the falling waters, which would have sunk the raft in a moment. Hans managed, with great skill, to bring us to the other end of the island. I jumped on the rock. My uncle followed me quickly, but the hunter stayed at his post like a man superior to such excitements.

We trod a granite soil mixed with silicious tufa. The ground vibrated beneath our feet, like the sides of a boiler full of superheated steam. The heat is intense. We came in sight of a small central basin, whence rises the geyser. I immersed our thermometer in the water, which runs away bubbling as it goes, and it marked 233°.

So this water must come from a burning center—contrary to the theory of Professor Lidenbrock. I could not refrain from giving utterance to this remark.

"Well," said he, "what does that prove against my doctrine?"

"Oh, nothing!" said I, perceiving that he was past reasoning with.

Nevertheless, I cannot deny that up to this time we have been singularly fortunate, and that for some reason unknown to me, we have made this voyage under peculiar conditions of temperature. But I look upon it as certain that we must, one time or other, arrive at the region where the central heat attains the greatest point, and leaves far behind all the gradations of our thermometers.

"We shall see." So the professor says. He has given his nephew's name to this volcanic isle, and now orders us to re-embark.

I stayed a few minutes longer to watch the geyser. I remark that its jets are irregular—sometimes the force is diminished, sometimes increased. And I attribute these variations to the fluctuating pressure of the vapors accumulated in the reservoir.

At last we start, making a circuit by the steep rocks at the southern end. Hans has taken advantage of our halt to repair the raft.

But before leaving I took some observation to ascertain the distance we had come, and I note them in my journal. We have made over 800 miles since leaving Port Gräuben, and we reckon that we are under England, 1,800 miles from Iceland.

XXXV

riday, August 21.—Next day the magnificent geyser was out of sight. The wind freshened, and carried us rapidly away from Axel Island. The roaring sound died away gradually.

The weather, if I may use the expression, will soon change. The atmosphere is dense with vapors charged with the electricity generated by saline evaporation; the clouds are slowly falling, and are of a uniform olive tint. The electric rays can scarcely penetrate them; they look like a dark curtain let down before the stage on which the drama of the Tempest is to be played.

I have the kind of premonitory sensation that animals have previous to a shock of earthquake. The "cumuli"* heaped up towards the south have a threatening look—they have the pitiless expression that I have so often noticed before a storm. The air is oppressive, and the sea calm.

In the distance the clouds resemble great bales of cotton piled up in picturesque disorder; gradually they swell, and lose in number what they gain in magnitude; they become so heavy that they lie close to the horizon, but the upper current seemed to melt them into a dark formless bank of cloud full of evil boding; now and then a ball of vapor, still illumined, will roll for a moment on the gray background, and then lose itself in the opaque mass.

The atmosphere is saturated with electric fluid, and my body also. My hair stands up as if an electric machine were at hand. I feel as if I should give a violent shock to my companions if they touched me.

At ten o'clock this morning the signs of a storm became more decisive—the wind seemed as if it paused to take breath. The cloud looked like a great bag in which the tempests were collected together. I tried not to believe in the stormy promise of the sky, but I could not help saying:

"Bad weather is brewing there!"

The professor did not answer. He is in an insufferably bad humor at seeing the sea extending farther and farther as we go. He shrugged his shoulders at my words.

"We shall have a storm," said I, pointing to the horizon. "Those clouds bear down on the sea as if they would crush it."

General silence. The wind has now died away. Nature has a death-like appearance, and seems not to draw a breath. From the mast, where I already see a faint halo like St. Elmo's fire, the sail is hanging in heavy folds. The raft lies motionless on the deep wave-less sea. But

---

*Clouds of a rounded form.

if we are not stirring, why keep our sail up, and thus run the risk of destruction at the first blast of the storm?

"Let us take in the sail and lower the mast," said I. "It would only be prudence."

"No! by all the powers!" said my uncle; "a hundred times no! Let me only behold the rocks of the shore, and I care not if the raft is shivered into a thousand pieces."

He had scarcely said the words, when the southern horizon underwent a change. The accumulated vapors descended in rain, and the air, rushing in to fill their place, produced a hurricane. It came from every quarter of the cavern. The darkness increased. I could do no more than make a few imperfect notes.

Suddenly the raft rises—makes a bound—my uncle is thrown down. He takes firm hold of a cable, and watches with delight the spectacle of the elements at war!

Hans does not stir. His long hair, beaten by the wind and driven across his stolid face, gives him a weird look, for at the end of every hair is a luminous tuft. He looks like an antediluvian man, a contemporary of the ichthyosaurus and the megatherium. The mast still survives. The sail swells out like a bubble on the verge of bursting. The raft spins along with a speed I cannot attempt to estimate; the water rushing past seems to fly faster still; it describes sharp, clear, arrowy lines.

"The sail! the sail!" I exclaim, making signs to lower it.

"No," said my uncle.

"*Nej,*" said Hans, gently shaking his head.

The rain is like a roaring cataract between us and the horizon to which we are madly rushing. But before it reaches us, the cloud curtain tears apart and reveals the boiling sea; and now the electricity, disengaged by the chemical action in the upper cloud strata, comes into play. Loud claps of thunder; dazzling coruscations; networks of vivid lightnings; ceaseless detonations; masses of incandescent vapor; hailstones, like a fiery shower, rattling among our tools and firearms. The heaving waves look like craters full of interior fire, every crevice darting a little tongue of flame.

My eyes are dazzled by the intensity of the light, my ears deafened by the crash of the thunder. I have to hold firmly by the mast, which is bending like a reed before the tornado.

· · · · ·

[Here my notes of the voyage become very fragmentary. I can only find a few fugitive remarks, which appear to have been written almost mechanically. But in their brevity, and even in their obscurity, they bear the impress of the excitement of the time, and portray my feelings better than I could do from memory.]

· · · · ·

XXXVI

Wither are we going? We are carried along with inconceivable rapidity.

The night has been appalling, and the storm gives no sign of abating. We live in an atmosphere of deafening sound—a ceaseless thunder. Our ears are bleeding. We cannot hear each other speak.

The lightning is incessant. I see flashes which describe a kind of backward zigzag, and, after a rapid course, seemed to return upward as if they would rive the granite vault above us. If that vault should be rent, what would become of us! Sometimes the lightning is forked, and sometimes takes the form of fiery globes which explode like so many bomb-shells, but whose report is lost amid the roar of the elements.

The human ear can no longer measure the increment of sound. If all the powder magazines in the world were to blow up, I believe we should fail to perceive the shock. The surface of the clouds is constantly emitting scintillations of electric light. Their molecules seem continually to disengage electricity. The air seems parched, and countless jets of water are thrown up into the atmosphere and fall again in foam. Again I ask myself, "Whither are we tending?"

My uncle lies stretched at full length on the raft.

The heat increases. On consulting the thermometer I find it marks. . . . [the figures are effaced].

Monday, August 24.—The storm has not ceased. It seems strange that after any modification in this dense atmosphere there does not come some definitive change.

We are broken down with fatigue. Hans is much as usual. The raft keeps driving to the south-east. We have already made more than 600 miles since leaving Axel Island.

At mid-day, the hurricane acquired tenfold force. We were obliged to make fast every article of cargo, and also to lash ourselves to the raft. The sea was washing over us.

For three whole days we had been unable to exchange a syllable. Even a word shouted in the ear was inaudible. My uncle leaned over to me, and said something. I fancied it was "We are lost!"

I am not certain. It occurred to me to write the words, "Let us take in our sail." He nodded assent.

He had scarcely raised his head again, when a fiery disc appeared on the edge of the raft. The mast and the sail were swept away together, and I saw them flying at an immense distance above, looking like a pterodactyl, the primeval bird of whom geologists tell us.

We were petrified with fear. The great ball, half fiery white, half azure blue, the size of a ten-inch shell, moved slowly, spinning with great velocity. It was now here, now there—up on the timbers of the raft, over on the bag of provisions; then it glanced lightly down, made a bound, grazed the case of gunpowder. Horror! we shall be blown to atoms! No! the dazzling disc retreated, approached Hans, who stared calmly at it; then my uncle, who crouched on his knees to avoid it; then myself, pale and shuddering at the glare and the glow; it gyrated close to my foot, which I was powerless to withdraw.

An odor of nitrous gas filled the air. It attacked the throat and lungs; we were all but suffocated.

What can it be that hinders me from moving my foot? It feels as if riveted to the raft! I have it! The contact of this electric body has magnetized all the iron on board. Our tools, our firearms were stirred, clicking as they touched each other; the nails of my boots had forcibly adhered to a plate of iron sunk in the timber. I cannot stir my foot!

At length, by a violent effort, I succeeded in tearing it away, just as the ball was preparing to strike me in its next gyration, if—

Oh, what intensity of light! The ball bursts! We are covered with jets of flame. Then all was dark. I had just time to discern my uncle stretched on the raft, Hans motionless at the tiller, and "spitting fire" under the influence of the electricity which pervaded his body.

Again I exclaim, "Where are we going?"

Tuesday, August 25.—I have just recovered from a prolonged swoon; the lightnings are let loose in the atmosphere like a brood of serpents.

Are we still at sea? Yes, driving on with incredible swiftness. We have passed under England, under the British Channel, under France, perhaps under all Europe!

. . . . .

A new sound greets our ears. Surely the roar of breakers! But in that case

. . . . .

XXXVII

Here ends what I call "my journal on board," which fortunately has been saved from the wreck. I take up my narrative as before.

What happened after the raft struck on the rocks I can scarcely tell. I felt that I was thrown among the breakers, and if I escaped death, if my body was not mangled by the pointed rocks, it was the strong arm of Hans that plucked me from the waters.

The courageous Icelander carried me beyond the reach of the waves, and laid me on a burning, sandy shore, where I found myself side by side with my uncle.

Then he returned to the rocks, where the angry sea was dashing, in order to try and save some waifs from the wreck. I could not speak. I was worn out with excitement and fatigue; it was more than an hour before I recovered my faculties.

Even at this time a deluge of rain was falling, but with that accumulated force that betokens the end of the storm. Some rocks piled on others afforded us a shelter from the torrent. Hans prepared some food which I could not touch, and then, exhausted by our three nights' watch, we fell into a troubled sleep.

Next day the weather was glorious. Sky and sea united in soft repose. All trace of the tempest was dissipated. Such was the joyful news with which the professor greeted me on awaking. His gaiety jarred on my nerves.

"Well, my lad," said he, "I hope you slept well."

He spoke as if we were at home in the Königstrasse, and that I had just come down to breakfast on my wedding morning with poor Gräuben. Alas! if the storm has only impelled the raft to the eastward we should have passed under Germany—under my beloved town of

Hamburg—perhaps under the very street where dwells all that is dearest to me in the world. Then there would only have been 120 miles between us—but 120 vertical miles through a granite wall, and in reality we had more than 3,000 miles to travel!

All these melancholy thoughts flashed through my mind before I replied to my uncle's question.

"Well," said he. "I asked you how you slept?"

"Very well," said I. "I am knocked up; but that is nothing."

"Nothing at all; merely a little fatigue."

"You seem in great spirits this morning, uncle," said I.

"Delighted, my lad! Delighted! We have arrived!"

"At the end of our expedition?"

"No, but at the end of the weary sea. We shall now resume our land journey; and, this time, we shall penetrate into the bowels of the earth."

"But, uncle, may I ask you a question?"

"You may, Axel."

"How are we to get back?"

"Get back! Is your mind on getting back before we have even arrived at our journey's end?"

"No; I merely wanted to know how it is to be accomplished."

"The simplest thing in the world. Once arrived at the center of the spheroid, we shall discover a new route whereby to regain the surface; or else we shall return in a commonplace manner by the same road by which we came. It will not be closed behind us, that is one comfort."

"In that case the raft must be made tight."

"Of course."

"But have we provision for all this traveling?"

"We have. Hans is a right clever fellow, and I am sure he has saved the greatest part of our cargo. However, come and let us see."

We left the windy grotto. I had a hope, which was almost a fear. It seemed to me impossible that anything on board the raft could have survived that terrible landing. I was wrong. When I reached the beach, Hans was in the midst of a mass of objects arranged in order. My uncle pressed his hand with the liveliest gratitude. This man, whose super-human devotion is probably without a parallel, had toiled while we slept, and had saved all that was most precious to us, at the risk of his own life.

Not that we had not serious losses. Our firearms, for example; but those we could do without. The powder was uninjured, having missed explosion during the storm.

"Well," exclaimed the professor, "as the guns are gone, we cannot be expected to go hunting; that is something."

"That is all very well," said I, "but what of our instruments?"

"Here is the manometer, the most useful of all, and for which I would have given all the rest. Having that, I can calculate our depth, and ascertain when we are at the center. Without it we should run the risk of coming out at the antipodes."

His joking manner appeared to me ferocious.

"And the compass?" said I.

"Here it is on the rock, quite unharmed, and the chronometer and thermometer. Oh, the hunter is an invaluable fellow!"

This could not be gainsayed. Not one of our Instruments was miss-ing. As to tools and Implements, I saw scattered on the sand, ladders, ropes, pickaxes, mattocks, &c.

There only remained the victualing question. "And the provi-sions?" said I.

"Ay! let me see the provisions," said my uncle. The cases which contained them were lying In a row on the strand in a perfect state of preservation. The sea had spared them for the most part; and taking everything together—biscuit, salt meat, geneva, and dried fish—we had sufficient for four months.

"Four months!" cried the professor. "Why, we have enough to go and come back; and with what Is left I will give a grand dinner to my colleagues at the Johannæum."

I ought to have been used to my uncle's eccentricities by this time, but still they never ceased to surprise me.

"Now," said he, "we can replenish our water stores from the granite basins which the storm has filled with rain; so we are in no danger of suffering from thirst. As to the raft, I should recommend Hans to make the best job he can of it, although I do not at all expect to want it again."

"Why not?" said I.

"A fancy of mine, my boy. I do not think we shall come out where we came in."

I looked at the professor with great misgiving. I wondered if he had gone crazed, but he spoke quite collectedly.

"Let us go to breakfast," said he.

I followed him to a high promontory after he had given directions to the hunter.

There, dried meat, biscuit, and tea made up an excellent meal, one of the best I ever made in my life. Fasting, the fresh air, and rest following strong excitement, all combined to give me an appetite.

During breakfast I questioned my uncle as to the means of ascertaining where we were at this moment.

"That," said I, "seems to me very difficult to calculate."

"Well, yes; to calculate exactly," he answered; "in fact it would be impossible, because during the three days' storm, I could take no note of the rate or direction of our course; but still, by reckoning, we can estimate our position approximately."

"Our last observation was taken at the Geyser Island—"

"At Axel Island, my lad. Do not decline the honor of giving your name to the first island discovered in the center of the earth."

"Be it so. At Axel Island we had crossed 810 miles of sea, and we were more than 1,800 miles from Iceland."

"Just so; therefore, starting from that point, let us reckon four days of storm, during which our speed was certainly not less than 240 miles in the twenty-four hours."

"I think that is about it. So that will be 900 miles to add."

"Yes, the 'Sea of Lidenbrock' must be 1,800 miles across! Do you know, Axel, it will rival the Mediterranean."

"Yes, especially if we have only crossed the breadth."

"Which is quite possible."

"Another curious thing," said I, "if our calculations are correct, the Mediterranean must be just over our heads."

"Really!"

"Yes, for we are 2,700 miles from Reikiavik!"

"That is a good step from here, my lad; but whether we are under the Mediterranean rather than under Turkey or under the Atlantic, we cannot decide unless we are sure that we have not deviated from our course."

"Well, it is easy to ascertain by looking at the compass. Let us go and see."

The professor made for the rock on which Hans had arranged the instruments. He was lively, sprightly, rubbed his hands, threw himself into attitudes as he went! He was young again. I followed him, anxious to know if my calculation was correct.

Arrived at the rock, my uncle took up the compass, laid it horizontally, and watched the needle, which, after a few oscillations, settled itself into its place. My uncle gazed; he rubbed his eyes, and looked again. Then he turned to me with a bewildered air.

"What ails you, uncle?" said I.

He motioned me to look at the instrument. I uttered an exclamation of astonishment. The needle indicated north, where we had believed the south to be. It turned to the shore instead of to the open sea.

I shook the compass. I examined it; it was in good order. No matter which way I turned it, it persisted in making this unexpected declaration.

We could only conclude that during the tempest we had failed to note the change of wind which had brought back the raft to the shore, which my uncle hoped he had left behind him.

XXXVIII

No words could depict the succession of emotions which agitated the professor-bewilderment, incredulity, rage. I never saw a man so discomfited at first or so enraged afterwards. After all the fatigues of the journey, all the risks we had run, all must be done over again! We had gone back instead of forward.

My uncle soon recovered himself.

"What a trick fate has played me! The very elements are against me. The air, the fire, the water conspire to bar my passage. Well! they shall know what my will can accomplish! I will not yield. I will not go back a step, and we shall see whether man or nature will win."

Standing upright on the rock, betraying his irritation by his menacing attitude, Otto Lidenbrock reminded me of Ajax defying the gods. I thought it time to interpose and put a check on his mad enthusiasm.

"Listen to me, uncle," said I, in a steadfast voice. "There is a limit to human ambition; it is useless to struggle after the impossible; we are badly equipped for a sea-voyage; 1,500 miles cannot be done on a raft of unsound timbers, with a rag of blanket for a sail and a stick for a mast, and in the face of all the winds of heaven let loose. We have no means of steering, we are the plaything of the storm, and it is the height of madness to attempt the voyage a second time."

I set forth all this without interruption for about ten minutes, but this was owing solely to the inattention of the professor, who did not hear one word of my arguments.

"To the raft!" cried he.

That was his answer. In vain I entreated him to desist. In vain I stormed, in vain I spent my strength in warring against a will harder than granite. Hans had just completed his repairs of the raft. It was as if this whimsical being had divined my uncle's plans. With some pieces of surtur-brand, he had strengthened the vessel. A sail was already spread, and was flapping in the breeze.

The professor gave a few directions to the guide, who immediately put our belongings on board, and made everything ready for a start. The air was pretty clear, and the north-west wind held.

What could I do? How could I alone make head against these two? Impossible, even if Hans had sided with me. But the Icelander seemed to have put away all individual will, and taken a vow of abnegation. I could do nothing with a servant so enslaved to his master. There was nothing for it but to go on. Accordingly, I proceeded to take my usual place on the raft, when my uncle put out his hand to stop me.

"We shall not start till to-morrow," said he.

I made a gesture of resignation to everything that might be in store for me.

"I must omit nothing," said he. "Since fate has thrown me on this part of the coast, I will not leave it without a full examination."

This remark will be intelligible when it is understood that we had returned to the north coast, but not to the part from which we had started. Port Gräuben must be more to the west. So that, after all, there was nothing unreasonable in the professor's desire to explore carefully this new region. "Let us go then and reconnoitre," said I.

And leaving Hans to his occupations, we set out. The space between the beach and the foot of the sea-rampart was very extensive. We walked for a good half-hour before reaching the rocky wall. Our feet crushed innumerable shells of every form and size, the former homes of extinct species. I also observed countless numbers of carapaces whose diameter often exceeded fifteen feet. They had belonged to those giant glyptodons of the pliocene period, of which the tortoise of our day is but a miniature copy.

The ground was also strewn with an immense quantity of rocky *débris*, a sort of pebbles rounded by the action of water and arranged in successive ridgy lines. I judged from this that the sea had at some time occupied this space. On the scattered rocks, now out of their reach, the billows had left evident traces of their passage.

This might account in some degree for the existence of an ocean 120 miles below the surface of the earth. But, according to my theory, this liquid mass must little by little lose itself in the bowels of the earth, and it is evidently replenished from the waters of the ocean which find their way through some fissure. Just now, however, the fissure must be closed, otherwise this cavern, or rather this immense reservoir, would be filled in a very short time. Or perhaps this body of water struggling against subterranean fires may be partly vaporized, which would account for the clouds suspended overhead, and for the electric disturbances which convulse the interior of the globe.

This seemed to me an adequate theory of the phenomena we ourselves had witnessed, for however vast the wonders of nature, they are always referable to physical causes.

We were walking on a kind of sedimentary stratum, formed by water, like all the strata of that period, so widely distributed over the earth. The professor pored attentively into every chink in the rock. He was convinced that some opening must exist, and it was vital to him to ascertain its depth.

We had followed the coast of the "Sea of Lidenbrock" for a mile, when suddenly the surface exhibited a change. It seemed to have been turned upside down—torn up by the convulsive heaving of the under-lying strata. In many places the extent of the disturbance was attested by deep chasms and corresponding elevations.

We made but slow progress over these fragments of granite, min-gled here and there with silex, quartz, and alluvial deposits, when we came in sight of a vast plain covered with bones.

It was like an immense cemetery, where the generations of twenty centuries mingled their dust. Piles of remains rose behind each other in the distance, undulating like a sea towards the horizon, where they were lost in a soft haze. Here, on an extent of probably 3,000 square miles, was concentrated the whole history of animal life—a history scarcely traceable in the too recent soil of the inhabited world.

An insatiable curiosity urged us on. Our feet crushed the remains of pre-historic animals and fossils, whose rare and interesting relics are eagerly competed for by the museums of great cities. The lives of a thousand Cuviers would not suffice to reconstruct the skeletons that lie in this magnificent assemblage of organic remains.

I was speechless with amazement. My uncle threw up his arms towards the impenetrable vault that stood for a sky. His mouth wildly open—his eyes gleaming under his spectacles; his head moving up and down, right and left—his whole demeanor indicated how intense was his astonishment. He found himself in a priceless collection of leptotherium, mericotherium, lophodion, anoplotherium, megatherium, mastodon, protopithecus, pterodactyles—all the antediluvian monsters gathered together for his private gratification. Just fancy an enthusiastic bibliomaniac transported in an instant into that Alexandrian library which Omar burnt, and which some miracle had reproduced from its ashes. Such was my uncle Lidenbrock at this moment.

But there came a new phase of astonishment, when hurrying across this organic dust, he seized a skull, and, in a voice full of emotion, he cried:

"Axel, Axel!—a human head!"

"A human head, uncle!" said I, equally surprised.

"Yes, my lad. Ah! Milne-Edwards. Ah! Quatrefages, why are you not here with me to behold it?"

XXXIX

To understand why my uncle invoked these illustrious *savants*, it should be understood that a fact of great importance in palaeontology had been announced some time before we left.

On March 28, 1863, some workmen, under the direction of M. Boucher de Perthes, excavating in the quarries of Moulin-Quignon, near Abbeville, in the department of the Somme, in France, found a human jaw-bone fourteen feet below the surface. It was the first fossil of that kind ever brought to light. Near it were found stone axes and cut flints, clothed by time with a uniform coating of green.

This discovery made a great noise, not only in France, but in England and Germany. Many learned men of the French Institute, among others, Messrs. Milne-Edwards and Quatrefages, took up the matter warmly, proved the incontestable authenticity of the bone in question, and became the ardent partisans of the "maxillary process."

The learned men of the United Kingdom who accepted the fact as authentic, such as Messrs. Falconer, Busk, Carpenter, &c., were supported by the German *savants*, and foremost among these—the warmest enthusiast—was my uncle Lidenbrock.

The authenticity of a human fossil of the fourth epoch was thus incontestably established and admitted.

Their theory, it is true, had an implacable opponent in Monsieur Elie de Beaumont. This high authority held that the formation at Moulin-Quignon did not belong to the "diluvium," but to a less remote stratum, and, so far in accordance with Cuvier, he denied that the human race was contemporary with the animals of the fourth epoch. My uncle Lidenbrock and the great majority of geologists had maintained the opposite by discussion and controversy, and Monsieur Elie de Beaumont was left almost alone on the other side of the argument.

All these details were familiar to us, but we were not aware of the progress which the question had made since our departure. Other jawbones, identical in species, though belonging to other types and nations, had been found in the light soils of certain caves in France, Switzerland, and Belgium, as well as weapons, utensils, tools, bones of children, youths, men, and aged persons. The existence of man during the fourth epoch was daily confirmed.

And this was not all. New remains, exhumed from the tertiary pliocene, had enabled still bolder spirits to assign an antiquity even more remote to the human species. These remains, it is true, were not actually human, but relics of man's industry, tibias and thigh-bones of animals regularly striated—carved, so to speak—and which told clearly of human work.

Thus, at a bound, our species gained many steps on the ladder of time; he took precedence of the mastodon; he became contemporary with the "elephas meridionalis;" he dated 100,000 years back, for that is the figure assigned by the best geologists to the tertiary pliocene.

Such was the state of palaeontological science, and the extent of our knowledge of it will account or our attitude as we gazed at this vast ossuary of the "Sea of Lidenbrock," and also for the bewilderment of joy with which—twenty paces farther—my uncle found himself face to face with an individual man of the fourth epoch.

It was a perfectly recognizable human body. Perhaps some peculiarity in the soil, as in St. Michael's cemetery at Bordeaux, had thus preserved it. Who can tell? But this corpse, the skin tightened and dried like parchment, the limbs still soft to all appearance, the teeth perfect, the hair abundant, the finger and toe-nails of a hideous length, stood before us as in life.

I was dumb before this apparition of another age. My uncle, generally so loquacious, so full of energetic talk, was silent too. We had lifted the corpse and set it upright. He looked at us from his hollow orbits. We handled his body, which sounded at our touch.

After some minutes of silence, the uncle was superseded by the professor! Otto Lidenbrock, carried away by his ardent temperament, forgot the circumstances of our voyage, the place we were in, the great cavern that held us. No doubt he fancied himself in the Johannæum, standing before his pupils, for he took the lecturer's tone, and addressing an imaginary audience, said:

"Gentlemen, I have the honor to introduce to you a man of the fourth epoch. Great *savants* have denied his existence; others equally great have maintained it. The Saint Thomas of palæontology, were he here, would touch him with the finger and believe! I know how necessary it is for science to be on her guard against discoveries of this kind. I am aware of the contrivances of Barnum, and others of the same class, to impose on the world a fossil man. I know about the knee cap of Ajax the pretended body of Orestes, discovered by the Spartans, and the body of Asterius, nine cubits long, of which Pausanias tells. I have read the reports on the skeleton of Trapani, found in the fourteenth century, which it was sought to identify as Polyphemus, and the history of the giant disinterred near Palermo, in the sixteenth century. You also, gentlemen, are acquainted with the analysis made near Lucerne, in 1577, of those gigantic bones which the celebrated physician Felix Plater declared were those of a giant, nineteen feet high! I have read eagerly the treatises of Cassanio, and all the memoirs, pamphlets, essays and counter-essays published *à propos* of the skeleton of the Cimbrian king Teutobochus, the invader of Gaul, exhumed in a gravel-pit in Dauphiné in 1613. In the eighteenth century I would have contested with Pierre Campet the existence of the pre-adamites of Scheuchzer! I have in my hands the monograph called Gigan—."

Here was my uncle's natural infirmity; he could not in public pronounce difficult words without stumbling.

"The monograph called Gigan—," he repeated.

He got no farther.

"Giganto—"

No, the unfortunate word would stick there. How they would have laughed at the Johannæum!

"Gigantosteology!" At last he brought it out between two imprecations.

Then, more fluently than ever he went on:

"Yes, gentlemen, all that is familiar to me! I am aware that Cuvier and Blumenbach see in these bones simply the remains of the mammoth and other animals of the fourth epoch! But here, to doubt would be an insult to science! The body is there! You can see it, touch it! It is no skeleton, it is a perfect form, preserved for the purposes of anthropology!"

I had no desire to contravene the assertion.

"If I could wash it in a solution of sulphuric acid, I could free it from these earthy particles and glistening shells that encrust it. But the precious solvent is wanting. But, as he is, let him tell us his story."

Here the professor took the fossil corpse, and handled it with the dexterity of a showman.

"You see," said he, "it is not six feet long, far from giant proportions. As to the race it belongs to, there can be no doubt it is Caucasian, the white race; the race to which we ourselves belong. The cranium of this fossil is ovoid; without projecting cheek-bones, or protruding jaw. It presents no indication of prognathism, which modifies the facial angle.* If we measure this angle we find it almost 90°. But I will go farther with my deductions; I will venture to assert that this specimen of the human race is of the family of Japheth, which extends from India to the boundary of Eastern Europe. Do not smile, gentlemen!"

Nobody was smiling, but the professor was used to seeing faces relax during his learned dissertations:

"Yes," he continued, with renewed energy, "we have here a fossil man, a contemporary of the monsters who fill this vast amphitheater. As to how he came here, how the layers of *débris* in which he was embedded came into this vast cavern, I cannot offer a speculation. No one can doubt that, during the quaternary epoch, there was considerable disturbance of the earth's crust. The gradual cooling of the globe produces gaps, chasms, faults, into which portions of the upper strata must fall. I assert nothing, but this much is certain. Here is the man

---

* The facial angle is formed by two lines, one (more or less vertical), which touches the forehead and the incisors, the other horizontal, passing from the auditory opening to the lower bone of the nasal sinus. The projection of the jaw, which modifies the facial angle, is called in scientific language—prognathism.

surrounded by his handiwork, these axes, these wrought flints, which mark the Stone Age; and unless he came here as a tourist like myself, a pioneer of science, I cannot entertain a doubt of his origin."

The professor was silent, and I uttered my "unanimous applause." My uncle was perfectly right, and wiser people than his nephew would have found it difficult to controvert his statements.

Another point is, that this was not the only corpse in the great bed of bones. We met with others at every few steps in the dust, and my uncle had a choice of wonderful specimens wherewith to convince unbelievers. In truth it was an amazing sight to behold generations of men and animals in one mass of confusion in this great cemetery. But here came an important question to which we had no solution. Were these beings already dust when, by some throe of nature, they were brought down to the shores of the "sea of Lidenbrock," or had they lived here, in this subterranean world, with this false sky, in birth and death like the inhabitants of the earth? Up to the present time we had only seen sea-monsters and fish alive! Were we yet to meet some man of the abyss wandering on this lonely shore?

XL

For another half-hour we wandered over these deposits of bones. We pressed on, impelled by intense curiosity. What other wonders would this cavern reveal? what new treasures for science? My eyes were on the watch for surprises, and my mind prepared for any degree of astonishment.

The sea-shore had long been shut out by the hills formed by the ossuary. The imprudent professor, little dreaming of losing his way, drew me on to a distance. We went on silently bathed in waves of electric light. By a phenomenon I cannot explain, the light seemed uniformly dispersed, not radiating from any center, nor casting any shade. It was as if we were in the summer noon of the equatorial region, under the vertical rays of the sun. All vapor had disappeared. The rocks, the distant mountains, confused outlines of distant forests, presented a singular aspect under the equally diffused light. We were like the fantastic creation of Hoffman, the man who lost his shadow.

After walking about a mile we found ourselves on the skirts of an immense forest, but not of a fungoid growth like those we had seen in the neighborhood of Port Gräuben.

It was the vegetation of the tertiary epoch in all its magnificence—great palms of a species now extinct, superb palmacites, yews, cypresses. Thujas represented the conifers, and were interlaced with an impenetrable network of lianas. The ground was thickly carpeted with mosses and hepaticas. Some small streams trickled through the groves, scarce worthy of the name, as they gave no shade. At the sides of the streams grew tree-ferns, like those of our hot-houses. But color was wanting to trees and shrubs alike, debarred from the vivifying light of the sun. Everything was of a uniform brown, or faded tint. The leaves had no greenness, and the flowers themselves, so numerous at that epoch, now colorless and scentless, looked as if made of paper, and discolored by the action of the air.

My uncle ventured into this gigantic labyrinth. I followed, not without apprehension. As nature had spread a vegetable banquet, why should we not meet with some of the terrible mammifers? In some openings, left by decayed and fallen trees, I saw leguminous plants, and acers and rubias and a thousand other shrubs dear to the ruminants of all ages. Then, blended in one group, I beheld the trees of dissimilar climates—the oak growing beside the palm, the eucalyptus of Australia elbowing the Norwegian pine, the birch of the North min-gling its branches with the kauri of New Zealand. It would puzzle the most scientific botanist of the upper earth.

Suddenly I came to a stop. I held back my uncle. The diffused light made the smallest objects visible in the depths of the forest. I thought I saw—No! my eyes did not deceive me. I did see immense forms mov-ing under the trees! They were the giant animals, a herd of mastodons, not fossil but living, of the kind whose remains were discovered in 1801 in the swamps of the Ohio River. I distinctly saw great elephants, whose trunks were coiling among the branches like a legion of ser-pents. I could hear the noise of their ivory tusks as they struck the bark of the trees. The branches cracked, and the leaves, torn off in masses, disappeared down the mighty throats of these monsters.

The dream, in which I seemed to see revived that pre-historic world—the third and fourth epochs—that dream was realized!

My uncle looked.

"Come!" said he, seizing my arm. "Come on; we will go on."

"No!" said I. "No! We are unarmed. What could we do in the midst of a herd of giant quadrupeds? Come, uncle, come! No human crea-ture could brave the fury of those monsters."

"No human creature!" said my uncle, in a subdued voice. "You are wrong, Axel! Look down there! I think I see a human form! A being like ourselves! A man!"

I shrugged my shoulders while I looked, and resolved not to believe it unless belief was inevitable. But, in spite of myself, I was convinced. About a quarter of a mile off, leaning against the branch of an enor-mous kauri pine, a human being—a Proteus of these subterranean regions—a new son of Neptune, was herding that vast troop of mast-odons.

Immanis pecoris custos, immanior ipse!

Yes, *immanior ipse!* It was no longer the fossil being whose corpse we had picked up on the ossuary, it was a living giant capable of commanding these monsters. His stature was over twelve feet. His head, as large as that of a buffalo, was lost in the mass of his tangled hair. It was a mane like that of the primeval elephant. He brandished an enormous limb of a tree, a fit crook for such a shepherd.

We stood motionless, petrified. But we ran the risk of being seen. We must fly.

"Come, come!" cried I, dragging my uncle, who for the first time in his life, allowed himself to be led.

A quarter of an hour after we were out of sight of this formidable enemy.

Now that I think of it all quietly; now that my mind is calm again, and that months have elapsed since that wonderful, supernatural apparition, what am I to think? What am I to believe? It seems impossible. Our senses must have played us false. Our eyes did not see what they showed to us! No human creature lives in that subterranean world. No generation of men inhabits those lower caverns of the globe without an idea of the inhabitants above, and without communication with them. It is madness—the height of madness.

I would rather admit the existence of some animal whose structure approximates to ours: some ape of a remote geological period, some protopithecus; some mesopithecus, like that which Lartet discovered in the bone-deposit of Sansau.

But this one which we saw exceeded in size all the species known in modern palæontology. No matter! One can imagine an ape, however improbable.

But a whole generation of living men, shut up in the bowels of the earth! Never can I believe it.

However, we left the light and luminous forest dumb with astonishment, overcome by a stupefaction which bordered on insensibility. We ran mechanically. It was a mad flight—an irresistible impulse, such as pervades some kinds of nightmare. Instinctively we returned to the "Sea of Lidenbrock," and I do not know into what vagaries my reason might have been betrayed, but that I was forcibly recalled to practical matters.

Although I was certain that we were treading virgin ground, I frequently noticed groups of rock that recalled to me those of Port Gräuben. This was further confirmation of the indication of the compass, and of our involuntary return to the north of the "Sea of Lidenbrock." It was sometimes very confusing. Hundreds of rills and cascades fell from the crags. I seemed to recognize the stratum of Surtar-brandur, our faithful Hansbach, and the grotto where I first regained my senses. Then again, at a little distance, lay the rocky sea-wall; the appearance of a streamlet, the striking outline of a rock, threw me into a state of indecision as to our whereabouts.

I imparted my doubts to my uncle. He, too, was in a maze. In a panorama so vast and so monotonous there was nothing the mind could fix on as a landmark.

"At any rate," said I, "we have not landed at our point of embarkation. The storm has led us lower down, and if we follow the shore we shall come to Port Gräuben."

"If that is so," said my uncle, "we need explore no further. The best thing we can do is to get back to the raft. But are you sure you are correct, Axel?"

"It is difficult to say positively, uncle; all the rocks are alike. And yet I fancy I recognize the promontory at whose foot Hans put our raft together. We ought to be near the little port; unless, indeed, this is it," added I, scrutinizing the small creek.

"No, Axel. If that were so, we should find our own tracks; and I see nothing of the kind."

"But I see!" said I, darting towards something that shone on the sand.

"What is it?"

"Look!" said I.

And I showed my uncle the dagger stained with rust which I had picked up.

"Steady, now," said he. "Did you bring this weapon with you?"

"I! No, indeed. But you—"

"Not to my knowledge," replied the professor. "I never had such a thing in my possession."

"How strange!"

"Well, no! After all, it is simple enough, Axel. The Icelanders often have poniards of this kind. Hans must have dropped this one. No doubt it is his."

I shook my head. Hans never had anything of the kind.

"Is it the weapon," cried I, "of some antediluvian warrior—of a living man, a contemporary of the giant herdsman? But no! it does not belong to the Stone Age, nor to the Age of Bronze either. This blade is steel—"

My uncle stopped me short in this new digression, and in his coldest tone he said:

"Calm yourself, Axel, and collect your wits. This poniard is a weapon of the sixteenth century, a true 'dagger,' such as noblemen used to carry in their belt to give the *coup-de-grâce*. It belongs neither to you, nor me, nor the hunter, nor even to the human beings who may live in the bowels of the earth."

"Would you venture to say—"

"See! That notch never came from cutting throats; the blade is covered with rust that dates not from a day, nor a year, nor an age."

The professor grew warm, as usual, when he gave the reins to his imagination.

"Axel," said he, "we are on the road to the great discovery! This blade has lain on the sand one, two, perhaps three hundred years, and that notch was made by the rocks of this subterranean sea."

"But," said I, "it did not come here by itself; it did not give itself this twist. Some one has been here before us."

"Yes! a man."

"And this man has graven his name with this dagger! He wanted to mark once more the road to the central point. Let us search everywhere!"

Intensely interested, we kept close along the high wall, prying into the narrowest crevices that looked like the entrance to a gallery. At last we came to a place where the shore narrowed. The sea almost washed the foot of the cliff, leaving a passage not more than six feet wide. Between two projecting points of rock we saw the entrance to a dark tunnel.

There, on a block of granite, stood the mysterious letters, half effaced, the initials of the bold traveler—

$$\centerdot \; \text{ᛑ} \centerdot \text{ᚼ} \centerdot$$

"A. S.!" cried my uncle, "Arne Saknussemm! Always Arne Saknussemm!"

XLI

Since the commencement of our travels I had passed through so many phases of wonder and surprise that I thought nothing could startle me any more, or excite a feeling of astonishment; but when I beheld these two letters, cut three hundred years ago, I stood there in a state of bewilderment akin to idiocy. Not only was the signature of the great alchemist before my eyes, but his stylet was in my hands. It would be an unbeliever indeed who could doubt the existence of the traveler and the reality of his travels.

While these thoughts were racking my brain, the professor went off into dithyrambics on Arne Saknussemm. "Wonderful genius!" cried he. "You neglected nothing that could open to other mortals the channels through the earth's crust; and your fellow-men can follow your traces, after three centuries, in the depths of these dark caves. You have done everything to enable others to behold these marvels. Your name, engraved from stage to stage, is an unfailing guide to any one bold enough to tread in your footsteps; and I believe your autograph will be found at the center of our planet. Well, I too will write my name on this last page of granite. But henceforth this Cape, discovered by you near this sea, shall be called Cape Saknussemm."

That is the substance of what I heard, and my own enthusiasm was rising with his words. A fire seemed to burn in my breast. I forgot everything, the dangers of the voyage and the perils of the return. What another had done I would dare, and nothing appeared to me impossible.

"Forward! forward!" I exclaimed.

As I spoke I sprang forward toward the dark gallery, when the professor, usually so prone to hasty action, restrained me, and advised coolness and patience.

"First let us go back to Hans," said he, "and bring the raft round to this point."

I obeyed with a bad grace, and hastened to the beach.

"Uncle," said I, "do you know that circumstances have been very much in our favor up to now?"

"Do you think so, Axel?"

"I do. Why everything, even the storm, combined to set us in the right track. Blessings on the hurricane! It landed us on the very coast from which fine weather would have carried us far away. Just fancy if our prow (a raft with a prow!) had touched the southern shore of the Lidenbrock Sea, what would have become of us. The name of Saknussemm would never have greeted our eyes, we should be wandering on a shore without an outlet."

"Yes, Axel, there is really some providential guidance which brought us, going to the south, back to the north, and to Cape Saknussemm. I may say it is more than astonishing, and there is something in it that baffles my sagacity to explain."

"What does it matter?" said I. "We do not need to account for facts, only to make the most of them."

"Certainly, my boy, but—"

"But we are going northward again. We shall pass under the northernmost countries in Europe—Sweden, Russia, Siberia, who knows? instead of penetrating under the deserts of Africa or the waves of the ocean; and what more do I want to know?"

"Yes, Axel, you are right, and it is all for the best, as we shall leave this horizontal sea, which can lead nowhere. We shall go down, down, always down! Do you know that before we reach the center we have only 4,500 miles to travel?"

"Bah!" said I, "that is not worth mentioning. Let us start at once!"

We talked on in this mad tone till we returned to the hunter. Everything was ready for an immediate start. Every package was on board. We took our stations on the raft, and, the sail being hoisted, Hans steered for Cape Saknussemm, following the coast-line.

The wind was not very favorable to a craft that could not sail very close. In some places we had to resort to poles to assist our progress: often low submerged rocks compelled us to go far out of our course. At last, after about three hours of navigation, that is, about six o'clock in the evening, we reached a point that offered a good landing-place.

I leaped on shore, followed by my uncle and the Icelander. The short passage had not calmed my spirits. On the contrary, I proposed "burning our ship" to cut off all temptation to retreat. My uncle would not hear of it. I thought him very lukewarm.

"At any rate, let us lose no time in starting," said I.

"Yes," said my uncle; "but, as a preliminary, we must examine this new gallery, to ascertain whether we must prepare our ladders."

My uncle got ready his Ruhmkorff apparatus, the raft, fastened to the shore, was left alone, the mouth of the gallery was not twenty paces off, and our little party bent their steps thither, myself leading the way.

The almost circular opening was about five feet in diameter; this dark tunnel was hollowed out of the living rock and carefully cleared by the eruptive matter to which it had once formed the outlet, so that we could enter without difficulty.

We followed an almost horizontal direction, when, after about six paces, our progress was cut short by an enormous block of stone.

I uttered an exclamation which was not a blessing when I found myself stopped by an insurmountable obstacle.

In vain we searched to the right and to the left, above and below, there was no passage, no outlet. I was bitterly disappointed; I would not allow the reality of the obstacle. I bent down, looked under the block. Not a chink! Above, the same granite barrier. Hans passed the lamp along every part of the wall, but found no solution of the difficulty. We had no alternative but to abandon all hope of passing.

I had seated myself on the ground. My uncle strode up and down the passage.

"What did Saknussemm do?" I exclaimed.

"Yes!" said my uncle. "Was he baffled by this stone barrier?"

"No! no!" said I, with warmth. "This rocky fragment must have suddenly closed this passage, set in motion by some shock, or by one of those magnetic phenomena which disturb the crust of the earth. Many years have gone by since the return of Saknussemm and the fall of that block. There can be no doubt that this gallery was once a channel for lava, and that the eruptive matters had a free circulation. Look, there are recent fissures furrowing the granite roof. It is composed of an assemblage of blocks, enormous stones that are arranged as if a giant had toiled to form it; but some sudden shock has displaced the mass, and, as if the keystone of the arch had been dislodged, the falling stones have obstructed all passage. It is a fortuitous obstacle which Saknussemm did not encounter, and if we do not remove it we are unworthy to reach the center of the earth!"

That was my speech! The soul of the professor had passed into me. The spirit of a discoverer pervaded me. I forgot the past, I disdained the future! Nothing existed for me on the face of our planet, in whose bosom I was plunged, neither town nor country, neither Hamburg nor Königstrasse, nor my poor Gräuben, who must think me lost for ever in the bowels of the earth!

"Well," said my uncle, "with the mattock and the pickax let us cut our way! Let us break down this wall."

"It is too hard for the pick!" cried I.

"Well, then, the mattock!"

"Too tedious!"

"But—"

"Well, powder! Let us mine, and blow up the barrier."

"Powder! of course!" said my uncle. "Hans, set to work at once!"

The Icelander returned to the raft, and came back with a pickax, wherewith to dig a trench for the powder. It was no easy task. We had to make a hole large enough to contain fifty pounds of gun-cotton, whose expansive power is four times greater than that of gunpowder.

I was in a state of feverish excitement. While Hans was at work I helped my uncle to prepare a slow-match, made of damp powder in a tube of cloth.

"We shall pass it!" said I.

"We shall!" said my uncle.

At midnight we had finished. The charge of gun-cotton was put in, and the slow-match was brought along the gallery to the outside. A spark only was wanting to set this powerful agent in operation.

"To-morrow!" said the professor.

There was no help for it. I had to resign myself to wait six long hours.

XLII

The next day, Thursday, August 27, was a notable date in this subterranean voyage. When I think of it my heart still beats with terror. From that moment our reason, our judgment, our ingenuity went for nothing, we were to be the playthings of the elements.

At six o'clock we were afoot. The moment was at hand when we were to force a passage through the granite crust by means of powder.

I begged to be allowed the honor of setting light to the match. That done I was to rejoin my companions on the raft, which had not been unloaded: then we intended to sheer off a little, lest the explosion should not confine its effects to the interior of the rocky mass.

We reckoned that the match would take about ten minutes before reaching the chamber where the powder was; I should therefore have time to regain the raft.

I prepared to fulfill my part, not without trepidation.

After a hurried meal, my uncle and the hunter went on board, while I stayed on the beach. I was equipped with a lighted lantern with which to fire the train.

"Go now, my lad," said my uncle, "and come back immediately to us."

"Never fear," said I, "I am not likely to loiter on the way."

And I turned my steps to the entrance of the gallery; I opened my lantern, took up the end of the match, the professor held his chronometer in his hand.

"Ready!" cried he.

"Ready!"

"Well, fire! my boy."

I quickly put the match into the flame, which crackled at the contact, and running as quickly as f could, I regained the beach.

"Jump on board," said my uncle, "and let us push off!"

Hans, with a powerful stroke, impelled us from the land; the raft was about twenty fathoms from the shore.

It was an exciting moment. The professor watched the hand of the chronometer.

"Five minutes more!" said he. "Four! three!"

My pulse beat twice in a second.

"Two! One—Crumble ye hills of granite!"

What happened? I do not think I heard the explosion. But the form of the rocks seemed to change before my eyes; they opened like a curtain.

An unfathomable abyss seemed to open on the shore. The sea seemed to become dizzy, and only formed one great wave, on whose back the raft rose perpendicularly.

We were all three thrown down. In less than a second the light was swallowed up in utter darkness. Presently I felt our support give way from beneath the raft. First I thought we were falling vertically, but I was mistaken. I thought of speaking to my uncle, but the hoarse roar of the waters would have prevented his hearing me.

In spite of the darkness, the shock, the emotion, I was able to understand what had happened.

Beyond the block which we had blown up, there was an abyss. The explosion had produced a kind of earthquake in this fissured rock, and now the gulf was laid open, and the sea, changed into a torrent, was carrying us away in its course.

I gave myself up for lost. An hour, two hours, who knows how much longer passed thus. We pressed closely together, holding hands so as not to be thrown from the raft. We felt shocks of great violence when the raft touched the wall, but this was rarely, from which I drew the inference that the gallery had widened. Beyond a doubt this was the passage of Saknussemm; but instead of traveling along it by ourselves, we had, by our imprudence, brought a sea along with us.

It will be understood that these ideas passed vaguely and darkly through my mind. It was difficult to think at all in this giddy journey, which was so like a fall. Judging by the wind that lashed our faces, our pace must have far exceeded that of the most rapid train. To light a torch under these conditions would have been impossible, and our last electric apparatus was broken at the moment of the explosion.

My surprise was great, therefore, at seeing a bright light shine out suddenly beside me. The stolid face of Hans was illuminated. The undaunted hunter had succeeded in lighting the lantern, and although its flame flickered almost to extinction, it threw some gleams into the appalling darkness.

The gallery was wide, as I had judged. The faint light did not allow us to perceive both walls at a time. The steepness of the waterfall which carried us off was greater than the great cataracts of America. The surface was like a shower of arrows, launched with the utmost force. No comparison can convey my impression. Sometimes, caught by an eddy, the raft would veer to the right or left in its whirling course. When it neared the wall of the gallery I threw the light of the lantern on the rock, and could form an estimate of our speed by the fact that little points of rock seemed to form continuous lines, so that we appeared to be enclosed in a network of moving threads. I judged our speed to be ninety miles an hour.

My uncle and I looked at each other with haggard faces as we clung to the butt of the mast, which was broken short off at the moment of the catastrophe. We turned our backs to the current of air, so as not to be choked by the rapidity of a motion which no human power could slacken.

But still the hours passed. The situation was unchanged, except for a complication.

In trying to get our cargo in order, I found that the greatest part of our stores must have disappeared at the moment of the explosion, when the sea had been so violently agitated. I wanted to know exactly what we had to rely on, and, lantern in hand, I began my investigation. Of our instruments nothing was left but the compass and the chronometer. The ladders and ropes were represented by an end of cable round the remnant of the mast. Not a pickax, nor a mattock, not a hammer, and, irreparable loss! we had provisions only for a day.

I searched the interstices of the raft, the crevices formed by the beams and the floor-joints. Nothing! Our store consisted of a morsel of dried meat and some biscuits. I stared about me with a stupefied air. I was loath to believe it. And yet, what did it matter? If the provisions would have sufficed for months, how were we to escape from the abyss or from the irresistible torrent that was hurrying us down? Why fear the torments of hunger, when so many forms of death were presenting themselves? Could we even count on time enough to die of inanition?

And yet, by an extraordinary freak of imagination, I overlooked the immediate peril, and was overwhelmed with the future, which looked to me so terrible. Besides, it seemed just possible that we might escape the fury of the torrent, and regain the surface of the globe. How, I know not. Where, I cared not. What matter? A chance is a chance, even if it is only one to a thousand; while death by hunger left us no ray of hope, ever so faint.

I thought of telling my uncle, and showing him the destitution to which we were reduced, and to show exactly how long we had to live. But I summoned courage to be silent. I thought it best to leave him his self-possession.

At this moment the light of the lantern gradually sank, and then went out. The wick was burnt out.

The darkness became absolute. No hope remained of illuminating it. We had a torch left, but it could not be kept alight. So, like a child, I shut my eyes to keep the darkness out.

A considerable time elapsed, and then our speed was increased twofold. I knew it by the current of air as it struck my face. The slope of the water became greater and greater. I think we no longer slid, we fell. It was to my sensations an almost vertical descent. The hands of my uncle and of Hans holding fast to my arms held me firmly down.

Suddenly, after a period whose duration was quite inappreciable, I felt a kind of shock, the raft had struck nothing solid, but its course was suddenly arrested. A waterspout, an immense liquid column, was falling. I was suffocated—I was drowning!

But this sudden flood did not last long. In a few seconds I was inhaling long breaths of pure air. My uncle and Hans squeezed my arms almost to breaking, and the raft still bore us all three.

XLIII

I suppose it was now about ten o'clock at night. The first of my senses that began to act was that of hearing. Strange as the expression may appear, I heard first the silence produced in the gallery, after the roaring which for hours had filled my ears. At last I heard my uncle say, in a voice that sounded like a far-off murmur:

"We are ascending!"

"What do you say?" I cried.

"We are ascending, I say!"

I put out my hand, I touched the wall; my hand was bathed in blood. We were ascending with extreme rapidity.

"Now for the torch!" exclaimed the professor. Hans, not without difficulty, succeeded in lighting it, and the flame was able to burn even with the ascending motion, and to throw light enough to illuminate the scene.

"Just as I thought," said the professor. "We are in a narrow well, not twenty-four feet in diameter; the water, arrived at the bottom of the gulf, regains its level, and we are ascending with it."

"Whither?"

"I do not know, but we must hold ourselves in readiness for any emergency. We are ascending at the rate of twelve feet per second—say 720 per minute, or nine and a half miles per hour. At that rate we shall make some way."

"Yes, if nothing stops us, and if the well has an outlet; but if it is closed, the air will be more and more compressed, and we shall end by being crushed."

"Axel," said the professor very calmly, "our situation is all but desperate; but there are chances of salvation, and those I contemplate. We may perish at any moment, but at any moment we may be saved. Therefore let us be on the alert to take advantage of any circumstance."

"What is there that we can do?"

"Recruit our strength by eating."

At these words I glanced sadly at my uncle. At last I should have to reveal my secret.

"Eat?" said I.

"Yes, without a delay."

The professor added some words in Danish.

Hans shook his head.

"What!" said my uncle; "our provisions are lost?"

"Yes, there is all that remains—a piece of dried meat for the three of us."

My uncle looked vacantly at me.

"Well," said I, "do you still think we may be saved?"

My question received no answer.

An hour passed. I was suffering the pangs of hunger. My companions suffered also; but none of us would touch the miserable remnant of food. We continued to ascend with extreme rapidity. Sometimes the air cut off our respiration, as happens to aeronauts rising too swiftly. But as they experience cold as they rise, we experienced, on the contrary, an ever-increasing heat, and at this moment it must certainly have reached 70°.

What does this change indicate? Up till now the facts had confirmed the theories of Davy and of Lidenbrock; till now the peculiar

conditions of refractory rocks, electricity, and magnetism had modi-
fied the general laws of nature, and given us a moderate temperature,
for the central-fire theory still seemed to me the only true or explicable
one. Were we hastening towards a medium where these phenomena
were developed strictly in accordance with that theory, and in which
the heat reduced the rocks to a state of fusion? This fear took hold of
me, and I said to the professor:

"If we are neither drowned nor crushed, and if hunger does not put
an end to us, we have still the chance of being burnt alive."

He merely shrugged his shoulders, and relapsed into meditation.

An hour passed, and no change save in the temperature, which
kept increasing. At last my uncle broke the silence.

"Come," said he, "we must make up our minds."

"Make up our minds?" said I.

"Yes; we must recruit our strength. If we husband our little store in
order to have a few more hours of life, we shall make ourselves weaker
at the last."

"Yes, at the last! That will be very soon."

"Well, well! suppose a chance of safety presented itself, and that
a sudden effort was necessary, how shall we have strength for it if we
weaken ourselves by fasting?"

"Uncle," said I, "when that bit of meat is gone, what have we?"

"Nothing, Axel, nothing. But what good does it do you to devour it
with your eyes? You reason like a being without will or energy!"

"Do you not despair?" cried I, exasperated at his coolness.

"No," replied he firmly.

"What! you shall believe we have a chance?"

"Yes, a thousand time, yes! While the heart beats and the flesh
palpitates, a creature endowed with will should never give place to
despair."

What a speech. The man that could utter it under such circumstances was of no ordinary mold.

"Well," said I, "what is your plan?"

"To eat what remains, to the last crumb, and regain our lost strength. It may be our last meal, it is true, but at least we shall be strengthened to meet our fate."

"Well," said I, "let us fall to."

My uncle took the piece of meat and the few biscuits that had escaped the wreck; he divided them into three equal portions, and distributed them. That gave about a pound of food to each. The professor ate heartily, with a sort of feverish appetite; I ate my portion with loathing rather than relish, in spite of my hunger; Hans took his moderately, tranquilly, masticating little mouthfuls, eating with the indifference of a man whom no thought for the future disturbed. He had discovered a gourd half full of geneva; he offered it to us, and the vivifying liquor reanimated me a little.

"*Fortrefflig!*" said Hans, drinking in his turn.

"Excellent!" rejoined my uncle.

Hope revived in me a little. But our last meal was ended. It was now five o'clock in the morning.

Man is so constituted that his health is a purely negative result; once the desire for food is satisfied, he scarcely conceives the horrors of starvation; to understand them he must be suffering them. So in our case, a few mouthfuls of biscuit and meat triumphed over all our past troubles.

Still, after our repast, each one gave himself up to his own thoughts. What were the reflections of Hans, this man of the extreme West, possessed with the fatalism of the orientals? As for me, my thoughts were nothing but memories, and they carried me to the surface of the globe, which I ought never to have left. The home in the Königstrasse, my poor Gräuben, our good Martha, passed before me like dreams, and in the melancholy rumblings that echoed in the rock I fancied I could hear the hum of cities.

My uncle, always busy, was occupied, torch in hand, examining the nature of the formation; he was trying to ascertain our position by observing how the strata were grouped. Such a calculation could only be a very rough one; but a *savant* is always a *savant*, as long as he keeps his self-possession, and Professor Lidenbrock had that faculty in no common degree.

I heard him mutter geological terms; I understood them, and in spite of myself I was interested.

"Eruptive granite," said he. "We are still in the primitive period. But we ascend still! Who knows?"

He still hoped. He felt along the wall, and in a few minutes later he exclaimed:

"There is the gneiss! There are the mica-schists; soon we shall come to the transition rocks, and then—"

What did he mean? Could he measure the thickness of the crust suspended over head? What means had he of calculating? The manometer was gone, and nothing could supply its place.

The temperature rose rapidly, and I felt bathed in a burning atmosphere. The heat was comparable to nothing but the blast from a foundry furnace where melting is going on.

"Are we approaching a burning mass?" cried I, at a moment when the heat seemed to acquire double intensity.

"No," said my uncle; "it is impossible."

"And yet," said I, touching the wall, "this rock is burning hot."

As I spoke, my hand touched the water, and I quickly withdrew it.

"The water is burning hot, too."

This time the professor only replied by an angry gesture. From that moment I became the victim of terror I could not shake off. I apprehended a speedy catastrophe, such as the wildest imagination could not have conceived. First it was a vague idea which soon changed to certainty in my mind. I repulsed it, it returned with unabated strength. I could not put it into words. But some involuntary observations confirmed my conviction. By the uncertain light of the torch I remarked some fitful movement of the beds of granite; something was going to happen in which electricity would play a part; then this excessive heat, this boiling water. . . I looked at the compass. It was stationary nowhere.

XLIV

Yes; it went round and round. The needle turned from pole to pole with abrupt movements, pointed to all the points of the compass, and turned as if touched by vertigo.

I was aware that, according to the most generally received theories, the mineral crust of the earth is never in a state of absolute repose. The changes brought about by internal decomposition, the agitation produced by great currents of fluid, the action of magnetism, tend to shake it incessantly, even when the beings scattered on its surface are not aware of any disturbance. This phenomenon, therefore, would not have filled me with terror taken alone.

But other facts, details quite *sui generis*, left me no room to doubt. The sounds of detonations became very frequent. I could only liken them to the sound of a multitude of carriages driven rapidly over a paved street. It was one continuous thunder.

Then the revolving compass, disturbed by electric shocks, confirmed my opinion.

The mineral crust threatened to break, the granite masses to close in again, the fissure to close up, and then, poor mortals! we should perish in the close embrace.

"Uncle! uncle!" said I, "we are lost!"

"What new terror has seized you?" said he, with amazing calmness. "What ails you?"

"What ails me? Look at those heaving walls, the dislocation that is gradually taking place in the mass, this torrid heat, this boiling water—every sign of an earthquake!"

My uncle only shook his head gently.

"An earthquake?" said he.

"Yes."

"My boy, I think you are mistaken."

"What! do you not perceive the signs?"

"Of an earthquake? No! I expect something better than that."

"What do you mean?"

"An eruption, Axel!"

"An eruption!" said I. "Then we are in the outlet of an active volcano?"

"So I think," said the professor, smiling, "and perhaps that is the best thing that could befall us."

The best thing! Was my uncle mad? What could he mean? Why this unnatural smiling calmness?

"What?" said I. "We are caught in an eruption; fate has thrown us into the track of the burning lava, the rocks of fire, the boiling torrents, all the eruptive materials. We shall be shot up into the air with rocky fragments, amid a rain of cinders and scoria, in a whirlwind of flame, and that is the best thing that can befall us!"

"Yes," said the professor, looking at me over his spectacles, "it is our only chance of reaching the surface again."

I passed all my ideas rapidly in review. My uncle was perfectly right, and I never saw him more confident or more satisfied than at this moment, as he waited and counted the chances of an eruption.

Still we were rising; the night passed in the same ascending movement; the surrounding noises increased; I was all but stifled; I thought my last hour had surely come, and still, imagination is such a strange faculty, I gave myself up to a childish curiosity. But I was the slave of my fancies, not their master.

It was evident that we were being forced upwards by an eruptive pressure; under the raft was boiling water, and under these waters a lava-mass, a collection of rocks which, on leaving the crater, would be scattered in every direction. We were in the chimney of a volcano. Not a doubt of it.

But this time, instead of Snäfell, an extinct volcano, it was a volcano in full operation. And I began to speculate what mountain it might be and on what part of the world we might be vomited forth.

Undoubtedly we were in the north. Before its derangement, the compass had never varied in that respect. Ever since Cape Saknus-semm we had been carried directly northward for hundreds of miles. Had we returned under Iceland? Were we to make our exit by Hecla or one of the seven other craters of the island? Within a radius of 500 miles to the westward I recalled only the imperfectly known volcanoes of the north-west coast of America. Eastward, the only one existing under the 84th parallel of latitude was the Esk, in Jan Mayen Island, not far from Spitzbergen! There was no scarcity of craters spacious enough to belch forth an army! But what I wanted to know was, which one would serve our turn.

Towards morning the ascending motion was accelerated. The heat increased instead of diminishing as we approached the surface, but this was a local phenomenon, and due to volcanic influences. The quality of our locomotion was quite certain in my mind. We were undoubtedly propelled by an enormous force—a force of many thousand atmospheres produced by the vapors accumulated in the center of the earth. But to what perils this force exposed us!

Presently reddish reflections penetrated the vertical gallery, which began to widen. I perceived, to right and left, deep passages like vast tunnels, whence arose thick vapors; tongues of flame coruscated as they licked the walls.

"Look, look, uncle!" cried I.

"Well," said he, "those are sulfurous flames, quite natural in an eruption."

"But if they close in upon us?"

"But they will not close in upon us."

"Suppose they stifle us?"

"They will not stifle us. The gallery is widening, and, if necessary, we can leave the raft and take refuge in some hollow of the rock."

"And the water still rising?"

"Axel, there is no more water—only a volcanic, pasty fluid, which is carrying us up on its surface to the crater mouth."

It was true: the liquid column had given place to eruptive matters, still dense, though boiling. The temperature became insufferable, and a thermometer exposed to this atmosphere would have marked more than 118°. I was bathed in perspiration. But for the rapidity of our upward movement we should have been suffocated.

However, the professor did not put into practice his proposition to abandon the raft, and he was right. Those ill-joined beams gave us a solid foothold, which we could not have found elsewhere.

About eight o'clock in the morning a novel incident occurred. The ascending movement ceased in an instant. The raft was absolutely motionless.

"What is it?" asked I, shaken by the sudden stoppage, as by a shock.

"A halt," replied my uncle.

"Is the eruption diminishing?"

"I hope not, indeed."

I rose. I tried to look about me. Perhaps the raft had caught on a point of rock, and offered a momentary resistance to the eruptive mass, in which case we must disengage it without delay.

Nothing of the kind. The column of cinders, scoria, and stony débris had itself ceased to rise.

"Has the eruption stopped?" cried I.

"Ah!" muttered my uncle, between his closed teeth, "you fear so, my boy; be consoled, this calm will not last long. Five minutes have already elapsed, and very soon we shall resume our ascent to the mouth of the crater."

As he spoke he continued to watch his chronometer, and he was destined to be right in his prognostication. Soon the raft began to move again in a rapid but irregular manner, which lasted about two minutes, and then stopped again.

"Good!" remarked my uncle. "In ten minutes we shall start again."

"Ten minutes?"

"Yes, this is an intermittent volcano. It lets us take breath also."

Nothing truer. At the appointed minute we started afresh with extreme rapidity. We had to cling to the raft, to avoid being thrown off. Then the pressure stopped again.

I have since reflected on this singular phenomenon, without finding any satisfactory solution. But I think it is clear that we were not in the main shaft of the volcano, but in an accessory passage, where the counter-shocks are felt.

How often this movement was repeated I cannot say, I only know that at each succeeding start the force was greater, and at last like the force of a projectile. During the intervals of rest we were stifled. I thought for a moment of the delight of finding one's self in a hyperborean region, at a temperature of thirty below zero. My overwrought imagination wandered on snowy plains in the Arctic regions, and I longed for the moment when I should roll myself on the frozen ground of the Pole. Gradually my senses, weakened by repeated shocks, gave way. But for the protecting arm of Hans I should more than once have had my head crushed against the granite wall.

I have no accurate recollection of what took place in the hours that followed. I have a confused idea of continuous detonation, of general convulsion, of a gyratory movement of the raft. It rocked on the lava sea in the midst of a rain of ashes. The roaring flames enveloped it. A hurricane like the blast of a furnace fed the subterranean fires. The last thing I recall is the face of Hans, lit up by the flames; and I felt like one of those poor wretches bound to the mouth of a cannon at the moment when the gun is fired and their dismembered atoms are shot into space.

XLV

When I came to myself again, and opened my eyes, I felt my waist pressed by the powerful hand of our guide. With the other hand he supported my uncle. I was not seriously injured, but worn out by exhaustion. I was lying on the slope of a mountain, two steps from an abyss, into which the least movement would have precipitated me. Hans had saved me from death, while I rolled on the sides of the crater.

"Where are we?" said my uncle, who seemed rather put out at having returned to the surface.

The hunter shrugged his shoulders in token of ignorance.

"In Iceland?" said I.

"*Nej!*"

"What! no!" cried the professor.

"Hans is mistaken," said I, raising myself.

After the innumerable surprises of our voyage, yet another was in store for us. I expected to see a cone covered with eternal snows, in the midst of the barren wastes of the northern regions, lighted by the pale light of a polar sun, up in the higher latitudes, and now, contrary to these previsions, my uncle, the Icelander, and myself, were stretched on a mountain side, dried and burnt up by the heat of the sun, which was even now scorching us.

I could not believe my senses; but the roasting process my body was undergoing did not admit of a doubt. We had come out of the crater half naked, and the glorious orb from whom we had received nothing for two months, now lavished upon us his light and heat, and threw around us a flood of radiance.

When my eyes grew accustomed to the splendor, I endeavored to correct the error of my imagination. I expected at least to be at Spitz-bergen, and I felt it hard to give up the idea.

The professor was the first to speak:

"After all, it is not like Iceland."

"But Jan Mayen, perhaps?" said I.

"Not even that, my lad. This is no northern volcano, with its granite sides and cap of snow."

"Still—"

"Look, Axel, look!"

Above our heads, 500 feet at least, was a crater, by which escaped, at intervals of a quarter of an hour, with a loud report, a tall column of flame, mixed with pumice-stones, ashes, and lava. I could feel the convulsive movement of the mountain, which panted like a whale, casting up fire and hot air from its enormous blow-holes. Lower down and on a very steep slope lay sheets of eruptive matter, covering a declivity 700 or 800 feet in extent, which gave the volcano a height of not quite 1,800 feet. Its base was lost in a basket-like mass of foliage, among which were distinguishable olives, figs, and vines, loaded with rosy grapes.

Not very like the Arctic regions, certainly.

Glancing across this belt of green, the eye was charmed with a lovely lake or sea, which made of this enchanted spot an island not many miles in extent. Eastward were a few houses, and then a little harbor, on whose blue waves there rode some vessels of peculiar form. Beyond these, groups of islands rose from the liquid plain, so numerous as to resemble a vast ant-hill. Looking towards the west, distant shores sloped to the horizon; on some there stood out the lovely outlines of blue mountains; on another more distant still, there towered a gigantic cone, on whose summit hovered a canopy of smoke. In the north an immense expanse of water sparkled in the sunlight, dotted here and there with tops of masts or the curves of a swelling sail.

The beauty of the scene was multiplied a hundred-fold by our entire unpreparedness for anything of the kind.

"Where are we? where are we?" I kept muttering to myself.

Hans closed his eyes, and was indifferent; my uncle gazed vacantly before him.

At last he remarked:

"Whatever mountain this is, it is rather warm quarters; the eruption is going on, and it would be a pity to have escaped a volcano to be crushed by a boulder. Let us go down, and then we shall find out all about it. Besides, I am dying of hunger and thirst."

Certainly, the professor was not of a reflective turn of mind. For my part, I was insensible to hunger or fatigue, and would have remained there for hours longer, but of course I had to follow my companions.

We encountered some very precipitous slopes in our descent from the volcano. We lost our footing among the ashes, and barely escaped the rivers of lava which ran along like fiery serpents. All the time we were coming down, I talked rapidly—my imagination was too much excited to let me be silent.

"We must be in Asia," cried I, "on the shores of India, or the Malay Islands, or Oceanica! We have crossed half the globe to come out at the antipodes of Europe."

"But how about the compass?" said my uncle.

"Yes, indeed! according to that we have gone uniformly northward."

"Then the compass lied!"

"Oh, uncle! Lied!"

"Yes, unless this is the North Pole!"

"Well, not the Pole; but—"

I had no solution to offer. I could think of nothing.

And now we were near the lovely vegetation, hunger assailed me, and thirst too. Fortunately, after two hours' walking, we came to a lovely plantation covered with olives, pomegranates, and vines, which looked as if they belonged to everybody. And indeed, in our state of destitution, we were not disposed to be too particular. How delightful we thought that fruit, and how eagerly we devoured the great bunches of rosy grapes. Not far among the shady trees we found a spring of water in the grass, and we bathed face and hands with the greatest enjoyment.

While thus reveling in the delights of rest, a child appeared between two clumps of olives.

"Ah!" exclaimed I, "behold an inhabitant of this happy land!"

It was a poor child, miserably clothed, scared-looking, and evidently frightened at our appearance; and in fact, half naked as we were, and unshaved, we must have looked rather queer, and unless the country was a nest of robbers, we were very likely to strike terror into the inhabitants.

Just as the little urchin was running off, Hans went and brought him back in spite of his kicks and cries.

My uncle began by comforting him, and asked him in German:

"My little friend, what is the name of this country?"

No answer.

"Very good," said my uncle; "we are not in Germany," and he repeated his question in English.

No answer. I was puzzled.

"Let us try Italian," said my uncle, and he asked, *"Dove noi siamo?"*

"Yes, where are we?" I repeated impatiently.

No answer.

"What! you won't speak," said my uncle, who was getting angry. He pulled the child's ears and asked:

"What do you call this island?"

"Stromboli," said the little herd-boy, and fled through the olives till he reached the plain.

We did not need him. Stromboli! How I was startled at this unexpected name. We were in the midst of the Mediterranean, in the Æolian archipelago of mythological memory—the ancient Strongyle, where Æolus held the wind and storms in fetters. And the blue mountains curving toward the east were the mountains of Calabria! And the volcano that rose on the southern horizon was Etna, the fierce Etna itself.

"Stromboli! Stromboli!" I repeated.

My uncle accompanied my gestures and words as if we were a chorus.

What a wondrous voyage! In by one volcano, out by another, and this other situated more than 3,000 miles from Snäfell; and from that arid Iceland, at the extreme end of the world. The chances of the expedition had brought us to the heart of the loveliest countries in existence. We had left the region of eternal snows for those of infinite verdure; and exchanged the gray fogs of the frozen zone for the azure blue of a Sicilian sky!

After an exquisite banquet of fruit and spring water, we set out again for the port of Stromboli. We did not think it prudent to divulge the manner of our arrival in the island; the superstitious minds of the Italians would certainly have looked on us as demons vomited forth from the infernal regions, so we made up our minds to pass as shipwrecked mariners. The glory was less, but the safety greater.

As we journeyed I heard my uncle mutter:

"But the compass—it always marked the north. How can we explain it?"

"Don't explain it!" said I, with a contemptuous air, "that is the easiest plan."

"What an idea! A professor at the Johannæum who could not find the reason of a cosmical phenomenon! It would be a scandal."

And as he spoke, my uncle, half naked as he was, girt with his leathern belt, and spectacles on nose, was once more the Professor of mineralogy.

An hour after leaving the olive wood we arrived at Port San Vicenzo, where Hans claimed the pay for his thirteenth week of service, which was paid to him with hearty good-will.

At this moment, if he did not participate in our emotion, he gave way to an expansion very unusual

With the tips of his fingers he lightly pressed our hands and broke into a smile.

XLVI

H ere ends a story to which no credence will be given even by those who are astonished at nothing. But I am fore-armed against human incredulity.

We were received by the fishermen of Stromboli with the attention due to shipwrecked travelers.

They clothed and fed us. On the 31st of August, after a delay of forty-eight hours, we set sail in a speronar for the port of Messina, where a few days of rest made us forget our fatigues.

On Friday, September the 4th, we embarked on board the *Volturne*, one of the mail-packets of the *Messageries Impériales* of France, and, three days later, landed at Marseilles, having only one drawback to our satisfaction, namely, our mysterious compass. This inexplicable phenomenon worried me greatly. On September the 9th, late in the evening, we arrived in Hamburg.

I will not attempt to describe the amazement of Martha or the joy of Gräuben.

"Now that you are a hero," said my beloved, "you will not want to leave me again, Axel!"

I looked at her. She smiled through tears. The return of Professor Lidenbrock, I need not say, made a sensation in Hamburg. Owing to Martha's imprudent talk everybody had heard of his journey to the center of the earth. Nobody believed it, and now that he had come back they believed it less than ever.

Still the appearance of Hans, and some reports received from Iceland, were not without effect on public opinion.

And thus my uncle became a great man, and I became the nephew of a great man, which is something. Hamburg gave a *fête* in our honor. A public meeting was held in the Johannæum, and my uncle related the history of the expedition, only omitting the facts about the compass.

The same day he deposited in the archives of the city the document of Saknussemm, and recorded his regret that circumstances stronger than his will had prevented him from following to the center of the earth the footsteps of the Icelandic traveler. He was modest as to his achievement, and thereby increased his reputation.

So much honor of course raised up enemies, and as his theories, based on certainties, were opposed to scientific systems, on the question of central fire, he was engaged by tongue and pen in controversy with the *savants* of every country.

For my part, I cannot admit the theory of cooling. In spite of all I have seen I still cling to the doctrine of central fire; but I do not deny that certain circumstances, only dimly defined as yet, may cooperate with natural phenomena to modify this law.

While these questions were fermenting in the public mind my uncle had a great trial. Hans had left Hamburg, in spite of his entreaties. The man to whom we owed everything would not allow us to pay our debt. He was the victim of home-sickness.

"*Farväl*," said he one day, and with that little word of adieu he set out for Iceland, where he arrived safely.

We were deeply attached to our brave eider-duck hunter. Even in absence he will never be forgotten by the men whose lives he saved, and I certainly will see him again before I die.

In conclusion, I ought to add that this "Voyage to the Center of the Earth" made a great noise in the world. It was printed and translated into all languages; the leading journals extracted the principal episodes, which excited comment, discussion, and attack, sustained with great animation in the believing and unbelieving camps. My uncle had the rare felicity of being famous during his life, and Barnum, himself, proposed to exhibit him in the United States on very handsome terms.

Still, amid all this glory, there was an annoyance, I may say a torment; it was the one inexplicable fact—the compass. To a man of science, such a phenomenon unexplained is a mental torment. But my uncle was destined to be made entirely happy.

One day, in arranging a collection of minerals in his study, the well-known compass caught my eye, and I took a glance at it. It had lain there for six months, unconscious of the mischief it had done.

Suddenly, what was my surprise. I exclaimed—

The professor hastened to me.

"What is it?" said he.

"That compass!"

"Its needle is pointing south, not north!"

"What do you say?"

"Its pole is changed!"

My uncle looked, compared it, and then made a jump that shook the house.

What a light now broke upon us!

"Well then," said he, when he regained his speech, "after our arrival at Cape Saknussemm the needle of this confounded compass marked south for north."

"Clearly."

"Then our mistake is explained. What could have produced the change of polarity?"

"I think that is easy to explain," said I. "During the storm on the sea of Lidenbrock that fire-ball that magnetized all the iron in the raft, disorganized our compass!"

"Ha, ha!" laughed the professor, "then it was a prank of electricity?"

From that day my uncle was the happiest of sages, and I the happiest of men; for my lovely Virlandaise, abdicating her position of pupil, was installed in the Königstrasse house in double quality of niece and wife. I need not add that her uncle was the illustrious professor Otto Lidenbrock, corresponding member of all the scientific societies, geographical, and mineralogical, in the five quarters of the globe.

Milton Keynes UK
Ingram Content Group UK Ltd.
UKHW021437211123
432985UK00035B/508